SHADOWS OF DESTINY

THE SHADOW REALMS
BOOK 5

BRENDA K DAVIES

Brenda K. Davies

CHAPTER ONE

LEXI'S HEART thumped like a rabbit's hind leg while scratching at fleas. It took everything she had not to turn and bolt away from the cave looming before her like a dinosaur looking to swallow her whole.

And many might consider what was inside the cave a dinosaur. Lexi refused to shiver as the chill running up her spine cooled her overheated skin.

She took a deep breath and worked to control her emotions before glancing back at Orin. He still wore that damn, smug smile he'd had since announcing he caught a dragon.

He didn't realize how punchable that smile made him... or he didn't care. The not caring was probably more like it.

Standing beside Orin, Cole's eyes were the color of liquid mercury as he stared into the cave. Behind his clamped lips, she saw the outline of his lycan fangs.

Her father and Sahira stood behind Cole with their jaws clenched. Lexi wondered if they were contemplating punching Orin too. It was a very good possibility.

Behind them, Maverick, Brokk, Kaylia, Varo, and Niall stared at the cave with different expressions of curiosity, unease, and awe.

This situation amused Orin, but it had the rest of them on pins and needles.

Lexi flexed her fingers as a bead of sweat ran down her nape. The unrelenting sun of this outer realm baked the rocks of the barren world. The jagged formations decorating the land were the color of apricots as they spread endlessly onward. She had no idea if this outer realm had a name, and she didn't care.

Something stirred deep within the cave. She couldn't see it, but what sounded like a knife scraping against stone came from the darkness.

Instinctively, Lexi knew a stone hadn't made the noise; it had been a claw that could decapitate her in one swipe. The image of such a thing happening was so clear she almost placed a hand against her throat to make sure her head remained attached.

She settled for wiping away the sweat that was starting to stick her green tunic to her flesh. *What am I doing here? Why are we* all *here? This is insane.*

But she already knew the answers to those questions. She *had* to be here. She needed to learn how this dragon would react to her. But not everyone else had to put their lives at risk.

However, they had all refused to remain behind once Orin dropped his dragon bomb. Not that she could blame them; she would be curious to see what happened if a dragon met an arach after all these years.

And she *did* want to know. It was essential and might be what helped them defeat the Lord. But she did *not* want to face a creature who could eat or squish her before she blinked.

At least it can't roast me.

Her immunity to fire was little consolation right now. Lexi gulped. She hoped it didn't kill her. She enjoyed her life and was in no rush to become splattered arach bits all over the cave.

"You don't have to do this," Cole said.

The gravelly tone of his voice was the one she'd come to

recognize as what came through when he was fighting against shifting into a wolf.

"I know," she muttered.

But they both knew that was a lie. She didn't have a choice in this, and everyone here knew it. She had to face the dragon.

She tugged at the collar of her shirt as she gulped again. Her eyes met her dad's; the disapproval and fury were evident in his red eyes.

A small snort and a rustling from inside the cave drew her attention back to it. It almost sounded like the dragon was settling in to sleep or something.

For a second, her shield crumbled beneath the weight of her terror and uncertainty. To her, that was worse than facing a dragon.

Her secret was out; the Lord knew an arach still lived and was a threat to his claim on *her* homeland, but she couldn't lose control. The Lord and those at the ball had seen her. She was sure images of her were circulating throughout the realms while the Lord hunted her, but she could remain hidden from those who didn't know who she was.

She couldn't do that while walking around glowing like an overcharged Glo Worm. Lexi scrambled to get her shield back into place, but it was difficult to concentrate while on the verge of going to meet the creature within.

Finally, she managed to regain control, and her glow completely vanished as she mentally erected her shield once more.

"I should go alone," she said. "It's probably scared and angry and will do better if it only has to face one of us."

It was probably *pissed*, and having this group tromping in to see it wouldn't make things better for the frightened, murderous creature. She tugged at the collar of her tunic again before meeting Cole's eyes. He would never let her walk in there alone, but they didn't *all* have to go.

"I'm coming with you; everyone else will stay here," Cole commanded.

"The dragons don't like you," Lexi reminded him.

"I don't care."

Of course he didn't, and it was probably best if he stayed out here, but he wouldn't relent. They would only waste time arguing over it, and she'd prefer to get this over with.

"Keep her safe," her dad said to Cole.

"Always."

When Cole turned toward her, she swore the silver of his eyes burned hotter, but at least the shadows weren't swarming him. They stirred on the ground but didn't creep any closer.

She didn't make the mistake of thinking Cole wouldn't turn them loose on the dragon if it attacked. She wouldn't let that happen. It was a murderous beast, but *no* one would hurt it.

When they stepped into the cave, Orin followed.

"Go back," Lexi said sharply to him.

"I put my ass on the line for this; I'm going to see what happens," Orin replied.

When Cole rounded on his brother, Lexi's hand shot out and caught his arm. "Don't," she whispered. "Leave him be. It's not worth it."

She hated Orin's arrogant grin, but Lexi wouldn't stand there and fight with him when she had a dragon to meet.

CHAPTER TWO

LEXI CLASPED her hands and squeezed as she put one foot in front of the other through the dark. After the heat outside, the cave's cool air was a balm on her skin.

Somewhere in the distance, water dripped from the rocks into a pool she couldn't see. Like a pot of gold at the end of a rainbow, the flicker of a distant torch drew her onward. Except, at the end of this rainbow was a dragon who would smash her to bits with the pot.

Stop it!

Freaking herself out wasn't going to do her any good. She had no idea what lay ahead or what would happen, but her turbulent thoughts weren't helping. When they got to the dragon, she might have her answers, and until then, she had to stop picturing this ending with her in pieces.

She didn't ask Orin how he'd managed to catch and restrain a dragon in this cave. She couldn't listen to his arrogant reply right now.

Another snort and scrape came from ahead as the dragon shifted. Did it know they were coming? Had it smelled or heard them?

She suspected, like most animals, it had amazing senses to help keep it alive, so it had to know they were on their way. Somehow, that made this worse.

Though, it was probably worse to *surprise* a dragon. She doubted that ever went over well.

When the dragon shifted again and the torchlight illuminated more of the gray stone rocks of the cave, the shadows on the walls twisted as Cole drew them closer.

"Don't," Lexi said to him. "There's no reason to call on them."

"I'll do whatever it takes to keep you safe," Cole replied.

"We don't need them."

He grunted in response. Orin wisely remained silent as a stone crunched beneath her foot. If the dragon hadn't known they were coming, it did now.

Her foot caught the corner of a stone, and her ankle rolled. Staggering to the side, she nearly went down, but Cole grasped her elbow and held her up. She rested her hand against the wall to steady herself as the throbbing in her ankle eased.

"Are you okay?" he inquired.

"Yeah," she muttered. "Stupid rock."

When she pushed away from the wall, Cole kept her arm. Desperate to connect with him and the calmness his presence brought her, she wrapped the fingers of her free hand around his on her arm while they continued.

As Cole's skin warmed beneath hers, love swelled in her, but so did a growing certainty... if they didn't walk out of here with answers, they would never get them.

With every step, the torchlight grew brighter, and the dragon released another snuff. She glanced back to see the faint light of day fading to a pinpoint at the end of the tunnel before focusing forward again.

She didn't think she'd looked back for long, but she almost gasped when they turned a corner. Her hand flew to her mouth as she spotted the beautiful creature in chains. The chains went to stakes embedded in the ground and cave walls and didn't give the dragon much room to move.

This should never be!

The protective, hostile emotions crashing over her were so fierce it took her a few seconds to breathe again. No one should ever treat a dragon like this!

These magnificent creatures should *never* be bound in such a way. They should always be free.

However, they hadn't been free in centuries as the Lord had also bound them, maybe not with chains, but in other ways. These poor beasts had been held captive for millennia… and it was time to set them free.

It wouldn't hurl a wave of fire at them as thick chains pinched its mouth shut. A padlock locked the chains over its snout together.

"What did you do?" she demanded.

"I caught a dragon," Orin replied.

"No shit! But *why* did you do this to it?"

"To avoid being eaten," he said slowly, like she was an idiot.

Lexi's hands fisted. He smiled and crossed his arms over his chest as he leaned casually against the wall.

"You're an asshole," she told him.

"But I'm an asshole who's still in one piece and didn't get torched by *a dragon*."

"Where is the key for the locks?" Lexi demanded. "I'm going to set it free."

"Like hell you are."

"How can I learn anything about what I can and can't do with dragons if this one is chained like a prisoner?"

"It *is* a prisoner," Orin replied. "And you can work with that monster while it's in chains."

"You're more of a monster than it is."

Orin shrugged. "I'm fine with that."

Turning to Cole, Lexi decided to ignore Orin. "I have to go closer, and I have to do it alone. It has to be *just* me."

"That's not going to happen," Cole said.

Lexi rolled her eyes over his stubborn nature, but she would argue about this because she was right. "I have to. Stay back and watch, but don't come any closer."

"Lexi—"

"I'm not arguing about this. It's already chained, scared, and angry; it doesn't need all of us approaching at once. I *am* going alone."

A muscle jumped in his cheek, the shadows shifted, and the dragon snuffed again before jerking on its chains. Lexi's heart raced as she forced a serene smile to her face. She wasn't fooling Cole.

"Cole, I have to go alone."

"Lexi—"

Rising onto her toes, she clasped his cheeks and kissed him before releasing his face and stepping back. "I'm going alone."

Before he could protest further, she stepped away. His jaw locked, and a muscle twitched in his cheek, but he didn't come after her as she edged further away. Lexi wiped her sweaty palms on her pants before striding toward the dragon.

"Don't get too close," Orin cautioned. "Those chains have some range to them."

CHAPTER THREE

As LEXI cautiously approached the dragon, it lifted its head and narrowed its eyes until she was staring into the black, glistening center of its slitted pupils. The sound it released was a cross between an irate cobra and a cornered tiger.

Her bladder clenched in response, and she almost crossed her legs, but Orin would snicker if she did. And if he did, she might torch his ass.

When she was only twenty feet away, the creature lunged forward. Lexi stumbled away from the snout coming toward her, but the chains bolted into the wall caught when it was ten feet away. They jerked the dragon back.

A startled hiss escaped the dragon when it slammed into the ground and its impact shook the cave. Without thinking and instinctively seeking to help it, Lexi sprang forward before catching herself and skidding to a stop.

She felt sorry for the poor thing; no one should treat a creature like this, but she'd prefer not to be its breakfast. Though the chains around its jaws should hold, she wasn't taking any chances.

The dragon lifted its head to glower at her. A puff of smoke flowed from its nostrils; each one of them was the size of her head.

The dragon was smaller than most of the others she'd seen, making her think it might be younger, but it could just be smaller than the others. Either way, that didn't make it any less lethal.

Its green scales, shimmering with yellows and oranges, resembled a starburst of color when it moved certain ways in the torchlight. The dragon was enraged... *and gorgeous.*

Her fingers twitched with the urge to pet it, comfort it, and connect with it, but she balled them into fists to keep from reaching out to the creature. That would probably be a surefire way to end up dead.

"Hi," she whispered, and the dragon released another puff of smoke. "My name is Elexiandra. Most call me Lexi; my dad sometimes calls me Andi."

She didn't tell it the rebels she helped save also called her Andi. The dragon wasn't overly impressed with her words as another puff of smoke issued from its nostrils.

Its talons scoured the stone when it tried to wiggle closer, stretching its chains as far as they would go. Lexi gulped as she eyed the chains. They didn't look like they were about to break, but she doubted she'd get much warning.

As the dragon tested the bounds of its restraints, the nails-on-a-chalkboard sound its talons created made her wince, and she resisted the impulse to run. She didn't know much about dragons, but they wouldn't respect cowardice.

It moved closer until its nostrils were only feet away when another puff of smoke billowed into her face. If there was some connection between her and the dragons, this one sure didn't care about it.

But then, she wouldn't be too receptive if someone tossed her into chains and locked her in a cave so others could explore with her.

∾

COLE'S CLAWS dug into his palms, drawing blood that filled his hands as Lexi inched closer to the dragon. His shoulders hunched as the creature lunged at her with another rattle of chains.

Once again, its bound legs gave out beneath it, and the cave's floor heaved when it hit the ground. Lexi's hand flew out as if seeking to comfort it, and the dragon surged toward her.

Around the dragon, the shadows on the walls crept closer while Cole kept his focus on the beast who would love to eat his fiancée. Those shadows would tear this thing apart before it got the chance to attack her. He'd make sure of it.

"I worked hard to catch this dragon; don't you dare destroy it," Orin muttered to him.

"Then you better hope those chains hold," Cole growled.

"They will."

Lexi's head spun toward him, and her shoulders went back as she frowned at the encroaching shadows. "We don't need the shadows."

"If it doesn't hurt you, I won't hurt it," he replied.

His voice sounded far calmer than he felt. This was a necessary evil, but he didn't have to like it.

"You shouldn't be calling on the shadows," Lexi said.

Because the more he did, the deeper they dug into his soul and the more their darkness spread through him. They were both aware of that, but he would use them to keep her safe no matter how much they affected him.

No matter the cost to his soul.

"I'm not a concern right now; *you* are," he told her.

Her slender nose wrinkled in annoyance. He had excellent vision, but from here, he couldn't see the freckles dotting the bridge of her nose. Freckles he knew were all scrunched up in the adorable way they did when she was irritated with him.

In the torchlight, the deep red strands of her auburn hair were the color of blood. The ominous hue made his claws dig in deeper as he resisted the impulse to shift into a wolf.

Or what if it landed on top, knocked a lot of the rocks above them free, and crushed them all?

Race cars went slower than her heart, but as she attempted to get some saliva back into her suddenly parched throat, she realized the dragon outside most likely wouldn't want to kill the chained one. So squishing was probably out, but fire was still in.

As the others gathered around her and Cole, the dragon at the front of the cave stuck its head back in. It snorted once before retreating.

They could always open a portal out of here, but they would have to leave the chained dragon behind and forfeit their chance at answers. They could always try to take the dragon through a portal, but she imagined that would be about as easy as catching a cloud.

"Come out, child. I will not harm you."

Lexi's eyes widened as the sweet, feminine voice drifted through the cave. It sounded kind, but its commanding tone refused disobedience. That voice demanded respect and obedience, and there was no *way* it came from a *dragon*.

"Who else is out there?" Cole demanded of the others.

"I didn't see anyone else," Niall said; his face had lost some coloring as he stood and gawked at the end of the cave.

"A dragon would have eaten anyone else," Brokk said.

"There has to be someone else; dragons can't speak," Cole stated.

"Have you ever tried talking to one?" Orin asked. When Cole shot him a look, he shrugged. "I'm just saying, I doubt it's something anyone, other than maybe an arach, has tried before. They don't exactly come across as conversationalists."

When the dragon behind them scraped its claws against the rocks, they turned to discover it had inched close enough that its snout was only feet away. The audible gulp of the others was loud in the hush of the cave.

"If you seek answers, child, then you should come out," the sweet, steely voice said from the front of the cave.

"I have to go talk to her," Lexi said.

"She might not be talking to you," Kaylia said.

"Who else would she be talking to?"

"It can't be a dragon talking," Maverick muttered as he ran a hand through his dark, wavy, brown hair. His chestnut-colored eyes were troubled, his broad shoulders back, and at six foot nine, he was the tallest in the cave. "Dragons don't talk."

"And again, have you ever tried?" Orin inquired.

"Shut up, Orin," her dad said as he studied the front of the cave. "I don't like this."

"None of us do," Sahira said.

Lexi took a deep breath as she tried to calm her chaotic thoughts. If it *was* the dragon talking to her, there were so many answers they could get from the creature… if it didn't eat her or stomp her first.

"I will not ask again, child. Come out, or I will come in," the voice stated.

And if it was the dragon and it decided to come in, judging by its size, it would tear this cave down around itself before they ever got any answers.

"I'm coming!" Lexi called before she could think about it any further.

Besides, there wasn't anything to think about. She didn't have any other choices. They'd come here for answers, and this creature was promising them.

"Wait," Cole grasped her arm before she could take a step. "You're not going out there."

"I don't have a choice," she told him.

"There are always choices," Kaylia replied.

"Do you see a different one in this scenario? Besides, we're all here to learn how I get along with dragons, and this one"—she thrust her thumb over her shoulder at the chained dragon behind them— "couldn't care less about what I am."

"You haven't had much time with it," Varo said. "Perhaps with more—"

"There is no more," Lexi said. "The one out there will make sure of that."

"Dragons can't talk," her dad said. "Let whoever's out there come in."

Lexi glanced back at the front of the cave; it made no sense to her, but he was wrong. "There is *no* one else out there. I have to go."

When Cole's hand tightened on her arm, Lexi glanced nervously at the shadows as they edged closer to him.

"Cole," she whispered.

"If they're what's necessary to keep you safe, then so be it," he stated.

Lexi's entire being protested his words. She did *not* want this. She didn't want *them*.

But she had no other choice; they came with Cole now. They were dark, twisted, and vicious, but they were a part of *him*. Nothing could change that.

She loved him too much to lose him to the malevolence and power the shadows brought. But she couldn't fight that battle right now, not while she was dealing with talking dragons. She only had so much room for crazy, and talking dragons won over the shadows.

"I have to go see what she has to say," Lexi said in a voice she hoped would calm him, but none of his tension eased.

"It's necessary." Varo's calm voice and soothing presence normally took some of the edge off a tense situation; it did nothing now. "She must learn of her destiny, Cole. You can't stand in her way."

"I'm not standing in her way!" Cole snapped at his youngest brother. "I'm making sure she stays safe."

"Then you have to let her go."

"Fuck off, Varo!" Cole exploded.

Lexi winced, and Varo's head bowed. She'd never expected Cole to talk to Varo in such a way; Orin definitely, Brokk on a rare occasion, but *never* Varo.

He was closer to the brink of losing it than she'd realized—a fact emphasized by the popping of his joints as the fingers around her arm lengthened and cracked. His claws flexed, and hair emerged from his knuckles as the lycan part of him, the one seeking to protect its mate, tried to take over.

"Easy," she murmured as she rested her free hand over his. "It's okay."

"I will not harm her... or you... Shadow Reaver," the voice said from the front.

"Oh, Hecate," Kaylia whispered. "The dragons know about the Reaver."

Which was *more* of a reason to talk to the dragon. *No* one else knew much about the powers inhabiting Cole since he survived the trials making him the dark fae king.

"*I* know," the voice from outside replied.

"It *is* the dragon," Orin breathed.

"Maybe *you* should go talk to it then," her dad suggested, and Maverick snickered.

"I'm good," Orin replied.

"I have to go," Lexi said again.

Cole's claws retracted, and his broad shoulders rose and fell as he bowed his head. When his black hair fell onto his forehead, she tenderly brushed it away before running her fingers over the tip of a pointed ear.

"You're not going without me," he said.

CHAPTER FIVE

COLE DREW the shadows closer around him and Lexi as they walked toward the front of the cave. He ignored Lexi's nervous glance at them as they swelled up to surround them like bees erupting from their hive to take out a predator.

The shadows swirled around them to create a wall that blocked out the sun streaming through the open end of the cave. The wind kicked up pebbles outside and sent dust swirling through the air. The dust blowing across the cave entrance briefly obscured his view of what lay beyond, but then the dragon lowered its head and peered inside again.

When the creature vanished, anger rippled up Cole's spine as his teeth ground together. He'd prefer nothing more than to destroy the overgrown lizard before Lexi got anywhere near it, but he had to see what would happen between them.

And they had to hear what this thing could tell them... if it didn't try to kill them. If that happened, he and the shadows would keep her protected.

"Let the shadows go, Cole," Lexi whispered. "Release them. She's not going to attack us."

"I'll release them when I'm certain of that."

Lexi didn't protest any further, but they were also at the end of the cave. Drawing her close against his side, he locked his arm around her waist as the shadows enclosed them.

Reluctantly, he stepped out of the cave with her at his side. The dragon's head coiled, so its chin tucked against its long neck; it peered down at them from golden eyes with slitted pupils.

He recognized the massive beast, with its brilliant red coloring and flecks of yellow along its belly, as the dragon in the throne room when he killed Malakai. It was also the one who entered the Gloaming. He'd become too familiar with the powerful creature recently.

"Release the shadows, Reaver," the dragon said. "She is safe with me."

This thing *was* talking and might know something about this Shadow Reaver bullshit. It was all too fantastic and good to be true, but if a dragon could speak, it certainly had to possess more knowledge and power.

"And as much as I don't like it and would prefer to kill you, you are also safe with me," the dragon continued.

Cole didn't lower the barrier.

"I see," the dragon murmured before shifting its attention to Lexi.

"You know about the Shadow Reaver?" Lexi asked.

"I do," the dragon replied.

It lowered its head to examine Lexi. Shifting toward it, the shadows sought to defend and protect her, but the dragon didn't move closer.

"Let me see you more clearly," the dragon said.

"I'm not releasing the shadows," Cole stated.

"I didn't expect you would. But I want to see her arach form."

Lexi frowned. "My arach form?"

"Yes, show me yourself in the sunlight."

Lexi glanced at him before closing her eyes and releasing the shield she'd erected around herself. Golden light and silver scale-like markings spread across her until she stood before them, bathed in a golden glow.

When she opened her eyes, they were the same striking gold color as the dragons, and her pupils had become slitted. She was always beautiful, but seeing her like this was breathtaking.

The dragon breathed out what could only be considered a sigh; it blew Lexi's hair back from her face and stirred her clothes. Its face softened as much as a dragon's face could, and an "Oh" issued from it.

Then, like a dog rolling over to expose its belly, the creature rested its chin on the ground as it gazed at Lexi with longing.

"It *is* true," the beast murmured. "You *are* real. An arach still lives."

"I'm real," Lexi whispered. "But are *you*? How is it possible a dragon can *talk?* Do you all do so?"

Cole swore the corners of the dragon's mouth pulled into a smile. *The thing is smiling.*

After hearing a dragon talk, he didn't think anything could astound him anymore; he was wrong.

"Not all of us do so," the dragon replied.

The dragon lifted its head from the ground and curled it above them in a proud gesture and—as much as he hated to admit it—a beautiful one. The sun glittering on its scales emphasized its radiant coloring.

"I, alone, am the speaker," the dragon continued. "Many, *many* millennia ago, the arach imbued my great-grandfather with the ability to talk with them. When he perished, it passed to my grand-mother, then it went to my mother, and on to me when she died. I am Alina… the speaker of dragons. Though, no one has heard my voice in a thousand years."

"It's a pleasure to meet you, Alina," Lexi replied. "I'm Elexiandra, but almost everyone calls me Lexi. Why has no one heard your voice?"

"I talk with the arach and the arach only."

"But you don't report to the Lord?"

"I would *never* share my voice with that usurper. He may control us, but he is *not* privy to us."

"I see," Lexi murmured.

The dragon lowered her head again and tilted it to the side while studying Lexi. "How is it you exist, child?"

"I suppose the same way as everyone else. My parents had a little too much fun one night."

The dragon tipped her head to the other side but didn't come any closer, and Cole didn't get any ill intent from her. She was simply curious.

"Your parents," the creature murmured. "Who are your parents, child?"

"I've been told my mother was Galeah. I don't know the name of my father," Lexi replied.

"Galeah," the dragon breathed and closed her eyes. "I have not heard that name in millennia."

Cole could have sworn the dragon was both happy and sad about this, but these creatures had no such emotions. They were monstrous, killing machines...

Except, this one wasn't killing. She was *talking* to them, and she knew things about them, and she was *smiling*!

Cole glanced back at the cave to discover the others had crept closer to hover in the shadows. Orin was the only one not focused solely on the dragon as he looked at Lexi and him too. Disbelief filled his brother's black eyes when Orin's gaze met his gaze.

"I should have known," the dragon murmured and opened her eyes again. "You look much like your mother. She was a powerful woman, beautiful, and a princess. And if your mother was Galeah, then your father was Irad."

When Lexi tried to surge toward the dragon, Cole restrained her against him. He chose to ignore the irritated look she shot him.

"You knew my father?" Lexi inquired.

"I did," Alina replied. "He was part of the reason the war, that ultimately led to the fall of the arach, started."

CHAPTER SIX

LEXI SWALLOWED the lump lodged in her throat. Alina's words repeatedly ran through her mind as she tried to figure out her next question. Hundreds of them formed on the tip of her tongue, but Alina's revelation froze her mouth as she tried to process that her *father* was responsible for the mess they were in now.

"That's not possible," Lexi croaked.

Despite her denial, she had no idea why it *couldn't* be possible. She'd never met the man, and he never had a hand in raising her. She existed because he once did, but she had no right to say what he could and couldn't be capable of doing.

"It is," Alina said.

Her tender voice should have been soothing, but it only irritated Lexi. She didn't want to be soothed, coddled, or treated like a child. She sought answers, but she couldn't get those answers if she didn't ask the damn questions.

She took a deep breath and lifted her chin to meet Alina's inquisitive gaze. "How? *Why?*"

"For your mother."

"I don't understand."

"You understand love," Alina said. When her eyes flashed

toward Cole, they hardened, but they softened when her attention shifted back to Lexi. "You understand the lengths others will go to in order to protect their loved ones and be with them."

"Of course I do, but why would that start a war?"

"Someone told me disagreements on ruling the Shadow Realms resulted in a civil war that dethroned the ruling family and sent them into exile. But the war didn't end after that, and eventually, the arachs all destroyed each other," Cole said.

"That is true," Alina said. "Except there were many who didn't want the ruling family banished from Dragonia and worked to bring them back. They all fought to the death over who should and would rule. Well... apparently not *all* of them."

Alina shifted her attention to Lexi. "Your mother was one of the most powerful beings in Dragonia. She had years of fine breeding and the best bloodlines flowing through her to make her such.

"It was always known she would wed a nobleman, which your father most assuredly was *not*. He was a commoner. Someone of low birth, a blacksmith by trade. He was extremely talented, the best in all the land, but not worthy of a princess."

"She disagreed," Lexi retorted.

She hadn't known her birth father, but she wouldn't stand to hear him considered as *lesser*. Alina's mouth curved into a smile.

"She did. I assume they met by chance one day at the market, fell in love, and when your grandmother discovered that love, she forbade your mother from seeing him again. Of course, we all know how forbidding someone works out. Your father was sentenced to death when their continued affair was uncovered."

"For what?" Lexi gasped.

"For disobeying the queen. What the queen didn't see coming was her daughter pleading for his life, fighting for his life, and ultimately saving him from the dungeons. Nor did she expect an uprising amongst the peasants to be a direct result of her actions.

"The commoners weren't as powerful as the royalty of Dragonia, but there were a lot more of them, and they were tired of being treated as lesser. Combine that with an increasing movement amid the nobility to take more control of the Shadow Realms and to exert the arach dominance further over the other immortals, and that spark lit the powder keg.

"Some of those dissatisfied nobility saw the rising rebellion among the peasants as their opportunity to fuel the fires so they could seize control from the queen who did *not* want to exert further dominance over the realms. But they whispered that if she couldn't control her daughter, she wasn't strong enough to rule the land.

"I don't think your mother or father saw what happened coming and never meant to become the catalyst. I believe they simply wanted to be left alone so they could love each other."

Lexi's heart ached, and she blinked away the tears burning her eyes as she rested her hand over Cole's. What she wouldn't give to be left alone to love him, in peace. She feared it would never happen, but she would fight with every fiber of her being to make it so.

"What happened afterward?" she asked.

CHAPTER SEVEN

"It spiraled out of control until a full-blown war raged," Alina said. "And that war wiped out all the arach. Or, not quite all, as *your* parents escaped for at least some time. Maybe for quite a *long* time, as you feel quite young to me, child."

Lexi really didn't appreciate being called a child, but considering this dragon was probably hundreds, if not *thousands*, of years older than her, she could suck it up for now. Besides, they required more answers.

"I'm twenty-four," Lexi said.

"A mere babe," Alina whispered.

"I'm stronger than my age would make you think," Lexi replied with more anger than she'd anticipated. They could *not* let Alina stop talking to them.

Alina nodded and rose over them again. She gazed down through the shadows surrounding them.

"What do you know about the Shadow Reaver?" Lexi inquired. While she was fascinated by her parents' history and the adversity and sadness they endured, they had more important things to focus on now. "Why won't you kill Cole? It's obvious the two of you don't like each other."

"I would gladly kill him… if I could. He murdered Tanis, one of my brethren."

"That fucking *monster* ate my father," Cole retorted.

If dragons could look indifferent, then this was the expression they'd be wearing.

"She was commanded to do so," Alina replied blandly.

"Didn't mean she had to do it," Cole snarled.

Lexi squeezed his hand as the shadows shifted. Her touch didn't calm him as it usually did, and from the corner of her eye, she saw Orin and Brokk creeping closer. The last thing she needed was their rage over their father's death to fuel Cole's.

Varo moved to intercept his brothers. He nudged them back toward the cave, but neither retreated. Thankfully, they didn't come any closer either.

"Yes, she did," Alina replied. "We must obey whoever sits on the throne. We are bound to do so."

"What about Lexi?" Orin demanded. "Will you obey her too?"

"If she manages to reclaim the throne that is her birthright, I shall obey her too, but not before then."

"What about the other dragons?" Brokk inquired.

"We all are bound by the laws of the arach and the dragons. Those laws require us to obey the ruler of Dragonia. Those same laws expressly forbid us from *ever* hurting any arach, which is the dragon's supreme law. The Lord can command us to turn on Lexi, but we will not do so."

"I guess that's something," Brokk muttered.

"The Lord can command us to kill whoever stands by her side, except the Reaver," Alina continued. "We are also forbidden from killing the Reaver."

"How is that possible when Cole *just* became the Shadow Reaver?" Lexi demanded. "Those laws have to be thousands of years old."

"More years than any of us could begin to grasp," Alina

confirmed. "But we are forbidden from killing anyone forged with arach powers."

It took too many seconds for the implications of her words to sink in. When they did, the air left Lexi's lungs in a rush. She felt like an idiot for not grasping the meaning behind Alina's words the second they left the dragon's mouth, but her mind still refused to process it fully.

Before Lexi could respond, Maverick eloquently put her question into words, "What the fuck?"

"Are you saying my increased control over the shadows came from arach magic?" Cole asked.

"Your control of the shadows came from a dark fae's ability to manipulate them. Your ability to turn those shadows into a destructive, murderous force unlike anything the realms has seen before came from arach magic."

CHAPTER EIGHT

LEXI COULDN'T BREATHE as everything in her froze. The *shadows*, the things she feared more than the Lord, were a part of Cole now because of *arach* magic.

Her ancestors did this to Cole. *Her* ancestors infused him with this dark energy twisting him into someone different and making him think he was becoming a monster. *They* had given him the ability to tear the extremities from Malakai without touching him, before Cole beat him into a bloody pulp.

She'd always felt a little sorry for the arach for destroying themselves. She'd believed the realms were a better place when they held the throne because there wasn't so much violence and because the human world was intact, instead of the bloody, chaotic ruins that now reined there.

Believed things must have been better before a madman sat on the throne and controlled the dragons.

But the arach weren't any better!

They destroyed themselves because they couldn't accept the love between a princess and a commoner. They tore themselves apart because some of them sought more power over the realms when it wasn't theirs for the taking.

The arach were a race who forced magic onto a good man when he wasn't expecting it, and he *did not* deserve to bear its curse. They *never* had any right to decide that for Cole.

The arach were as monstrous as the Lord… maybe more so. When they made their destructive choices, their minds weren't rotten and corrupted by a throne that wasn't theirs.

And then a terrifying possibility occurred to her—had the throne corrupted the arach too?

"Were the arach also insane?" she whispered.

Alina blinked at her. "Insane?"

"Like the Lord? Were they completely crazed lunatics like him?"

"Not at all." Alina sounded astounded by the mere suggestion. "The Lord was corrupted by magic that doesn't belong to him and power that was never his to wield."

"Then *why* did they destroy themselves over a forbidden love and a thirst for more power?"

"Because that is what some immortals and mortals do. Immortals seek power they shouldn't have, and once they attain it, they thirst for more. And they will destroy anyone or anything who stands in their way of getting it.

"That is the way of the realms; it's always been so. Before your parents really lit the spark, there were occasional uprisings and murmurs of discontent in Dragonia. It was only a matter of time before it all went up in flames."

"How bleak," Lexi whispered.

But it was true. She wouldn't seek more power if she ever claimed the throne, but others would, and many would try to wrest it from her. Their battle wouldn't end with destroying the Lord.

"If they weren't crazy, *why* would the arach create a magic that could… could…." Lexi took a deep breath to control herself as her voice started to take on a hysterical tone.

A magic that could what? Destroy Cole or the realms if the

Shadow Reaver prophecy was true? And if it was real, then she was bound to die.

She glanced at Cole, who was studying her with eyes full of understanding. She yearned to drape her arms around his neck, bury her face there, and cling to him as she chased away all his shadows, but she couldn't shut this out.

There was no hiding from this.

"Why did they do something to create the Shadow Reaver?" she inquired in a voice far stronger than she'd anticipated. "Why would they *want* the Reaver to exist?"

Alina lowered her head again until her beautiful, golden eyes met Lexi's. The sadness in those eyes told Lexi she would *not* like what the dragon had to say.

"I believe it was to protect you," Alina replied. "Or I should say to protect the arach, but since you are the last one, then it is for *you*."

Lexi's lungs constricted like all the oxygen was sucked out of the air. She almost looked down to make sure the ground hadn't plummeted from under her, but she couldn't move her head.

The lump in her throat became a boulder; it would have choked her if there was any oxygen to breathe. Her hands clenched on Cole, but she couldn't bring herself to look at him again.

She was the reason he was battling this demon. Out of all the many things she could have imagined Alina saying, this appalling possibility hadn't occurred to her, and she would give anything not to have heard it.

"No!" she blurted as the air suddenly rushed back into her. "No! I don't need that kind of protection. Tell me how to fix it."

"And *I* don't want it fixed."

Cole's lethal tone caused the hair on her nape to rise. Gulping, she turned her head to look up at him. The shadows around him emphasized the coldness in his silver eyes.

"Cole—"

"I'll do whatever I can to protect you and use whatever means necessary."

"Even if it destroys you?" she cried.

"I won't allow that to happen, and neither will you."

Oh, how she wished it were so simple, but they both knew it was nowhere near that easy. She'd witnessed his recent unraveling after killing Malakai and the Lord's men. She'd stood on the balcony with him as he struggled against the shadows trying to take him over.

She'd stopped him from unraveling, but as his powers grew and the shadows corrupted him more, it wouldn't get easier for him. And it would become more difficult for her to pull him away from the shadows' enticing grip.

"*I* don't want this," she said.

"That doesn't matter; it is done," Alina said. "If I knew a way to change it, I wouldn't allow it, and neither would the Reaver. He exists to protect *you*. He exists because of the arach."

Lexi bit her lip against blurting *fuck you*, but it wouldn't stop Alina from calling her *child* if she started acting like one. And it wasn't the dragon's fault; she'd asked the question. Alina simply answered it.

Instead, Lexi worked to steady herself as she tried to piece together the scattered remnants of her chaotic thoughts.

CHAPTER NINE

"I DON'T UNDERSTAND. How did the arach know they should create the magic for the Shadow Reaver? And why hasn't there been a Reaver before Cole? The dark fae trials to crown their king or queen have been going on for...?" Kaylia's question trailed off.

"At least fifty thousand years," Cole said. "Not much is known before then."

"History has a way of being lost when there is so much of it," Varo said.

"Too true," Alina murmured.

"Could the arach see the future?" Kaylia inquired as she brushed back a strand of silvery blonde hair. Her pewter gray eyes were intent on Alina.

Good question. Lexi shifted her attention to Alina as she awaited the answer.

"And who are you?" Alina inquired.

"I am Kaylia, a crone."

"So, you are also old and have some power."

"I do."

"She's also a friend," Lexi said. "A good one who has been helping me try to learn my powers."

"And have you learned your powers?" Alina asked.

"I've learned to stop myself from glowing—"

"That's not glowing. That's your mark of the dragon," Alina interrupted.

"My what?"

"The mark of the dragon. The arach and dragons are inexplicably entwined. You bear our mark, and we bear yours. You become more like one of us when your shield comes down, and it draws us to you."

"You are?"

"Yes."

"What is my mark on you?"

"Our fire is the mark of the arach."

"Holy shit," Orin muttered.

Lexi lifted her hands to stare at the glow and silver markings on her palms. As she stared at them, she pictured all those she loved, and fire sputtered to life on her fingertips.

"The mark of the arach," she murmured. "And I bear the mark of the dragon."

"You do," Alina said.

"And could the arach see the future? Did they somehow glimpse something that made them decide to create the Reaver?" Lexi asked.

"I was not privy to all the arachs' secrets, just as they were not privy to all of ours. We are entwined, but we also live separate lives. But no, they couldn't see the future. They wouldn't have perished if they could, and I know *that* for certain," Alina replied. "They never saw their downfall coming."

"Why were there no Shadow Reavers before Cole if the magic to create the Reaver came from the trials?"

"I do not know," Alina said. "Perhaps the magic was only set to release when it sensed something from a certain dark fae."

"Like what?" Cole inquired.

"Like the ability to carry the magic; maybe it required a special brand of courage, strength, or power."

And Cole was the most powerful dark fae ever. A dark fae's ciphers indicated their power; all dark fae kept at least some of their ciphers hidden, but when he revealed them to her, Lexi learned Cole's covered him from head to toe.

If power was what triggered the release of the Shadow Reaver magic, then Cole's would most certainly have done it. Combine that with his courage and strength, and she couldn't think of anyone else it could have been.

"*How* did the arach know to create the Shadow Reaver to protect them?" Lexi asked.

"I do not know," Alina replied. "As I have said, I was not privy to all their secrets. The arach and the dark fae created the trials so long ago that I doubt many, if *any*, of the arach alive at the end knew the answer. They all knew of the legend of the Reaver, all in Dragonia did, but how many still believed in it by then is unknown to me. I did not believe it until I saw the Reaver, but now I know."

"The original arach who had a hand in helping the dark fae create the trials must have known something about Lexi and possibly Cole. There would be no prophecy otherwise," Kaylia said. "When the last light blooms, the Shadow Reaver shall rise. When the last light falls, the Shadow Reaver will destroy us all. Lexi is clearly the last light, and Cole is obviously the Reaver."

"No one believes in the prophecy," Cole stated.

Lexi saw the doubt on Kaylia's face, but she didn't argue with him.

"Prophecies are often foolish things," Alina agreed, "but this one has a ring of truth to it."

"I'm not going to let anything happen to her," Cole said.

"I'm happy to hear that."

"Who is *us?*" Maverick inquired.

"What?" Kaylia asked.

"The prophecy states the Shadow Reaver will destroy us all, but who is *us?* Is it all immortals? Is it humans and immortals? Is it the dark fae, the arach, the crones? Who is *us?*"

"And *that* is what makes prophecies such ridiculous, inane things," Cole said. "Their vagueness makes them pointless, and they notoriously never come true. People and immortals see what they want in their words and run with it."

"I agree with the Reaver." Alina looked pained to say so.

"How come the dragon in there didn't recognize her as an arach if she bears the mark of the dragon?" Orin demanded and pointed his finger at the cave.

"Was capturing him your doing?" Alina asked Lexi.

"No. I would never do that."

"Was it his?" she jerked her head toward Orin.

"Don't eat him!" Lexi blurted, startled by her instinct to keep Orin alive.

He drove her crazy, but he loved Cole, and Cole loved him, even if they would gladly beat each other bloody. But while she'd prefer it if Orin didn't die, it might be nice if Alina gargled him around her mouth like mouthwash before spitting him back out.

It might take Orin down a peg or two. But probably not. He'd start bragging about how he'd survived being eaten by a dragon and become more insufferable.

"I'll do whatever's necessary to defeat the Lord," Orin replied defiantly. "And we have to learn about her and the dragons."

That gargling thing might be worth it. When Lexi leaned forward and cupped her hand against her mouth, Alina lowered her head toward her. Though a wall of shadows separated them, a conspiring air surrounded them.

"Can you put him in your mouth and gargle him around a little before spitting him out?" she asked.

"I might swallow him if I did," Alina replied.

Lexi debated if it was worth the risk as she recalled all the things Orin had done, like imprisoning her father and keeping it from her, blackmailing her into helping him, and his overall shitty attitude. Was Alina accidentally eating him worth it to scare him?

"Lexi," Cole growled when she didn't immediately respond.

"I guess you shouldn't do it," she grumbled and pulled back.

"It's time to set Tymin free," Alina said.

"Who?" Lexi asked.

Alina's slender head twisted toward the cave, and her scales rippled like blood flowing over rocks in the sunlight. "Tymin, my friend. If we are to work together, you cannot imprison us. The Lord already has us in mental shackles."

"I would never... that's not...." Lexi stammered over her words before saying. "I'm sorry; we didn't know. We were trying to see how a dragon would react to me, and Tymin was *not* happy to see me."

"No one is happy to be in chains, but he also doesn't know what you are. All other dragons believe the arach are dead, and if your shield was up when you went in there, he wouldn't know what you are. To him, you are the enemy."

"Is *that* what the dragon marks are for? To let the dragons know what I am?"

"To let us know, call us to you, and show we are united. In the shadows, he has no idea what you are."

"So how do I set him free if the marks fade once I'm out of the sun?"

"They'll last for long enough for him to see. That should be enough."

"Okay," Lexi said, but she wasn't so crazy about that *should be enough* statement.

She'd prefer not to die in a cave if things went wrong. But she couldn't leave Tymin in chains either.

She threw her shoulders back as she turned away from Alina. Striding toward the cave, she prayed Alina wasn't simply trying to kill her off. Maybe Alina couldn't get past the shadows and this was her way of getting rid of Lexi and making the Lord happy.

She gulped, but she had no choice. If they were going to make any headway with the dragons and against the Lord, she had to return to that extremely angry dragon.

CHAPTER TEN

"I NEED the key to set him free," Lexi said to Orin and held out her hand.

He gawked at her before closing his jaw. "No. They could both eat us—"

"We have no right to imprison them, and if we're going to form an alliance with the dragons, then we have to give them a show of good faith."

Cole did *not* like her going anywhere near the pissed-off creature at the end of the cave, but he had to admit she was right. "I will set it free," he said.

"It's more likely to eat *you* than *me*," Lexi protested.

"The shadows will protect me."

When she leveled him with her most withering stare, even Orin stepped back.

"That dragon is here because of me. Orin brought it here to test my connection to them. Alina is here... wait." Lexi turned toward the dragon waiting behind them. "How did you know *where* we were?"

"I felt a break in your shield," Alina said. "Not long before I arrived. It was enough for me to latch on and follow you."

"But you didn't know where we were or what this place looked like?"

"But I felt *you*. That is enough for a dragon. Instead of imagining a place, I pictured the mark of the dragon, and it brought me to you. It is not the first time I've felt it recently."

"Then why only come now?" Brokk demanded. "Why didn't you come the other times?"

"She did," Lexi whispered. "That's why you went to the Gloaming."

"I sensed something from you in there," Alina confirmed.

"But that was before I ever started to glow."

"It was a weak spark I sensed, but it was something," Alina said. "No other dragon would have felt it, but I am the speaker. Arach magic also imbues me, and therefore we have a closer bond than you do with my brethren. But once I arrived in the Gloaming, I felt nothing from you."

"But the dragon mark came out for the first time after you left."

"I sensed it then too, but I didn't return."

"Why not?" Niall asked.

"Because after I failed to find her in the Gloaming, I believed it was a foolish longing I was chasing and not an arach. They were all supposed to be dead, so every time I've experienced the pull of the mark since then, I ignored it. I refused to chase silly things that couldn't possibly be real. It is not good for us under the Lord; we yearn for freedom, and I believed I was falsely seeking an impossible end to his oppression... until Lexi revealed herself at the ball."

Cole ignored the twinge of pity and understanding he felt toward the dragon and her friends. He couldn't imagine what it must be like for them to be chained to someone like the Lord, but he could vividly picture one of them swallowing his father. His sympathy was short-lived.

"Why didn't the other dragons feel the pull of her mark?" Varo asked.

"I cannot speak for all of them, but I imagine most never felt it. Even today, what brought me here wasn't strong. And if they did, they probably assumed, like me, it was simply a longing for the impossible. The call has grown stronger from her, but it is *not* what we are used to from the arach. I don't know if that's because she is unsure of her abilities. *Why* have I felt nothing from you until recently?" Alina asked Lexi.

"I had her powers bound to keep her safe and hidden from the Lord," Del said.

"*I* made the potion to do so," Sahira said.

"You bound an *arach?*" Alina sounded truly horrified by this revelation.

"I'd be dead if they didn't," Lexi said.

"Most likely. Now I understand why we did not know about you until recently and why your call is weak. You are new to your powers and learning, but they will grow. And now that we know of your existence and to acknowledge the call, we can find you."

"Amazing," Del breathed as Kaylia rested a hand over her heart.

"And you never felt the call from her parents over the years?" Cole asked.

"No. When they left Dragonia, they effectively shut us all out. We had all assumed they died in the war too. If your parents shut off their marks, we wouldn't be able to find them."

"So, if I'm glowing, I can call you to me?" Lexi asked.

"Yes. Me and any other dragon. When there were many arach, it was a beautiful spectacle when they all got together to reveal their marks. We had a celebration every year...."

Her wistful words trailed off, and she looked out over the rocky land. Her tail swished behind her on the ground, and her talons bit into the rock as sorrow emanated from her. Cole did *not* like these beasts, but he softened toward this one... a little.

The rest could rot in Hell, but they probably thought the same about him, including Alina. And for all he knew, she was setting them up to die. Once he was in the cave, he and the shadows would be away from her. She could try to kill them then.

Lexi wiggled her fingers at Orin. "The key."

His brother scowled as he dug it out of his pocket. "And if she tries to eat us after you enter the cave?"

"Give her the key," Cole commanded, and Orin hesitated before handing it over.

Lexi slid the key into her pocket. "You'll have to take your chances." Then she looked at all the others before glancing at Alina. "You'll be okay with her. I'm not so sure about the chained dragon; you should probably leave before I release it."

"We'll be fine," Del assured her as he squeezed her shoulder. "I'm not going anywhere until I know you're safe. Take care of yourself."

"I'm not leaving either," Sahira stated.

"I'll erect a shield around us," Kaylia said. "It will keep us safe."

"Good," Lexi said.

"You should all stay out here," Cole said before looking pointedly at Orin. "Especially *you*."

His brother crossed his arms over his chest. "Fine."

Cole glanced back at Alina; if she tried to kill them, he would make her pay for it. The mark of the dragon was still visible when Cole clasped Lexi's arm and they entered the cave. The dragon's talons scratched the rocky floor as they approached; it knew they were coming.

The further they progressed into the cave, the more Lexi's light dimmed. However, the silver marks and golden glow were still evident as they neared the imprisoned beast.

"What if the marks are gone by the time we get there and it doesn't recognize me?" she whispered.

"I don't think they'll be gone by then."

Lexi paused before replying. "What if it *does* recognize me and it's so pissed off it doesn't care what I am?"

"Then we'll have to destroy it."

She inhaled sharply, and her step faltered. Cole realized his words had come out colder than he'd intended, but the iciness of the shadows he drew to him was creeping through his blood and deeper into his soul.

Still, that was no reason to be so abrupt with her. The shadows already upset her; he couldn't add to it. And he couldn't let her know how much they were affecting him.

"We'll do whatever is necessary to protect you," he said more gently.

Her next words indicated she wasn't buying his warmer tone.

"Let the shadows go. We'll be fine without them."

"Once we finish with the dragons."

Lexi shook her head and pushed back a strand of hair that fell into her eye. She started to say more but stopped when the dragon came into view.

Little natural light pierced this deep into the cave, but it was enough for a small glow to emanate from Lexi. Her step slowed as they approached the dragon. The beast's eyes narrowed before widening. And then its head came off the ground.

The silver scale-like marks were nearly gone as they stopped before the dragon, and the last of them faded when her glow went out. Still, in the dragon's eyes, Cole saw it had seen them, and it *knew*.

What it did with that information would grant it freedom… or death.

CHAPTER ELEVEN

LEXI REMOVED the key from her pocket and held it before the dragon. "I'm Lexi, and Alina tells me that you're Tymin."

Nothing about the dragon's face changed; Lexi didn't know if it understood her or not. She should have asked Alina if the others could understand what she said. The dragons must understand; they obeyed the Lord's commands after all.

"I'll open the locks and set you free," Lexi explained.

She glanced at Cole, who remained rigid beside her. His face was an unreadable, cold mask. He looked so handsome yet harsh and unforgiving as the shadows swirled around him and the torch-light reflected in his silver eyes.

His joints popped as they shifted toward paws before he reined in his lycan side. She wasn't sure if she was more unnerved by the dragon or *him*. He would unleash hell in here if this went wrong.

Cautiously, she approached the chains around Tymin's front legs and snout. She wasn't sure which ones to unlock first; his talons were as lethal as his teeth.

Finally, she settled on his snout. Those chains had to be what was pissing him off the most as his mouth was pinched shut. He would probably be a lot happier without them on.

"Don't eat me," she said as she approached the mouth lock. "Please, don't eat me."

The inhuman sound Cole emitted caused the hair on her nape to rise as the dragon's gaze swung to him. The tension in the cave was so palpable it vibrated the stones. She glanced nervously at the jagged rocks above, but they appeared sturdy.

She hoped they remained that way.

Just keep going. Keep going.

She kept telling herself this, but she was in this cave with two extremely powerful, extremely tense immortal beings who would gladly destroy each other.

"Easy," Lexi encouraged when two puffs of smoke coiled from Tymin's nostrils.

She rested her hand on the dragon's scaly front paw, or was it a foot? She had no idea about correct dragon anatomy, but whatever it was, it was big enough to splat her like a fly, and she didn't feel like being splatted.

"I have to climb up you to get to the lock. I won't hurt you. Please don't eat me."

Maybe if she kept saying it, the dragon would refrain from turning her into a snack. With tender care, she pulled herself onto the dragon's leg and crept toward the lock. Its scales were hard beneath her hands, but not slippery, and smoother than expected.

The shadows shifted around her and gathered close but didn't touch her as she moved. When she glanced back at Cole, he stood near the dragon's mouth, but his attention remained riveted on her.

Gulping, Lexi focused her attention on the dragon as the shadows drifted only inches away from her. If she tried, she could touch them, but she'd prefer not to.

When she reached the lock, she settled in behind the thick spikes surrounding the dragon's head. This close, the spikes surrounding its head were far more lethal than she'd realized.

If she wasn't careful, she could spear herself on one of those spikes. She shuddered at the image and twisted to get better access to the lock. Turning it toward her, she steadied her hand and slid the key in.

"Please don't eat me," she whispered as she turned the key and the lock clicked.

The dragon didn't move. She leaned forward to pull the lock free, but when one of Tymin's spikes poked her arm, she jerked back. No blood trickled free, but a red mark marred her skin.

"Are you okay?" Cole demanded, and the shadows rose around her like they were preparing to strike.

"I'm fine," she said in a voice that sounded like someone was choking her.

Leaning around the dragon's spikes, she carefully grasped the lock and tugged it free. Off-balance, she couldn't keep hold of the lock, and it tumbled from her grasp.

She winced and braced herself as the lock bounced off the dragon's front legs before clattering to the ground. Unable to breathe, Lexi waited for it to toss her like a rodeo clown standing in front of the rampaging bull.

When nothing happened, she cracked one eye open. The dragon stared back at her as its tail swished across the ground. She could almost hear him telling her to get on with it.

"Okay, good dragon," she murmured as she ran her hand over its solid surface. It was as unyielding as steel beneath her, but there was something comforting about its warm, strong body. "Good dragon."

Crawling closer to its mouth, she worked the chains from its snout. "Please don't eat me."

And with those words, the chains fell free.

CHAPTER TWELVE

WHEN THE CHAINS hit the ground with an echoing clink, Cole didn't move. He pulled the shadows closer around Lexi as the dragon opened and closed its mouth like the creature was cracking its jaw.

Finally, its mouth remained closed, and its eyes swung toward her. Claws erupted from Cole's fingers; he'd slice the head off this beast just as he'd done to the one who ate his father. Every instinct he had screamed at him to pull her away from this thing, but he had to let her test her abilities and spread her wings, no matter how much he *loathed* it.

Prepared to launch onto the dragon, Cole remained riveted on the creature as it stared at Lexi. He waited for the dragon to attack and wouldn't give it a chance to hurt her. Between him and the shadows, they would tear this beast to pieces.

And then, it nudged her with its snout like a dog looking for a pet. Cole didn't relax, but his mouth parted, and he was sure a breeze could have pushed him over.

Lexi laughed as she tentatively rubbed the dragon's snout. When it snuffled, its breath blew the hair back from her face as it leaned into her touch.

What the fuck? Cole had expected a connection between them, but *this*?

This was insane, unheard of, and completely unpredictable. Alina hadn't been this tender with Lexi. Was that because they had her friend in chains, or was Tymin a kinder soul than the dragon outside? Would Alina have sought to connect with Lexi like this if he'd dropped the shadows?

Either way, it didn't matter as Tymin's eyes closed, and Cole swore happiness radiated from the creature. But Cole knew how the dragon felt; she'd often tamed the beast in him too.

But was this because she'd freed the dragon or because she was an arach?

Cole had no answers, but the phenomenon of what was unfolding between them wasn't lost on him. A crunch drew his attention toward Orin as he crept through the shadows toward them. When he spotted Lexi and Tymin, Orin froze.

But the crunch didn't just draw Cole's attention; it also alerted Tymin to Orin's approach. The dragon's head snapped around. Hatred emanated from the beast as Orin stumbled a couple of steps back but didn't run.

"No!" Lexi cried as she grabbed one of the dragon's two long spikes, which could also be considered its horns, and jerked its head toward her. The key tumbled from her hand and fell to the ground. "Don't kill him!"

"Lexi!" Cole shouted when the dragon roared.

Cole surged forward as the shadows swarmed around Lexi, encasing her in a protective barrier. His claws extended as he leapt onto the dragon's leg.

The dragon lurched toward Orin, but the chains binding its legs pulled taut and yanked it back. The whole cave quaked when it crashed to the ground.

"Get out of here!" Cole bellowed at his brother when the dragon lunged again. The creature wanted Orin dead, and his brother's presence had pushed it beyond reason. "*Get out!*"

Orin finally broke out of his stunned stupor and retreated into the shadows as Cole scrambled up to sit behind Lexi. Wrapping his arms around her, he grasped the dragon's horns above her hands as it lurched and jerked before collapsing again.

The beast's sides rose and fell as its breath heaved in and out. Smoke coiled from its nostrils, but it didn't try to break free again.

Cole released the shadows forming a wall between the dragon and Lexi as it remained unmoving beneath them. Then, he detected the coppery scent of Lexi's blood on the air.

"You're hurt," he said.

She lifted her hand and turned her palm over to reveal the slash across it. She fisted her hand against the blood, but it still seeped between her fingers.

He would kill Orin for this.

Cole's eyebrows shot up when the dragon released a sound more like a whimper. If he wasn't mistaken, this *thing* was upset it cut her.

"I'm fine." Lexi stroked the dragon's neck with her other hand as she stared at him. "I'm fine."

Cole cradled her injured hand and, pulling it close, tenderly kissed her palms. "Let me finish freeing him, and we'll get this bandaged."

"You'll get hurt."

"I'll be fine. It's not me this beast wants to kill... at least not today. Come on."

He clasped her good hand and slid it to the side. Carefully, he helped her climb down the dragon's side and front legs until they touched the ground. The beast studied them before nudging Lexi with its snout.

"It's okay," she said as she caressed its nose. "It doesn't hurt."

Cole knew that was a lie. It was a deep gash, and blood still seeped from between her closed fingers to splatter across the ground.

Lifting the key from where it had fallen, Cole studied the

dragon as he rose, but the creature only had eyes for Lexi. It was strange to realize he had a lot in common with this dragon.

Cautiously, he approached its back legs and undid the chains. He kept the shadows nearby but didn't believe they were necessary... not even when the dragon stretched its hind legs, its talons scraped the ground, and its tail swished.

He didn't sense animosity from the beast anymore, not like he had when Orin came into view. Lexi had calmed it once more, but her specialty was taming beasts.

When he returned to the front of the dragon, he unlocked the chains there and pulled them free.

"You can go now," Lexi said as she ran her hand over the dragon's snout.

It closed its eyes before opening them and rising. Though it was small, it barely fit in the cave now that it wasn't bound. The dragon remained hunched beneath the overhead rocks before it raced around the corner and disappeared.

CHAPTER THIRTEEN

LEXI BLINKED against the sun as they emerged from the cave. The others stood about fifteen feet away from the entrance; a clear wall of shimmering air encased them. Kaylia lowered the shield when she spotted Lexi and Cole.

Alina remained standing on the other side of the cave, but Tymin was gone. Lexi searched the air for him but didn't see him there either.

Her attention was drawn from the sky when Cole made a sound that would have petrified a giant. She lurched to grab his arm, but he was already beyond her reach. As Cole stalked toward them, Orin started backing away.

"Cole...." Orin's hands went up, but he froze when the shadows encircled his wrists.

"I told you to stay *out* of there!" Cole roared.

The shadows released Orin's wrists as Cole seized his brother by the throat. Cole propelled Orin backward and slammed him into the mountain surrounding the cave.

"You could have gotten her killed!" he shouted as he lifted Orin off the ground and thrust his face into his brother's.

"Cole, stop it!" Lexi cried as she raced toward them.

His fury battered her flesh and darkened the air as the shadows pulsed and swarmed in anticipation of blood. Orin's face turned red and then blue as he struggled to inhale; his feet kicked the rock, and his fingers clawed at Cole's hand.

Despite blood spilling from where Cole's fingers dug into his neck, Orin did nothing to ease Cole's grip. He swung at Cole, who caught his hand and bashed it against the rocks, before smashing his brother off them a few times.

"Easy, Cole," Varo said.

His normally soothing voice had little effect as the shadows encompassed Orin's waist. Brokk edged away but stopped and held up his hands when some of the shadows twisted toward him.

"I'm not coming any closer," Brokk assured them. "Let him go, Cole."

"You're my brother, but I won't tolerate this *shit* from you anymore," Cole snarled. "Do. You. Understand?"

He punctuated each of the last three words with a sharp shake of Orin.

"He can't answer you!" Lexi cried as she ran through the shadows. They parted to let her pass and hovered beside her as she grasped Cole's wrist and tried to yank him off Orin. "Let him go!"

Orin fell on his ass when Cole abruptly released him. But with a hand on his throat, he bounded up again.

"Do you understand?" Cole demanded.

Orin kept his hand against his throat as he choked out, "Yes."

"I've given you *too* many chances. You won't get another."

When Cole turned to her, he clasped her injured hand. Blood still oozed from the wound she'd forgotten about until now.

"She needs medical attention," he said to Sahira.

"My potions are at the prison."

"It's fine," Lexi said.

She tried to tug her hand free, but the tender caress of his thumb stopped her. Some of his rage finally dissipated as he lifted his silver eyes to hers. He was so tall, so broad and powerful, that any sign of vulnerability from him was shocking.

That vulnerability was there now as love filled his eyes while he stroked her skin. She doubted the others saw it, but she saw his need for her to understand in his eyes. She understood that he loved her, would always protect her, and destroy anyone who hurt her.

But his control was slipping as it became increasingly difficult to control the shadows. Resting her other hand over his, she squeezed it between her palms. No matter what happened, she would stand by his side.

A small smile curved the edge of his full lips before it fell away, and he leaned forward to kiss her forehead. He loved her, and she loved him. They would have to deal with all the other shit as it came. That was all they could do.

"I see why the shadows chose you," Alina murmured. The sun glinted in Alina's eyes as she examined Cole. "You are worthy."

Cole and Lexi both turned to glower at her. She should be nicer; Alina was their link to answers, and she'd already given them some, but Lexi was so tired of half-truths, secrets, always being in the dark, not knowing what she could do, and shadows.

She was over it *all*.

"Why do you say that?" she demanded.

"He will do whatever is necessary to keep you safe, even destroying someone he loves," Alina replied.

Lexi was about to argue, but since she was tired of half-truths, she wouldn't utter a lie. It would ruin him, but Cole would destroy anyone he deemed a threat to her... no matter who it was. No one here doubted it.

Unable to deal with the dragon right now, she turned to Cole and cradled his cheek with her hand as she smiled at him. Shadows continued to swirl around them, but they weren't as much of a barrier between them and Alina as they were before.

"I'm fine, and she's not going to hurt us," she assured him. "Let the shadows go."

Because the longer he kept them close to him, the more they corrupted him. They slipped away a little, but he didn't release them completely.

With a sigh of resignation, she turned back to Alina. "So, how do we defeat the Lord?"

"With an army."

"And you'll fight beside us?" Orin's voice was still hoarser than normal, but he stood proudly behind them.

"We cannot," Alina replied.

"Why not?"

"Whoever controls the throne controls the dragons. We are forbidden from harming the arach and Shadow Reaver, but we must obey the commands of our ruler. We will kill the rest of you, and we cannot fight against the Lord."

"Then what good are you to us?"

"Orin!" Lexi shot him a look over her shoulder. The man had no idea when to *shut up*. "Enough."

When Maverick rested a hand on Orin's shoulder, the dark fae shrugged it off.

"I caught a dragon because I believed we had hope of them helping us, or doing something for us, or against him, but we still have *nothing*," Orin snarled.

"I would not obey you anyway." Alina sounded affronted by the possibility he thought she might.

"I don't want you to obey *me*." Orin pointed a finger at Lexi. "I want you to obey *her*!"

"If she secures the throne, I will gladly follow her lead as our queen, as will the others."

"Why were the arach considered kings and queens while those who followed them have all been Lords?" Lexi inquired.

"The first usurper to sit on the throne declared himself the Lord of Dragonia. All those who followed him assumed the name too. I assume it was a way to differentiate themselves from the arach, but they had no reason to do so. They did not belong there, and that already made them different." Alina closed her eyes and tipped her head to the side. "The Lord calls. I must go."

"Wait!" Lexi blurted. She still had so many questions and no answers. "Is there anything else I can do? Do I have any other abilities besides the mark of the dragon and fire?"

That strange little smile tugged at Alina's mouth as she unfurled her wings. "Oh, child, there are *so* many things you can do. Now, I *have* to answer his call."

"How do I awaken those abilities?"

"That is for you to discover."

When Alina pushed herself into the air, Lexi rushed toward her, but all she received was a face full of wind as Alina flew away. "Will I see you again?" she shouted after the dragon.

"I hope so."

And with those final words, Alina opened a portal and left. Hope and frustration warred in Lexi. She'd *talked* to a dragon, but they weren't any closer to taking down the Lord, and she still had so many questions.

"We can still figure out a way to use the dragons to help us, and now we know more. This doesn't change our plan," her dad said. "We still have to recruit an army."

"We'll go to the sirens when Lexi is ready," Cole said.

CHAPTER FOURTEEN

ALINA SHOOK off the water still clinging to her from her bath as she crept into the dark recesses of her cave. She usually took a bath after being in the Lord's presence; the man, and the things he commanded them to do, always made her feel dirty.

She longed for a time when that didn't happen, but she didn't get her hopes up. Yes, an arach still lived, there was a chance she could free them from the Lord's tyrannical rule, but it was a small chance.

Taking over Dragonia and getting the usurper off the throne would not be an easy task. But there was an arach and the *Reaver*.

She didn't know what that meant, had no idea what the arach were thinking or what they intended, other than to protect themselves when they created the magic for the Reaver. But that magic had been unleashed, and if there was ever a time when they needed power, it was now.

She hoped the magic didn't end up taking a really bad turn and causing the Reaver to create more havoc on the realms than the Lord. But then she recalled the moment between the Reaver and the arach. The way she pulled him back from the brink.

Lexi could keep the Reaver in check... while she remained alive. Alina cursed the prophecy as she weaved through the cave.

The stones brushing against her sides massaged her sore muscles. She stopped to scratch an itch on her back against a particularly jagged rock hanging from the ceiling.

It was impossible to see anything this deep into the cave, but it had been her home since she was nothing more than a young wyrmling fresh from hatching. Her parents and siblings were all gone now, but she remained to take care of her home.

She knew every crevice, rock, and place where air crept in from outside this cave like they were a part of her. And this place was a part of her. It was her home.

She stopped scratching and continued toward her nest in the center of her cave. When she arrived at the center, she stopped to breathe fire onto the torches inside the open doorway.

The flames flickering to life illuminated the cavernous space of the domed room with its high, stone ceiling nearly fifty feet over her head. Jagged rocks that could spear through a dragon hung from above. She didn't fear the rocks; she'd lived beneath them for thousands of years.

The rocky walls of the circular room were smooth from years of dragons brushing against them. It was filled with laughter when she was young as she tumbled and played with her siblings beneath the watchful eyes of her parents. At one time, six of her family lived in this room.

And then, after they were gone, it became home to her and her mate, Sosho. But someone killed him hundreds of years ago, and she was left alone in her home.

Where love and laughter once filled it, now only silence and loneliness greeted her. She crept closer to the nest in the middle. Her great-great-great-grandparents, maybe even further back than them, built this nest.

It had housed many families over the years and was supposed

to have housed hers. Before laying her eggs, she and Sosho spent countless hours gathering more sticks, feathers, blankets, and other soft materials.

But those eggs remained a sad testament to a long-ago time. Alina peered in at the three eggs still safely secured in the center of the nest. All the eggs were a greenish-yellow color, but that had no bearing on the color of the dragons within.

When she first laid those eggs over a thousand years ago, she'd spent many countless hours dreaming about what colors her offspring would be. And she'd spent the past nine hundred years still wondering, but with the certainty that she would never know the answer.

It had taken her a hundred years after the arach were dethroned, and an outsider claimed the realm and the dragons, to realize her eggs weren't going to hatch. It should have only taken a couple of months for her young to hatch, but she kept waiting, hoping, and waiting some more until it finally sank in.

She was ashamed it had taken so long. Sosho accepted it before her, but she'd clung to the hope she would one day meet their babies.

And then her hope faded into nothingness. *No* dragon eggs had hatched since the arach fell, and *no* dragons had laid eggs since.

It wasn't common knowledge, and it never could be as it meant the dragons were dying out, but it was true. Her eggs had never hatched, and neither would any of the few others hidden in the land, trapped in a time before mad Lords ruled the realm.

She should have gotten rid of them; she should have moved on from the *tiny* hope still tugging at her heart, but she couldn't do either. Once Sosho died, these eggs were all she had left.

It was foolish, she was a brokenhearted idiot, but she curled up with her eggs and nudged each to rotate them. She told them about her day as she worked and sang a dragon lullaby while the torch-light reflected off the walls and the loneliness crept in.

Maybe an arach on the throne would bring some life back to the land and the dragons could start breeding again. It would do nothing for *her* as she'd lost her mate and the offspring within these eggs, but the dragons needed life again.

Lowering her head, Alina used her chin to draw the eggs closer and tucked them against her side before falling asleep.

CHAPTER FIFTEEN

LEXI KEPT HER SHOULDERS BACK, her chin held high, and a look of confidence on her face. It was a confidence she didn't feel as they strolled into the land of Aerie, home of the sirens.

Maybe she would feel more confident if she hadn't spent the past two days working on spells with Kaylia only to have it amount to nothing. She had no idea what the arach were entirely capable of, but it certainly wasn't casting spells like a witch.

Kaylia had managed to figure out how to help her erect her shield, but she couldn't figure out a way to unlock whatever other abilities Lexi might possess. Lexi was becoming increasingly frustrated by her lack of progress in *all* things, but at least her hand had healed while they worked.

And now they traversed this narrow pathway while eyes stared down at them from the high cliffs to their left. Lexi glanced at the sirens perched above them. She'd feel a *lot* more comfortable about the lethal creatures if she had something, besides fire, to counteract them should they attack.

The sirens sitting on their lofty perches didn't make any noise. They looked strangely indifferent to their presence, considering most of those who came to Aerie never left it.

Cole wasn't thrilled about bringing her here, but he didn't have much choice. A few sirens attended his ball, but the Lord had little to do with them for the most part. It was time to start recruiting an army, and their best option was to start with the immortals shoved aside or ignored by the Lord.

He never asked them to participate in the Lord's war. Lexi didn't know if that was because the sirens were all women, and therefore the Lord saw them as inferior, or if it was because no one trusted the beautiful, lethal creatures.

The sirens were known to lure mortals into Aerie with their beautiful voices and smash them against the jagged cliffs to her right… if they didn't keep them as slaves.

The sirens could also enslave immortals with their song but often preferred the easier prey of the mortals, which might be another reason the Lord shunned them. Many immortals saw the sirens as scavengers who could only take out those weaker than them. Therefore, many immortals deemed them pathetic.

Lexi didn't know what to think of the sirens, but they unnerved her. She did *not* want to be a slave to these women.

Lexi gulped. Cole told her he'd been here before and never had a problem with leaving—if one could resist the siren's song, they were allowed to go—but she'd never been here before and worried she might run into an issue.

However, they couldn't expect the sirens to follow the last living arach into a war against the Lord if they didn't *meet* her. So as much as he hated it, Cole couldn't deny she had to be here.

Afraid the others might be affected by the siren's song, they remained at the prison. Her dad and Orin weren't happy about it.

Above them, the half women, half birds cocked their heads as they strode higher along the path. When the sirens shifted, rocks broke away from beneath their talons.

The stones bounced down the cliffs to clatter against the rocky pathway she and Cole traversed. As they passed, the sirens took flight. Some of them flew ahead to land on the cliffs and settled in to watch her and Cole approach. The others vanished; she didn't know where they went, making her more nervous.

The wind howling down the pathway tore at her hair and battered her face. The higher they climbed, the colder it grew. When snow began to dot the tops of the cliffs, her fingers and nose went numb.

Despite the thick coat Cole told her to wear, the cold air crept in to ice her bones. Or maybe it was the hundreds of eerie eyes staring at them that chilled her so much.

Stay calm. Stay calm.

She restrained herself from tugging at the collar of her coat and the fae tunic a woman guard at the prison gave her. Sahira had tailored the green tunic and black pants to fit her better.

She may not look as royal or well dressed as she'd always imagined a queen, but she was okay with that. The heavy coat was too big, but she was glad as she huddled deeper into the hood while the wind battered them.

To their right, the purple water of the Sea of Demise crashed against the rocky cliffs and hammered the numerous broken ships below. The wooden remains of masts, bowsprits, and the shells of boats poked out of the high, crashing waves rolling in and out. There were so many skeletal ships out there she couldn't begin to count them, and she was sure the water hid thousands of others.

A wave roared before it crashed against the cliffs. It burst upward in giant plumes that dampened what little exposed skin she had.

She wiped away the water coating her lashes as, on the horizon, a ship appeared. Lexi's heart leapt into her throat. Was some unsuspecting soul approaching their death right now?

As if they were reading her mind, the sirens lifted their heads and started singing. Lexi resisted running to the edge of the cliffs and waving her arms as she screamed at the ship to turn away.

While she bit her tongue, the siren's haunting melody grew

louder on the air. The song was so haunting and enchanting, tears sprang to her eyes.

How could something be so beautiful and awful?

One of the sirens rose from the peaks and soared out over the sea. Lexi assumed she was flying out to the ship, but the siren folded her wings against her back and plunged into the water. She remerged with a fish that she brought back to the cliffs.

Her claws tore the fish apart, and she used her talons to shove it into her mouth while watching them. The sirens lured their unsuspecting prey to Aerie but didn't feed on them. They relied on fish from the sea to sustain them.

Another siren landed at the end of the pathway. With a shiver of motion, she transformed from a five-foot-tall woman/bird into a woman close to six feet tall. Feathers no longer covered her body… and neither did anything else.

The woman, completely unperturbed by her nudity, had a body that would make men steer their ships into a cliff. And she knew it as she stood with her shoulders back, her ample breasts thrust forward, and a smug smile on her beautiful face.

Lexi recognized her as the woman Cole danced with at the Lord's ball. And if this woman was at the ball, then that meant she held a lot of power in this realm, if not ruled it. She wasn't sure about the politics of Aerie.

"King Colburn of the dark fae," the woman greeted in a sultry voice so filled with promises of sex it probably made many trip over themselves to get to her.

Lexi glanced at Cole, but his eyes remained on the woman's face, and he seemed unaffected by her presence. Lexi knew he only loved her, but this woman was *gorgeous* with her honey-colored hair and eyes the color of an amethyst.

"We are at a disadvantage," he said. "I'm unaware of your name."

The woman arched an elegant brow. "And why would you

know it? You last visited our land years before I became ruler of the parliament here. I am Celaliana, but you may call me Cela."

Her striking eyes brimmed with curiosity when they landed on Lexi. "And you are Elexiandra Harper, fiancée to the king, a surprise to us all, and a bane to the Lord."

Lexi forced herself not to squirm beneath the woman's intense scrutiny. She didn't know how to respond, and she was glad Cole's next words spared her from having to reply.

"I assume you know why we're here."

The woman smiled at him. "You've come to grovel for help against the Lord."

CHAPTER SIXTEEN

COLE KEPT his smile in place, but there was no way he or Lexi would grovel for anything. He'd spend the rest of his life hiding on that rock of a prison realm before begging for anything.

This woman had to know that, but she was a siren, and they loved to play with others. She was playing with the wrong immortal today.

"Come with me," the woman said.

Her hair swayed against her back when she turned and sauntered forward. Cole focused on the sirens above them as the ship drew closer to the rocky cliffs. It was only a matter of time before it crashed against the jagged rocks and broken boats decorating the purple sea.

Cela took a left, taking them off the cliff pathway and leading them between the mountains of Aerie. The rocky trail curved up a steep incline as the snow grew thicker on the peaks. The rocks vanished as the crunch of snow replaced the dirt and stone.

When they turned another corner, an entanglement of branches swooped overhead. The branches were easily the size of a tree, and the crisscrossing pattern joined the mountains.

The thousands of shiny objects tangled within the branches

caught and reflected the sun so that light danced all around them. From his last visit, he knew those objects were the personal possessions of the countless sailors who lost their lives in Aerie.

The higher they climbed, the chillier it got as the shrieking wind blew up snow and whipped it around them. It clung to his skin in tiny crystals that froze his flesh, but he refused to acknowledge the cold as the shadows watched the sirens for any hint of an attack.

He draped his arm around Lexi's shoulders and pulled her against his side to warm her when she shivered. Cela remained unfazed by the cold as her bare feet crunched in the snow and it melted against her bare skin.

They were almost to the top of the mountain when the sirens released a series of loud shrieks like a maniacal beast's cackling laughter. Lexi shuddered, but this time it had nothing to do with the cold.

They both knew what caused the laughter; the ship had crashed.

In front of them, Cela's head tipped back, and she lifted her arms. A flutter started on the air, followed by a whooping sound he felt in his bones.

All around them, the sirens took flight. Their wings beat the air in a rising crescendo that thumped like drums as they rose higher.

There were so many they blocked out the sun as they soared overhead. They formed a V as they flew toward the massive nest at the top of the mountain Lexi and Cole climbed.

When the sirens reached the nest, they dove into its top and disappeared. Cela smiled as she led Cole and Lexi through a high arch comprised mostly of silver and gold watches, necklaces, jewels, brooches, and teeth.

Lexi's step faltered before she quickly regained control and lifted her chin to stride purposely forward. Then they were through the doorway and beneath the domed nest with its circular opening to the sky.

A large fire burned in the center of the room; its flames kept the nest warm. Most of the sirens settled on their perches high up on the walls. A few settled onto posts on the ground near the fire.

Cela sat on the largest perch. Unlike the other sirens, who all remained in half-bird/half-human shape, she sat and dangled her crossed legs before her. The others gazed down at them in disdain.

Cole ignored them as he strode forward to stop before Cela. She leaned back to drape her arm across the wooden beam. Vines and sticks created its intricate back.

Grinning, she plucked a fish from the plate beside her and swallowed it whole before speaking. "What will you give us if we fight for you?"

~

GAZING at the gathered sirens above and on the same level as them, Lexi was amazed that she wasn't blushing over the unabashed display of nudity from Cela. She was too angry to blush.

Or maybe she was getting used to being around immortals and their lack of inhibition about nudity. Either way, she didn't like this woman's arrogant attitude or that she acted like they were at her mercy.

She also didn't like the countless objects once belonging to humans glittering around them. Those people had deserved better than to end up a broken body or a trophy to these monsters.

But then, none of the Shadow Realms and few immortals were known for their kindness. The sirens were monsters, and she would have to deal with plenty more of them before all this was over.

You're being too tough on them. They have to survive too.

At one time, she considered the dark fae the worst creatures in the realms, outside of the Lord, and now she was engaged to their king. However, the sirens didn't have to kill their victims; they did it for fun.

And the dark fae don't have to shadow kiss some of their victims; they also do that *for fun.*

She would have to accept the ways of the other immortals and look past the things she disagreed with if they were going to gather an army, but she didn't have to like it. She certainly didn't like this woman as she kicked her leg and eyed Cole with far too much lust in her eyes. Lexi glared at her, but Cela didn't notice as she idly ran a hand between her breasts.

Two young, well-muscled, and handsome men entered the cavernous space. One carried two platters of fish and the other a couple of glass decanters of what she assumed was red wine. Another man emerged from a different direction with half a dozen golden goblets.

The only thing covering any part of them were the manacles clasped around their necks and wrists. The chains running from each of the manacles were long enough to allow them to easily carry their possessions toward Cela, who smirked at her and Cole.

Her smug look had Lexi contemplating setting this whole place on fire. Cela wouldn't smirk so much once her home was falling around her ears.

The men knelt as they offered the platters and wine to the woman. Lexi's stomach rolled. They'd made a mistake coming here. She'd rather have the Lord cut off her head and feed it to these monsters than ask them for help.

"Put them over there," Cela commanded and waved at a table beside her perch. "Can I interest either of you in a drink and some food?"

"No," Lexi said while Cole said, "I will have some wine."

Cela tilted her head as she studied Lexi. "You don't like me."

Lexi didn't respond.

"You grew up in the human realm and actually *pity* these creatures? Stop!" She grasped the arm of one of the men starting to retreat.

Alarm crossed a face that couldn't be much more than twenty-two years old. He'd probably just started working on one of the ships that sailed here, or perhaps his father was a fisherman and he'd grown up running around boats. Either way, he shouldn't be here.

"They're barely more than animals," Cela said.

"They're much more than that," Lexi retorted. "They're people with thoughts and feelings, and they deserve better than this."

Cela stroked the young man's wrist before releasing him. "So, you condemn us as the Lord has done?"

"I don't condemn anyone, but you don't have to do this to survive, so why would you?"

"For the same reason the dark fae leave mindless, shadow kissed, sex slaves in their wake... it's fun," Cela said. "But you're okay with them doing that."

Lexi wasn't okay with any of it, but she could no more change the dark fae than the sirens or any other immortals. This was the way of things in the realms. None of this would bother her if she'd been raised here, but she wasn't.

CHAPTER SEVENTEEN

As the tension in the nest ratcheted up, Cole prepared himself to get Lexi out of here as fast as possible. He didn't draw the shadows to him, but they danced and swayed across the walls as the ones inside him rose. He could unleash them faster than these creatures could descend on them.

He glanced at the sirens perched above. None of them looked pleased with Lexi. They'd come here for help, but he wouldn't beg for it, and he certainly wouldn't allow these women to attack her. He'd destroy all of Aerie before that happened.

He opened his senses to the wind creeping through the thousands of branches making up the nest. He could also use the air to batter them off their perches if necessary. The sirens wouldn't expect the attack from the wind, which would give Cole and Lexi more than enough time to get away.

He should have known this wouldn't go well. Lexi was too kindhearted for the siren's brutal ways.

"What do you do with the humans when you tire of them?" Lexi asked.

"We kill them," Cela replied without an ounce of remorse.

While Cole had no opinion on what the sirens did with the

humans, Lexi and the captive winced. The man whimpered and moved as if to run, but Cela grasped his chains to hold him in place.

Cela clasped his dick. "But we make sure they're happy until they die."

"Don't," Lexi commanded.

Cela grinned at her. "Don't? You forget yourself, little girl. This is *our* realm."

"I'm not a little girl, and I will *not* tolerate you abusing him while I'm here."

"Or you'll what?"

"Or I'll set this whole place on fire. Don't. Push. Me."

Despite probably losing a chance to align themselves with these women, pride bloomed in Cole's chest. Lexi had always been stronger than she believed, but she was finally starting to own her strength, and it was a sight to behold.

She was a leader, his fiancée, and he loved her. She'd also enraged an entire realm as the sirens released high-pitched screams in response.

Cole still didn't pull the shadows closer; he would if necessary, but he could still feel the lingering effects from when he drew them close to protect her from Alina. He would use other options first.

The shadows promised power and death. They also sought to gain more control of him, and he wouldn't let that happen.

Lexi looked at him, and as she did, fire emerged from her fingertips. The screams of the sirens increased until they rebounded off the wooden walls. Some of the glass in their stolen trinkets shattered and sprayed over the ground.

When some of the glass fell toward Lexi, he waved a hand, and a current of air knocked it aside. He ignored the glass settling on his hand and shoulders as he glowered at the winged beasts.

His eardrums throbbed as the awful screeching continued. If the stiff set of Lexi's jaw was any indication, she was resisting the impulse to cover her ears. The captive man didn't hesitate as he slapped his hands over his ears and knelt beside Cela.

After another minute, Cela held up her hand and gave a small wave. The screaming stopped. The ensuing hush emphasized the ringing of his ears as a single feather floated down. It landed between them and Cela.

"You need us to help you destroy the Lord," Cela grated. "You can't go up against him without an army."

"You need us more than we need you," Cole replied. "Once the Lord turns his dragons loose on Aerie, you won't be able to stop him. And he's going to come for you. He's never liked the sirens, and now that the Gloaming is gone, you will have moved up on his list of targets because he *knows* there's a chance you'll side with us against him. It's only a matter of time before he destroys everything here."

Cela's full lips turned white when they compressed into a flat line. The color drained from her face, and her cheekbones became sharper beneath her pale skin.

"And we may not have a massive army, but we have more fighters than you. You were at the ball. You saw what I can do, and you *know* what she is." Cole rested his hand on Lexi's shoulder. "She's the key to defeating him."

Cela's gaze flicked to Lexi. "We could take her to the Lord. He'd leave us alone if we handed her over."

With little more than a flicker of effort, Cole seized control of the shadows around Cela. He didn't care if their evil crept deeper in and gained more control; he'd destroy every one of these birds if they dared to attack Lexi.

A choked gasp escaped Cela as the shadows behind her rose to envelop her throat. Her head tipped back as they clamped down and pulled upward, drawing her onto her tiptoes. Cole's joints popped and cracked as his claws extended and the lycan sought to destroy the woman threatening his mate.

"Don't fuck with me," he snarled in a voice he barely recognized.

Beside him, Lexi stiffened. The other sirens shifted as if they were preparing to take flight from their perches.

The fire on Lexi's hands increased until it caught on her thick coat. Like a phoenix, her coat erupted into flames and crumbled at her feet until she stood bared to the waist beside him. He hated that they saw her in such a way, but he couldn't do anything about it now. He had to get her out of here alive.

One of the sirens took flight, but a shadow lashed out, caught her foot, and yanked her back. The shadows behind Cole alerted him to two more rising into the air.

Before they could dive-bomb them, he drew on the air and whipped it into a frenzy that threw the sirens into the wall. Shadows encircled the sirens to keep them there. The other sirens squawked but didn't take flight as shadows shifted and swayed all around the room.

"We came here to unite with you and help keep you safe," Cole growled as Cela tried to tear away the shadows encasing her throat. All she succeeded in doing was shredding her skin.

"And to take our slaves from us." A bird perched near Cela transformed into a tall, lithe woman with hair the color of a ruby and sable eyes.

"I wouldn't do that," Cole replied.

The woman pointed at Lexi. "But she would."

Lexi shifted uncomfortably beside him. When her gaze went to the young man, her eyes filled with sadness as she replied, "No, I wouldn't."

Lexi turned her head away as the man emitted a sound of anguish. Her dismay beat against Cole, but he couldn't take the time to comfort her. The enemy surrounded them, and she had to realize she couldn't take on everything she deemed an injustice in the realms.

She'd never stop fighting if she did. And, in the end, she'd be no better than the Lord if she tried to break the way of those she disagreed with. It was a hard lesson to learn, and he hated feeling more of her innocence slipping away.

But if Lexi was going to rule the realms, she had to decide what kind of leader to be… a tyrant who broke those different from her or one who listened to and accepted them, even if she didn't like it. Cole knew she would make an excellent queen, but she had to choose her path.

"I don't agree with what you're doing here, and I never will, but I'm not the Lord. I'm not out to break other immortals. I don't agree with the shadow kissed, but I won't take them from the dark fae. I will *not* break someone or take away their way of life because it's not what I would do," Lexi said.

"And how do I know you won't change your mind once we help you gain your rightful place on the throne?" the woman inquired.

Lexi didn't take offense to the woman's words. "I wouldn't do such a thing, but I have no way to prove it. You'll have to trust me."

The woman snorted. "You threatened to burn down our home."

"I won't take your lifestyle from you, but I also won't stand by and *watch* while you abuse others."

The woman studied Lexi before shifting her focus to Cole. "Let her go. I am Yamala and the real leader of Aerie."

Cole smiled as the shadows constricted around Cela's neck and she squeaked. "I don't like being toyed with."

Yamala edged closer to Cela. "This was my idea, not hers. She shouldn't pay for my mistake."

"If you're the true leader here, why weren't *you* at the ball?" he demanded.

The woman smiled, but it didn't reach her eyes and was more of a grimace. "Because the Lord only requested the presence of his daughter there."

CHAPTER EIGHTEEN

COLE KEPT his shock over this revelation hidden as he released the shadows around Cela's neck. He continued to make sure the others knew the shadows were there, watching and reporting on them.

He eyed Cela. Was there some way they could use her against the Lord? Would that madman care if they had his daughter?

"If you think you can use her against him, you're mistaken," Yamala said.

Cela bent over and placed her hand against her throat as she panted for air. "We should kill—"

"Shut up," Yamala hissed. "Do not be like your father."

Cela recoiled like her mother had slapped her. Red colored her cheeks as she gawked at Yamala before glaring at her.

"I am *nothing* like him," Cela spat.

"You seek blood," her mother replied.

"We *all* seek blood. We are sirens. We lure others to their deaths because it is *fun* for us. Is that *not* seeking blood?"

"That is who we are; it is what we have always done. You seek blood for spite," Yamala said. "That is not the way of the siren."

"There's not much of a difference," Cela muttered.

Cole couldn't help but agree, but who was he to judge the

morals of the sirens? Each immortal made their own rules and laws; many wouldn't agree with them, but that's how they lived.

Yamala scowled at her daughter until Cela's shoulders hunched and she ducked her head. Then she shifted her attention to Cole. "What is your plan for the Lord?"

Cole studied the mother and daughter. Yamala was right; they wouldn't be able to use Cela against the Lord. He was too much of a psychopath to care if they killed his daughter. However, he couldn't trust the Lord's daughter and ex-lover not to turn on them.

"We shouldn't have come here," he said.

Yamala held out her hand as she stepped toward him. "If you think there is any love between that bastard and me, you are mistaken. I love my daughter, but I will gladly see him dead."

"Isn't *that* spiteful?" Cela asked.

"The Lord's death is *necessary*," Yamala replied, and Cela rolled her eyes. "We will help you ensure it."

Careful to avoid the flames encircling her hands, Cole drew Lexi closer. He'd made a mistake bringing her here, but he hadn't known the Lord had a daughter, never mind one who was half siren. There hadn't been any rumors of such a thing, and though the Shadow Realms held many secrets, he was astonished this one didn't get out.

"It's time for us to go," Cole said.

"Wait," Yamala said.

When Cole opened a portal in front of him, the woman stepped in front of it.

"Wait," she said again. "Let us talk… alone."

"I'm not going anywhere without Lexi."

"I understand. I'm talking about my people. Everyone, please leave."

The sirens stirred over her command but remained roosted. He sensed their unwillingness to leave her alone with him and Lexi.

"Go!" Yamala commanded.

Cole released the air keeping the two of them pinned to the

wall. Their loud screech as they flew out was like nails on a chalkboard.

As the sirens fled the nest, feathers drifted through the air and settled on the ground around them. The different hues in the feathers caught and reflected the light.

They became a kaleidoscope of colorful brilliance until the last one fell from the sky. He didn't take his attention away from the mother and daughter as he brushed a couple from Lexi's hair.

"My daughter will also remain," Yamala said.

Cole nodded but didn't close his portal. He would hear what they had to say before leaving.

Yamala focused on Lexi. "My daughter told me what happened at the ball, but I didn't believe... I *couldn't* believe it. I believed there was *no* way an arach could still live, yet here you are." Then her sable eyes pinned him. "And here *you* are. Cela said someone at the ball called you the Shadow Reaver. Is that true? Are you the legend of the Reaver?"

"So I've been told," Cole replied dryly.

"And now that I've seen your shadows and her fire, I believe the two of you can bring the Lord down."

"You're the Lord's mistress. Why would you want to bring him down?"

"I was *never* his mistress," Yamala spat. "Everyone here knows what happened to me, and though I tried to hide it from her, even my daughter learned the truth of her heritage. But only one other outside of Aerie knows what happened, and that is the Lord. I plan to keep it that way."

CHAPTER NINETEEN

THE PANIC on Yamala's face melted some of Lexi's anger toward these vicious women. Taking a deep breath, Lexi smothered the fire engulfing her hands.

Without the flames to warm her, the cold crept in to caress the naked flesh of her torso. Suddenly aware she was nearly as on display as these women, Lexi almost shielded her breasts from view.

But it was too late for such modesty and would probably only earn her snickers from these women. She refused to appear weak in front of them, but she was freezing.

Cole grasped the bottom of his tunic, pulled it off, and slid it over her head. The material, still warm from his body, heated her.

The bottom of it nearly touched her knees; she pondered rolling the sleeves up to her wrists but was afraid she'd look too childish in front of these women. They would *not* respect that, and though most immortals derided them, the sirens were a proud group.

"What did the Lord do to you?" Cole asked Yamala.

The beautiful woman's eyes flashed as she lifted her chin. "He imprisoned me, raped me, and when I became pregnant, set me free."

Lexi showed no response to this revelation while she inwardly flinched and wept for the woman. It didn't shock her the Lord did it; he was a monster, and nothing he did astounded her.

"Why did he release you?" Cole asked.

"I assume it was because he was done with me, but I've never seen him again to ask; if I did, I'd kill him. He has called for his daughter to attend him over the years. During that time, I came to believe he set me free because he could still torture me through her.

"To him, taking my daughter from me, keeping her away, and leaving me with the worry he could kill her at any time, is more fun than the years of abuse he heaped on me. He's never finished fucking me."

"Why do you go when he calls?" Cole demanded of Cela.

"Do you think I can say no? He would set his dragons loose on us and destroy Aerie if I disobeyed him. He plays his games, and we jump through his hoops, like all the other realms. And those who don't play, pay the consequences... like the human realm and the Gloaming," Cela replied.

"I do what I must to keep those in Aerie safe, but it kills me every time my daughter walks out of here. I'm certain that one day she won't return. He'll grow tired of playing with us and deal the final, crushing blow by killing her. But if I refuse to let her go, I put so many other lives at risk."

"You know the sirens would stand by your refusal," Cela said.

"They would, but some, if not many, would die, and I cannot live with their blood on my hands. We would also lose our home..."

Yamala's voice trailed off as her head tipped back and she took in the nest surrounding them. Lexi's hand tightened on Cole's arm. It was the same reasoning that kept him and the Gloaming under the thumb of the Lord for years, but Cole always knew it would only be a matter of time before the Lord unleashed his wrath on them.

And when the lunatic finally went after the Gloaming, he destroyed much of the realm and took far too many innocent lives. But the dark fae were free of his oppressive tyranny, even if they were on the run.

The sirens knew he'd come for them too. Lexi ran the tunic sleeves between her fingers as she studied Yamala. She couldn't imagine anything more torturous than having the man who raped her take her child away whenever he found it amusing.

And Yamala and Cela couldn't say no, or the bastard would destroy Aerie. Lexi hadn't considered it possible for her to hate the Lord any more than she already did; she'd been wrong.

"The Lord will take our home from us, but we can and *will* rebuild," Yamala whispered.

"We can," Cela replied as she rested her hand on her mother's arm.

"I know the man's a complete lunatic, but why did he target you for such torment?" Lexi inquired.

"When we were young, years before he sat on that throne, Andreas pursued me, but I wasn't interested."

"He harbored a grudge against you for *that?*" Lexi asked incredulously.

"No, or at least I didn't think so at the time. At the time, he took my rebuff well, and we became good friends. We remained friends until he took the throne. Then, after nearly fifty years of ruling the realms, he ordered me to attend him. We hadn't seen each other in some time, but I had visited him five years before.

"When I arrived in Dragonia, I barely recognized the man staring back at me from the throne. His eyes had turned completely red, and spittle flew from his mouth as he berated me for denying him years ago. I wasn't there ten minutes before he ordered me locked away.

"I was convinced I'd never walk free of that place, but when I told him I was pregnant, he gave me my freedom... and our child. I am forever grateful for our daughter, no matter the circumstances of how I conceived her, but I will forever *hate* him."

CHAPTER TWENTY

Now Lexi understood why Cela pretended to be the one in charge when they first arrived. She was sure Yamala still helped wreck those ships, but she doubted the woman still took pleasure in the abuse the sirens inflicted upon those they took captive.

She didn't ask why Yamala stood by and watched the others abuse these men. What happened here was the way of the sirens, and even if Yamala didn't partake, she wouldn't change her people.

"I'm sorry you had to endure that," Lexi whispered.

Yamala said nothing as her mouth flattened into a thin line.

"You can't stay here," Cole said. "He's going to come for you *soon*. He's insane, but he must realize you hate him. That hatred makes you an enemy."

"He thinks very little of any of us," Cela replied. "Including me. I'm his daughter, but to him, I'm nothing. We're not a threat to him."

"You *weren't* a threat to him before he learned of Lexi. He's going to consider *everyone* a threat to him now. He'll come for you, and it will be soon."

"I know," Yamala replied. "We're preparing for that."

"Then why are you still here?" Lexi asked.

"We were waiting for you. We knew you would come. If you're going to take him down, then you need fighters. And where to start recruiting but at the bottom? Or at least what *he* would consider the bottom. So, we stayed... for now."

"Where are you going to go?" Lexi asked.

"We have a place."

"Then I would suggest going there. Soon," Cole said.

Yamala glanced over Cole's shoulder as one of the sirens returned to settle on an upper perch.

"We have discussed it and will agree to fight with you," Yamala said. "In return, we would like to be left alone in our realm... if the Lord doesn't destroy it. We also will not be shunned again. We're not asking to be a part of Dragonia and everything that goes with it, but we won't be humiliated or considered lesser anymore."

"Is that all you want?" Lexi asked.

"We won't change our way of life. Do you agree to that?"

Lexi felt all their gazes on her, including the curious, frightened one of the captives behind Yamala. Cole would stand by whatever decision she made here, but could she agree to let this kind of murder and abuse continue?

If it meant destroying the Lord, a man who killed more in a day than the sirens did in a year, then yes, she could do so. How could she turn away their help when the sirens might help them defeat such a monster?

Looking at the captive made her nauseous, but she couldn't pretend he didn't exist. That was somehow crueler to her.

The man deserved better than *this* fate, but she couldn't save everyone. She just couldn't... even if it broke her heart and stole little pieces of her soul every time she sacrificed someone.

The best she could do was try to save as many mortals and immortals as possible. Still, she couldn't be a coward who wouldn't look the man in the eye as she sacrificed him.

Lifting her head, she met the captive's pleading gaze. Tears burned her throat, but she didn't shed them.

"I agree," she said in a voice far stronger than she expected.

A tiny piece of her withered and died as the man's head bowed and his shoulders shook on a soundless sob. Lexi wished she could yank her words out of the air and tear them to pieces, but she didn't say anything.

Maybe they could win this war without the sirens, but at what cost?

And if you lose because you didn't have enough fighters?

Then it would be far more than the man standing here crying. It would be mothers and fathers, children, and siblings. Countless mortals and immortals would weep throughout the lands as the Lord tormented and destroyed them.

Or there wouldn't be any crying because they'd all be dead.

She could say no to the sirens now. They could walk away, but if they lost the war, she would always question if there was something more she could have done. And turning away the sirens would be one of those things.

Besides, what would she do if they did win the war? Declare war on the sirens because she didn't approve of how they lived and the things they did?

She would be no better than the Lord then. She hated everything about her acquiescence to their demands, but she would *not* be like the Lord.

Cole placed his hand on her back and pulled her closer. When she rested her hand on his chest, the rhythmic beat of his heart helped soothe her, but not as much as she would have liked.

Yamala and Cela stared at her before Yamala spoke again. "No one else can know the Lord is my daughter's father. They will use it against her, and they will try to use her against him... to no avail. He won't do anything to save her; he'd be the first to sacrifice her."

"I know," Cole said. "But the Lord has most likely told others what she is to him."

"Perhaps, but I don't think so. He enjoyed torturing me and continues to do so, but he believes the siren are beneath him. Even with as insane as he is, and maybe *because* of how insane he is, he wouldn't want others knowing he fathered a child with a species as low as us."

"We won't tell anyone else," Cole vowed. "But things like this have a way of getting out."

"That they do," Lexi muttered.

"We will take our chances with that, but if I find out the information came from either of you, our deal is off," Yamala said. "Understood?"

"And what if we reveal it after the war?" Lexi inquired.

"Would you?" Yamala questioned as she studied Lexi intently.

"No," Lexi said honestly. "But you're putting a lot of trust in us."

"Not trust. I'm putting a lot of *faith* into the hope you'll be better leaders than the Lord and the madmen who ruled before him."

"That shouldn't be too difficult," Cela murmured.

"One would think, but incompetence has followed incompetence before."

"True," Cole agreed. "But we're putting a lot of trust in you to fight when the time comes for war."

"We will be there," Yamala vowed.

"Do you plan to stay here much longer?" Cole inquired.

"No. We will be leaving soon."

Sadness laced her voice as her hand entwined with Cela's.

"How will we get in contact with you once you leave?" Cole asked.

Yamala turned and opened a portal behind her. "Send your shadows through, Reaver. Let them see the land where we plan to hide."

CHAPTER TWENTY-ONE

EVERYTHING INSIDE LEXI protested Cole doing such a thing. With the shadows, he could dismember, see behind him, and kill... but to send them on a reconnaissance mission?

That couldn't be possible. If it *was* possible, he was communicating at a much higher level with them than she'd realized.

Her fingers dug into Cole's chest as he stood unmoving against her. At first, he didn't do anything, and the shadows didn't move. She started to ponder if perhaps Yamala was wrong about this.

And then, those *things* glided forward and slipped into the portal.

No. No. NO! Lexi shouted in her head as she struggled to keep her face impassive and her spiraling panic under control.

When the shadows returned from the portal, they curled around Cole's leg, slid up his side, and into his eyes. Lexi forced herself not to shudder, but Cela did. Yamala remained unmoving.

"How do you know so much about the Reaver?" Lexi demanded of her.

"I know some of the legend stating the Reaver and the shadows are one. Did I know for sure he would be able to send them ahead to see our new land? No. But I suspected he could. Did you get what you needed, Reaver?"

A muscle in Cole's jaw twitched. "Yes. I can find the realm, and you, again."

"Then we're all learning more about the Reaver," Yamala said. "We will be there when you're ready for us."

Lexi didn't like the appraising way Yamala studied Cole. It wasn't lustful but more like she was searching for a weakness. Cole must have sensed it too, as the shadows stopped moving and, as one, turned toward her.

Yamala held her ground, but Lexi could see the strain on her face for her to do so. Lexi couldn't tell if it was admiration or apprehension in the woman's eyes.

"It's time for us to leave," Cole said.

"Wait!" Yamala held up her hand as Cole started toward the portal he'd left open.

She turned to the human captive and beckoned him forward. He bowed his head as he shuffled forward with his chains rattling. Yamala grasped the loose end of the chain and tugged him forward more quickly. She held out the chain as she stepped toward Lexi.

"We're not evil; we are simply immortals who have our way of doing things," Yamala said.

Lexi didn't point out they didn't have to kill and capture sailors to survive. The dark fae didn't need to create the shadow kissed, the vampires didn't have to feed on humans or immortals, the lycan could learn how to control their tempers, and all immortals could be different somehow.

But they were who they were, and they were each special and unique. Her ancestors were a bunch of inflexible idiots who destroyed each other.

If she became queen, all she could do was hope to make the Shadow Realms a better place and learn from past mistakes. That was probably easier said than done, but she would do her best.

"Here is a token to show we mean what we say. We will stand by you to bring down the Lord," Yamala said.

She held the chain out to Lexi, who hesitated before taking it.

"We will not give up our ways, but we are willing to work together," Yamala continued.

"And so are we," Lexi said.

Lexi hated that the man trailed her like a dog as she followed Cole through the portal, but she smiled as they returned to the prison realm.

CHAPTER TWENTY-TWO

WHEN THEY RETURNED, Varo gathered clothes for the man they brought back, and Cole broke off his chains. Lexi stayed nearby to ensure the man was safely ensconced in a room.

Free of his chains, clothed, and freshly washed, he turned toward her as she started to close the door. "I'm Johnny," he said as his blue eyes met hers. "And thank you for taking me from there."

Lexi winced as guilt pierced her heart. She was glad he was free, but she didn't deserve his gratitude. "I was going to leave you there."

"I know, but you didn't want to."

"That doesn't make it any better."

She closed the door before he could say anymore and stepped away as fresh tears burned her eyes. The truth of her words rang in her head.

She'd been willing to leave him there, to sacrifice him to win this war. It was something she *never* would have believed herself capable of only a few months ago.

So much had changed since then, and so many lives rode on

her and Cole's shoulders. She could barely remember the naïve girl she'd been when the invitation to the Gloaming first arrived.

What would she become when this was over? If it was *ever* over.

"Don't beat yourself up," Cole said as he squeezed her shoulder.

She hadn't heard him approach, but he was often as noiseless as the shadows he ruled.

"I was going to sacrifice him," she said.

"He would have been the first of many, unfortunately. We can't save them all, and there are some we'll have to choose to let die."

Including us. But she didn't voice those words.

Lexi rubbed at her eyes as she mumbled, "I know."

She turned into him and wrapped her arms around his waist. Resting her head on his chest, she closed her eyes as she leaned against him. "Where are we off to now?"

"Next stop is Verdan, the witches' realm," he said. "But we'll go after you get some rest."

"No, we have to keep recruiting. I can rest when this is over."

"Lexi—"

"We should go, Cole."

There were far too many people relying on her; she couldn't stand around feeling sorry for herself. She would never emerge the same as when she went in, but Lexi *would* emerge from this. And she would do everything she could to save as many immortals and mortals as possible.

"Kaylia wants to come with us when we go," he said.

"And Sahira?"

Her aunt was half vampire and half witch. It was an extremely rare combination. Many immortals didn't like the vampires, and the witches despised them.

"Sahira thinks it would be best if she didn't go," Cole said.

Lexi started to insist Sahira was wrong, but her aunt was probably right.

"Let's get you better fitting clothes," Cole said as he turned her toward their shared room.

She'd forgotten she was still swimming in his tunic until he reminded her. They walked side by side down the long hall. When they arrived at their room, he opened the door and waved her in. He followed and closed the door behind him.

Lexi located a clean shirt, pulled hers off, and tugged on a bra and new shirt before facing him. Cole leaned against the wall with his arms crossed over his chest. The muscles in his forearms bulged as he surveyed her.

The shadows weren't present now, but she sensed their power simmering beneath the surface of his calm exterior. He'd always been powerful, as evidenced by the ciphers covering his arms from his fingertips to across his shoulders.

The markings also licked at his chin, ran across his shoulder blades, and down his back to his waist. Their sharp edges caused the black ciphers to resemble flames.

And those were only the markings he allowed to be visible to the world. When revealed, as he'd only ever done for her, they covered every inch of him from head to toe.

Before becoming the Shadow Reaver, he was probably the most powerful dark fae ever. The shadows only enhanced his powers.

And her people were the ones who burdened him with the shadows that were more of a curse. Or at least she'd started considering them as a curse. Yes, he could use the shadows to save and protect them, and those shadows helped destroy Malakai, but their ruthlessness and their effect on Cole scared her.

She would *not* lose him to their power and malevolence.

When he shifted, her gaze was drawn back to his face. He was gorgeous with his square jaw and short, black beard lining it. His piercing, Persian blue eyes were filled with love and desire.

Her skin prickled in response, and her breath came a little

faster, but now wasn't the time for this. They had things to discuss and witches to recruit to their cause.

"Did you know the shadows could do what they did in Aerie? That they could enter another realm and report to you about it?"

"I didn't," he said. "But it makes sense. They see things I can't and are in places I can't be. They also alert me to danger when I don't know it's coming."

"If you're in this realm, can you communicate with the shadows in another realm?"

"No... or at least not yet."

That final word sent a chill down her spine. "Yet?"

"I think, with time, the power might grow enough to let me do so."

What had her ancestors done to him? What were they *thinking* when they created such vast power and set it up to one day release on the realms?

Had they considered or cared about what they were doing at all? She'd always felt sorry for the arach, but the more she learned about them, the more they came across as a bunch of maniacal assholes.

Or at least most of those who once ruled Dragonia seemed that way. She doubted they let the commoners help establish the Shadow Reaver after what she'd learned about her parents' history.

And now, the arachs' greed and malevolence resided inside Cole. He was the strongest man she'd ever met, and one of the best men she knew, but could he withstand the corruption of so much power?

None of the Lords, since the arach mostly killed each other off, had withstood the vast power of the arach throne. But then, had the arach been able to withstand it? They'd destroyed each other and unleashed these shadows on Cole and the realms.

Was the throne the source of all that?

CHAPTER TWENTY-THREE

"WHAT IS IT?" Cole demanded when the color drained from Lexi's face and she sat on the bed.

She clutched the shirt in her hands as she stared at the floor. He strode across the floor to kneel in front of her.

Clasping her hands, he leaned forward to look into her stunned eyes. "What is it?"

"What if the throne corrupted the arach too? Alina said they weren't crazy, but they destroyed each other and created the Shadow Reaver; what if they became as insane as the Lord?"

He didn't take offense to her thinking the Shadow Reaver was something that someone who was crazy would create. The unknown about his new abilities frightened her, and she worried about losing him.

And she was not alone in her fear, but she didn't know what he did, deep in his heart... no matter what happened, he would *not* lose her.

"What if they were insane, and we're fighting to put *me* on that throne?" she whispered.

"Alina is right; they weren't insane."

"But—"

"They were greedy, set in their ways, and careless with their powers, but they *weren't* insane. Power corrupts, but corruption doesn't equal insanity. The arach wanted different things for the realm. Some of them sought more power, the royal family fought not to lose what they had, and in the end, they destroyed everything. They didn't do it because of madness; they did it for greed."

"How can you be so sure?"

"The arach never did anything like the Lords who have claimed the throne did to the realms. They never wielded the dragons' power over the realms, and there was mostly peace in the lands when they ruled.

"Of course, there was fighting amongst the different species, but not like there is now, and there was never the mass destruction and death the Lord has unleashed. The arach destroyed themselves, but they were sane when they did it."

"That almost makes it worse," she muttered.

Cole squeezed her hands and leaned closer. He clasped her chin and lifted her head so their eyes met.

"And you're not them," he told her. "When we win this war, it will be a new beginning and a chance for something better. Together, we'll make the realms a better place."

"And we will win," she said.

"Yes, we will."

"Do you trust the sirens?"

"No. But I think they'll fight with us."

"You think they'll try something afterward?"

"They'd be foolish to try, but they're not known for their kindness, and they don't work well with others. They never have."

"Maybe they're changing. They gave us Johnny."

"Maybe, but I doubt it. They gave us their reasons for helping, and I believe they'll help *because* of those reasons. But I'll never trust them."

"It was a pretty good reason."

Lexi leaned closer until her lips rested against his forehead.

Cole bowed his head as her kiss warmed his flesh and chased away the ice the shadows left encased on his soul.

He would never be free of the shadows again, they resided permanently in him, but she could keep them at bay. They didn't try to break free to destroy and kill when he was with her. She gave him peace.

She stroked his beard, and he closed his eyes and savored the tenderness of her touch. When she moved to slide off the bed, he inched back a little so she could settle on his lap and slide her legs around his waist.

He loved her long legs locking around him, the warmth of her breath against his cheeks, and her body pressed against him. Slipping his arms around her waist, he pulled her closer as she kissed his cheeks, nose, and lips.

The shadows stirred inside him, seeking to connect with her, but he kept them suppressed. She was *his*. And his alone.

When she nipped at his bottom lip, his hands flattened against her back. She smiled against his mouth, and her fingers slid through his hair while she leaned back to look at him.

The concrete floor was cool beneath his knees, but he didn't feel it as she gave him a sultry smile that caused his cock to pulse in anticipation. His hands trailed up her back until he found her bra hooks and undid them.

The simple, black bra sprang open, and his mouth watered as he took in her lush breasts and hardened nipples begging for his attention. Bending his head to her, he took one into his mouth and nipped at it as she leaned into him.

Her fingers tugged his hair as she released a delicious moan. Excitement pulsed through his veins. It didn't matter how often he took her; he couldn't get enough of this beautiful creature, his mate, fiancée, and the woman who would one day be his wife.

She was his light, and he was her darkness, and they were so incredibly strong together.

He flattened his palms against her back before sliding them

down to the waistband of her pants. He undid the button and let it fall open before rising and lifting her off the ground. Tugging her pants down her hips, she wiggled before kicking them aside.

They had things to do, battles to fight, and an army to gather, but he didn't care about any of it as he carried her to the bed, pulled off his pants, and settled over the top of her. The feel of her warm, inviting body beneath his was like coming home.

Propping himself up on his elbows, he brushed the hair back from the beautiful contours of her face.

"Stay with me," she whispered.

"Always," he vowed.

She smiled, and then locking her leg around his waist, she shifted so they rolled to the side on the small mattress. Sensing what she wanted, he rolled onto his back, and she climbed on top.

When she planted her hands in the center of his chest, her hair tickled his skin as she bent to kiss him. Content to watch her even though his shaft ached, he folded his hands behind his head while she made her way lower down his body.

Everywhere she kissed, his skin prickled and rippled in reaction. Then she moved down to kneel between his legs. When her eyes met his, they twinkled as she bent her mouth to his dick.

Riveted, he watched while she moved leisurely up and down the rigid length of his cock. Her hand and mouth worked over him until he gritted his teeth against his increasing urge to come.

And then the temptress pulled her mouth away. He was reaching for her when she slid his shaft between her breasts and, clasping them together, started to fuck him. His fingers entwined in the sheets, pulling them up from the bed as pain and pleasure mixed until he was nearly out of his mind.

"Lexi," he groaned.

The mischievous smile she sent him was nearly his undoing. He grasped her hips, and she started to protest as he lifted her toward him, but her objections died when he brought her down over his face.

She gasped as he tormented her with the same eagerness she unleashed on him. He teased her with his tongue and fingers as he tasted her until she begged for him to end it.

Her fingers tugged at his hair, and she cried out. He smiled as she came before lifting her off him. She slid down his body and wiggled her hips to take him into her. Grasping the back of her head, he drew her down to kiss her again.

"I love fucking you," he whispered against her mouth.

She smiled. "I love when you fuck me harder."

He wrapped his arm around her waist and turned her over. Bracing himself between her legs, he lifted one of her legs as he plunged deeper into her.

Seeking to feed, the dark fae part of him rose to feast on the energy their joining created. His head fell back as the shadows stirred within him and his power grew. The potency of that energy seeped through his body, flooded his veins, and swelled his muscles.

When she released a loud cry and her sheath clenched around his cock, he thrust deep again and again before burying himself inside her. A tingle ran down his spine, and his back bowed as he came.

Completely sated, he almost collapsed on top of her but caught himself as he lowered his head to rest it in the hollow of her neck. Her sweet scent assailed him as she turned her mouth into his neck and bit deep to feed.

CHAPTER TWENTY-FOUR

A KNOCK on the door finally caused Lexi to stir in Cole's arms. She mentally slapped herself when she recalled they were supposed to go to the witches' realm, and instead, she was sleeping. She hadn't expected to fall asleep, but exhaustion won out.

Cole's arms tightened around her as she lifted her head from his chest. He'd managed to get the blankets out from under them at some point. He'd pulled them around her and tucked her in against his chest.

She nestled into the warmth and security he offered as his head turned toward the door. In this room, with no windows, it was impossible to tell what time it was, but it felt late.

"What is it?" Cole called.

"I came to see if Lexi wanted to work on spells before going to Verdan?" Kaylia called through the door.

It must not be too late if Kaylia was looking for her. When Lexi started to move, Cole's arms clamped around her and he growled.

"I have to practice," she reminded him. He grunted in response, and she smiled at him as she tapped her fingers on his chest. "It will make me stronger, and if I can master *something*, maybe the witches will respect me a little more and be willing to help us."

He grunted again.

"I'll be there in ten minutes!" Lexi called out.

"See you soon," Kaylia said.

Her footsteps faded swiftly away from their door.

"We have to go," Lexi said. "And when I'm done working with Kaylia, we're going to Verdan, and no arguments from you."

Cole quirked an eyebrow. "Bossy little thing, aren't you?"

She smiled as she tapped her fingers on his chest. "You know you like it."

"I do. You also need some more rest."

"I've rested far more than I planned already. We have to get back to recruiting. I hope I can figure out *something* else I can do before then."

He ran his fingers through her hair. "Stop being so hard on yourself. It will come in time, and you've already learned and mastered so much."

"Hmm."

"Lexi."

"Okay, okay," she relented.

He hugged her closer before reluctantly releasing her. She wasn't exactly thrilled to work on spells; it was an increasingly frustrating endeavor, but she possessed some kind of magic. She had to figure out what and how to make it work.

You figured out how to create a shield and activate your fire. You'll figure this out too, she reminded herself as she pulled on a bathrobe and hurried out of the room to take a shower.

She scrubbed herself, dried off, and returned to their room, where Cole remained in bed. His attention shifted from the ceiling to her when she entered.

Lexi tugged on a pair of brown pants that fit like a second skin. When she realized Cole wasn't getting out of bed, she glanced over to discover him with his arms propped behind his head while he watched her.

Judging by the gleam in his eyes, he was *not* thinking about working on figuring out her magic.

"Don't do that," she muttered as her body reacted to the hunger in his gaze.

"Don't do what?" he asked with fake innocence.

"You know what."

"I'm just admiring the view."

She huffed as she tugged on a bra and shirt. The clothing did little to deter his attention while she pulled her hair into a ponytail.

"I have to go," she said.

With a sigh, he tossed aside the blanket and climbed out of bed. He trusted Kaylia now, and the two of them worked alone as often as they worked with Cole present, but he often liked to watch.

She kept her gaze averted from him as he gathered his things for a shower. He wasn't the only one who liked to admire the view, but she couldn't be distracted by him right now.

"I'll see you there," she said as she kissed his cheek and left the room.

Lexi passed the closed doors of the other rooms as she made her way down the cold, barren hall. The prison was as hospitable as the Antarctic.

She climbed two flights before emerging into another hall. At the far end, a set of stairs led to a balcony overlooking this inhospitable land.

She and Kaylia used to practice in an outer realm with plenty of sunlight, but they stopped traveling there after the Lord's ball. They all decided it was better to do as little traveling as possible while being hunted.

They had no choice but to travel to other realms in search of recruits for their army, but they didn't go to that outer realm anymore. They couldn't take the chance the Lord would somehow hunt them down there.

He might find them here too, but at least they'd all be together, and they'd all agreed on a different outer realm to retreat to if necessary. Varo had taken them there so they would know what it looked like and where to go.

Lexi climbed the hundreds of steps to the balcony and stepped out into the endless night of this realm. Stars shone in the sky, and a sliver of a moon hung over the craggy rocks and desolate land.

She strode over to where Kaylia stood with her hands resting on the stone wall as she gazed at the land. Lexi smiled as she glanced at the spot where she and Cole made love less than a week ago. That had been a scary night, one in which she worried she would lose him to the shadows, but it was also a special moment between them and their secret.

Lexi tried not to let the bleak atmosphere of this realm drag her down, but she couldn't help feeling saddened by the darkness of this place. "I miss the sun."

"So do I." Kaylia brushed her knee-length, silvery blonde hair back from her beautiful face. Her pewter gray eyes were troubled as she studied the area. "But one day, we'll walk in it again without fear."

Lexi hoped so, but doubt reared its ugly head. She shoved it back down to the depths of Hell where it would fester and tear at her, but she refused to acknowledge it now.

Just like she wouldn't let the bleakness of this place get to her, she wouldn't let her uncertainty drag her down too. They wouldn't succeed if she didn't believe they could.

"How did it go with the sirens?" Sahira asked as she came to stand beside Lexi.

Lexi smiled at her aunt, who had twisted her mahogany-colored hair into a neat bun. "Joining us today?"

"Yeah," Sahira murmured.

Sahira's familiar, Shade, leapt up to walk the wall. The black cat kept his tail high in the air as he surveyed the land like it was a toy he planned to batter. Without thinking, Lexi absently rubbed his back. He repaid her with a look of utter disdain from his golden eyes.

Sahira rubbed at her amber eyes and yawned.

"Aren't you sleeping?" Lexi asked.

"I am," Sahira said.

"It sure doesn't look like it."

Sahira shrugged. "We've been going through our Books of Shadows to see if there's something about the arachs we might have missed. Maybe some way to get your magic to open up."

Lexi's heart leapt with excitement. "Any luck?"

But as she asked it, she knew the answer. Kaylia and Sahira wouldn't look so exhausted if they'd found something, and they would have told her as soon as they did.

"Not yet," Kaylia said.

"You should be taking care of yourselves," Lexi told them. "There's not going to be any answers in your books. Maybe there are some in Dragonia, but we'll never know while the Lord is on the throne."

"That doesn't mean there aren't answers somewhere. I might have a friend who can help. She knew the arach and worked with them."

"That would be great!" Lexi blurted at the same time Cole growled from behind them, "Who is it?"

Lexi turned to discover him a few feet away. She hadn't heard him arrive.

Kaylia's shoulders went back as she turned to face him. "A light fae who's nearly twice my age."

CHAPTER TWENTY-FIVE

IF SOMEONE HAD PUT their finger against her forehead and pushed, Lexi would have fallen over. As it was, she barely managed to keep her jaw from dropping. No one had mentioned working with the light fae simply because they knew the light fae wouldn't help them anyway.

Varo was half light fae, and even *he* hadn't suggested working with his people. But she also had no idea how close he was to his mom, how the light fae felt about him being half dark fae, or if he had any contact with them.

The witches shunned Sahira for being half vampire; maybe the light fae had done the same to Varo for being half dark fae. And they all knew the light fae would *not* fight. They made that clear during the last war the Lord waged.

"This fae was around the arach. She knew them better than I did; she may have some insights I don't have," Kaylia continued. "I'd like to go to Lumus to speak with her."

"Will she be willing to help?" Lexi asked.

Cole's upper lip curved into a sneer, but he didn't protest her words. At this point, they would take any help they got.

"I don't know," Kaylia admitted. "The light fae have locked themselves away. They know the Lord doesn't like them—"

"Does anyone?" Cole inquired.

"I do," Kaylia retorted. "They shouldn't be compelled to fight if they don't want to."

"No, but they also shouldn't sit idly by and watch as the Lord unleashes havoc on the realms. They may be against fighting, but they're okay with the Lord destroying others as he rolls over the realms. He'll go for them too. He no longer cares how much carisle they pay him in taxes; he's determined to destroy everyone."

"I agree, but I'm not light fae or privy to their beliefs on this. I'm just saying there's a woman who might be able to help us."

Cole looked to Lexi. "What do you think?"

"I think it's worth a shot," Lexi said. "What harm can it do?"

"The Lord could have spies in Lumus waiting for us to show up in the light fae realm."

Lexi bit her bottom lip as she pondered this. "I don't think we have a choice. If there's a chance this woman has answers, then we should speak with her."

"I think I'll have a better chance of getting her to work with us if Lexi goes with me to find her," Kaylia said.

"You want to take Lexi into Lumus?" Cole asked incredulously.

"They'll welcome her there, and maybe if they realize an arach really *is* still alive, they'll reconsider their position about fighting."

Lexi's heart raced as she looked between Kaylia and Cole. She *never* thought she'd enter the realm of the light fae. The light fae had been shunned since the war started, but they weren't known to welcome strangers into their land even before then.

Normally, if someone saw a light fae, it was because the fae was in another realm, but their home remained closed to others.

"Have you been there?" she asked Kaylia.

"A couple of times, but it's been many years."

"When was the last time you saw this woman? How do you know if she's still alive?" Cole demanded.

"It's been decades, but unless the light fae have started turning on each other, she should still be alive," Kaylia said.

"Will they let me stay there or kick me out?" Lexi asked.

"We won't know until we try," Kaylia replied.

"If this happens, I'm going too," Cole stated.

Kaylia shifted uncomfortably as she glanced between Cole and Lexi. "You know they're not going to welcome a dark fae there."

"It's not negotiable. She's not going without me. Don't," Cole said to Lexi when she opened her mouth to protest. "If the Lord has men there, then you'll need protection. And even if he doesn't have men there, I don't trust the light fae not to turn you over to him. They might not fight, but they'll do whatever's necessary to save their asses. You're *not* going in there with just Kaylia."

"I don't think it would happen, but I can't disagree with that," Kaylia said.

"Okay," Lexi said.

She had intended to go straight to the witches' realm after training, but she couldn't resist the possibility of getting some answers. Knowledge was power, and they had little of it when it came to her abilities.

We're getting there, she reminded herself. She knew more now than last month and could do more. Unfortunately, it wasn't enough to take down the Lord.

"Then we'll go to the woods of Lumus together," Kaylia said.

"I think it will be best if I stay behind," Sahira said.

"What about Varo?" Lexi inquired. "Should he go with us?"

"I'll ask him," Cole said.

CHAPTER TWENTY-SIX

LEXI COULDN'T STOP GAWKING at the surrounding land as soon as they exited the portal Kaylia created. She hadn't known what to expect from Lumus.

It was beautiful. Lush, green land stretched for thousands of acres to a white castle set high on cliffs and surrounded by water on three sides. The white sun burning down from the yellow sky reflected off the blue water in a dazzling display visible even from their distance.

Pixies zipped by, giggling as they left trails of vibrant color behind them. Their song filled the air, and though they weren't all singing the same thing, the melodies blended into a soothing, beautiful tune that warmed her heart.

Ever since the Lord had hundreds of pixies murdered and dumped on her front lawn to prove a point to Cole, she hadn't seen any of the beautiful, tiny creatures. But they'd probably scattered and fled to different realms to hide from the Lord.

They had found a safe place here, or maybe these had always resided in this realm. She had no way of knowing.

A couple of them stopped and fluttered near Cole and Varo. They giggled as they hovered before the dark fae, batting their eyelashes and wings as they cooed. Lexi rolled her eyes but staggered back when a tiny man stopped in front of her.

"Hello, beautiful," he said.

Before Lexi could reply, a tiny woman hit him in the side. She was yelling so loudly and talking so fast that Lexi barely understood what she said while chasing the man away. She suppressed a laugh when she caught something about kicking him in the ass and castration.

The ones flying around Cole and Varo took off too, and soon calm descended, though their songs still filled the air. Lexi turned to examine more of the realm.

A thick copse of trees stood to her left. They were the thickest trees she'd ever seen; each was easily five times the size of the biggest redwood on earth. She gaped at them as they towered over the land and cast their shadows across the earth.

"Wow." Her neck ached from being tipped back, yet she still couldn't see the tops of the trees. "Amazing."

"It is a pretty realm," Kaylia said.

Cole grunted, but Varo remained stone-faced. Lexi finally lowered her head and rubbed at her neck while studying the realm.

"This way," Kaylia said and started toward a path cutting through the forest. "Elfie lives in the woods."

Varo stopped dead at the edge of the woods. Beside her, Cole stiffened as his head turned toward his youngest brother. Varo paled further than normal, something she hadn't considered possible until now.

Varo had put on a little weight since she first met him, but he was still too thin, shadows haunted his eyes, and his cheekbones were too pronounced. His nearly white-blue eyes stood out starkly against his black eyebrows. The tips of his pointed ears poked through the black hair he'd brushed back from his face.

"You didn't tell me we were coming to see my mother," Varo stated.

Lexi's eyes widened, and she shot Kaylia a look. The crone appeared as stunned as she felt.

"I didn't know," Cole said as he stared accusatorily at Kaylia. "You said we were going to the woods."

"I... I... didn't know Elfie was your mother," Kaylia said to Varo. "And we *are* going to the woods."

"Of course you didn't. I doubt many, if *any*, know she has a son," Varo said.

The bitterness in his tone disturbed Lexi as much as it upset her. She didn't know Varo well, but she liked him. He was kind, soft-spoken, and willing to do whatever it took for his brothers. How anyone could toss him aside in such a way was beyond her.

"I should have asked who we were meeting," Cole said. "I *never* expected Elfie to be in the woods."

"No," Varo said. "*I* should have asked, but it doesn't matter. We're here to see if we can help Lexi, and that's what matters. Elfie is an ancient; she'll be at the castle with the other ancients."

"I've always met with her in the woods. She told me it's where she prefers to stay," Kaylia said.

"When was the last time you talked with her?" Cole asked.

"Fifty years ago, give or take."

"Things could have changed."

"I doubt it. Once someone decides they prefer peace and solitude over luxury, they're not likely to change."

"True," Cole agreed.

"The light fae live in the woods?" Lexi asked.

"They live in the *trees*," Varo said.

"They *what*?" Lexi blurted.

"Many make their homes inside the trees," Kaylia said. "They're quite beautiful."

"I bet they are," Lexi murmured.

She was more than intrigued by this revelation, and despite already disliking this Elfie, she was excited to see what awaited them in the forest.

"Let's hope she's here," Kaylia said as she turned and started toward the forest again. "There's *no* way they'll welcome two dark fae into the palace."

Lexi didn't bother to point out that Varo was half light fae; if it didn't matter to his mother, it wouldn't matter to anyone else. She stepped closer to him and rested her hand on his arm as they entered the forest.

"I'll understand if you decide to go back," she assured him.

His kind eyes shone as he smiled at her. "I know, but I'm fine. I haven't seen the woman since I was a child, and I came to terms with her absence centuries ago. Besides, I doubt she remembers me."

Lexi didn't see how any mother could forget their son or leave him behind, but there was a lot she didn't understand in *all* the realms. Her hand fell away from his arm as they went deeper into the woods.

Beside her, Cole was tense and his shoulders rigid as his eyes searched the forest. Despite the size of the trees, sunlight pierced through their thick canopies and danced across the ground as they walked.

Sticks crunched beneath their feet, and creatures scurried through the woods, but she didn't see them. At least they weren't like the animals who resided in the woods of the Gloaming. They were more intent on trying to eat them than playing.

Or at least, she hoped they weren't like the creatures in the Gloaming. For all she knew, these creatures were about to pounce, but since no one else seemed concerned about them, she tried not to be either.

And then, the cutest little animal she'd ever seen darted onto the path in front of them. It stopped when it spotted them and rose onto its hind legs. It had the face of a hedgehog but with brown fur and a fluffy tail like a fox. Its little button nose twitched as its tiny front paws rose to its chin, and it *smiled* at them.

"Oh," Lexi breathed.

Then, it dropped down and vanished into the woods. She almost chased after it, but they weren't here for her to find a new pet, even if it was freaking adorable.

She couldn't stop herself from grinning as she looked up at Cole. He smiled back and slid his hand into hers. Their fingers entwined as the path progressed until they started to pass trees with doors in them.

CHAPTER TWENTY-SEVEN

COLE STUDIED the doors and windows in the trees they passed. Each door had different decorations, and they were all different colors. Candles flickered behind the glass panes of many of the homes while others remained dark.

Light fae moved about behind some of the windows. In others, faces materialized behind the glass as the fae became aware of their presence in the woods. One of the doors opened, someone was shushed, and a child was pushed inside as a light fae man stood and gawked at them. He scurried back inside, and the door slammed shut.

He could imagine their frantic whispers to each other; the dark fae were in their realm. The stuff of nightmares and boogeymen was walking through their woods, and while the light fae were a powerful race, they didn't like confrontation.

So, they would hide their children and wait. They would prepare for an attack, but they wouldn't start the fight.

Kaylia stopped outside a tree with a colorful door. Painted stars and a crescent moon covered one side of the door; the sun and flowers were on the other side.

A wreath of yellow and red flowers hung right over the stained-glass pane in the center of the door. In vivid reds, oranges, and golds, a tree decorated the center of the pane.

Kaylia lifted her hand to knock, but the door opened before her knuckles touched wood. On the other side stood a slender, fair woman with pale blonde hair wrapped around her head in a crown of braids.

It had been centuries since Cole last saw Elfie, the woman who was once his father's mistress and his brother's mother. Her white-blue eyes widened on Kaylia before settling on him. The color drained from her face, and her smile vanished.

They hadn't interacted with each other much when she lived in the palace; there was no reason for them to, but he'd recognize her anywhere.

"Colburn," she said flatly before her eyes went past him. For a second, no recognition registered on her pretty face. Then her mouth parted.

"Alvaro?" she breathed.

His brother's face remained impassive as he gazed at the woman who left him when he was ten. As far as Cole knew, that was the last time they saw each other.

Elfie's fingers stretched toward Varo, but her hand fell back to her side when he didn't move. The muscles around her mouth twitched as her lips compressed into a flat line.

She pinned Kaylia with a look of fury that Cole hadn't considered possible for the light fae to pull off. That look made it clear she would skewer Kaylia if she got the chance.

"I didn't know he was your son until we were already here," Kaylia said.

Elfie winced, but it didn't ease her rage. "Why have you brought *dark fae*"—she spat the words like they were acid burning her tongue— "into *my* realm?"

"It's good to see you too, Elfie," Cole said. She didn't want them here, and he and Varo would prefer not to see her, but he'd be damned if he would let her act like *they* were the worst things to exist when she was the one who abandoned her child. "What's it been, four hundred and sixty years or so?"

When Kaylia waved a hand at him, he scowled at her, but she was too focused on Elfie to notice his irritation.

"Four hundred and sixty-seven," Varo said from behind him.

Beside him, Lexi winced at the sorrow in Varo's voice. His brother didn't want to speak with his mother, but he easily recalled how long it had been since he last saw her.

That knowledge, and the deep-seated sadness it represented, only irritated Cole more. His brothers all pissed him off, but *no* one else would hurt them.

When Cole glanced at Varo, the callous glint in his eyes didn't fool Cole as Lexi rested her hand on his arm. Varo's face showed no reaction to the sign of support, but his eyes softened.

Turning back to Elfie, Cole sneered at the woman who remained focused on Kaylia. "We don't need her help."

"But we do!" Kaylia protested. "We can't...." She broke off and glanced around before looking to Elfie again. "We have to talk privately."

"I don't want you, or *them*, in my home," Elfie stated.

"Oh, for fuck's sake!" Kaylia's rare show of temper caused Elfie's eyebrows to rise. "I don't care about your history with them. It's the past! We're talking about *all* our futures. If you plan on having one, then you'll speak with us. It's important, Elfie, or I wouldn't be here. I left the crone realm because of this!"

Elfie remained unmoved for a minute before reluctantly stepping aside. "Come in, but *only* you."

"You'll want to speak with all of us," Kaylia said.

"They're not coming into my home."

"This isn't going to work," Lexi said. "Let's go. She's not worth this."

Elfie looked down her nose at Lexi. "I am an ancient, girl. You best watch your tongue."

"And you best watch yours," Cole warned. "Or I'll tear it out so you can see it."

"Enough!" Kaylia snapped.

Stepping closer to Elfie, she bent and whispered something in the woman's ear that Cole didn't quite catch. Elfie didn't move, but her eyes flew to Lexi and her mouth parted.

Her hand trembled before tightening on the door. Eventually, she stepped back and waved a hand at the open doorway. "The two of you can enter, but not them."

"She's not going *anywhere* without me," Cole stated.

"I'm not allowing—"

"I'm not going anywhere without them," Lexi interjected. "I don't leave my family behind."

The dig had its intended effect as Elfie winced. Kaylia slapped her palm off her forehead and Cole grinned at Elfie when she looked at him again.

"Lexi is my fiancée," Cole told her.

"Oh, Colburn," Elfie breathed as she closed her eyes. "You were always so determined to walk in your father's footsteps. It will be your doom."

"What does *that* mean?" Varo demanded.

Cole didn't have time to get annoyed by Elfie's words as the angry, accusatory tone of Varo's question shocked any irritation from him. He'd never heard his brother speak to someone like that before.

Instead of answering, Elfie stepped aside and gestured for them to enter. "All of you, come inside."

CHAPTER TWENTY-EIGHT

KAYLIA AND LEXI ENTERED FIRST; Cole ducked under the doorframe to follow his fiancée inside, and Varo brought up the rear. Once they were all inside, Elfie closed the door.

It didn't shut out much light as more streamed down from the hole in the top of the tree. The light pouring down from above shone off the dozens of suncatchers hanging inside. A myriad of different hues from the suncatchers danced around the room and bathed it in color.

A winding set of stairs spiraled to the top of the tree. A couple of doors branched off the stairs, but they were all closed.

Elfie waved a hand at the round table, carved from wood, set in the center of the room. The thick knots in the table's wood were black, and many were nearly the size of his head. Four chairs surrounded the table.

"Please sit," Elfie said.

No one sat. From one of the thick, wooden beams running across the center of the tree, Elfie removed a shining copper pot. She filled it with water from the small spigot sticking out of the tree and positioned over a white basin.

When she finished, she placed the pot on the metal hook

hanging over the fire on the other side of the room. The small fire crackled in the hearth as its smoke spiraled up the chimney and out the side of the tree.

Elfie stood before the fire, her hands clasped and her head bowed like she was seeking strength. As he studied her, Cole realized she didn't appear as hungry or tired as he'd expected the light fae to be.

"I thought the light fae were starving after the war," Cole stated. "You look fine."

"You even *sound* like your father," she murmured.

"He did raise us." Refusing to be sidetracked from his observation, Cole asked. "Why aren't you starving?"

"Because we're not."

"How is that possible? There isn't much joy in the realms right now, and that *is* what you feed on."

Varo was barely getting by on food and what little joy there was in the prison. He could also feed on sex, but he still had to provide for his light fae half.

"We also eat food," Elfie said.

"Food isn't enough to keep you sustained."

"Do you think I'll give away the light fae secrets?"

Cole remembered her as being meeker, but things had changed. He didn't like it. "No."

She turned and pinned Lexi with her gaze. "Are you *really* an arach?"

Cole's eyes narrowed on the woman before he looked at Kaylia. Now he knew what he couldn't hear the crone tell her. They had come here for answers, and they couldn't get them without revealing what Lexi was, but he would have preferred to do it *his* way.

"I am," Lexi stated.

When Elfie continued to stare at her, Lexi lifted a hand and flames erupted from her fingertips. Elfie remained unmoving, but something akin to yearning bloomed in her eyes... no, not yearning, *hope*.

And then the hope swiftly deflated as her shoulders sagged. Cole stepped closer to Lexi. Elfie wouldn't go after her, the light fae were selfish twats, but they didn't provoke attacks. However, he still didn't like having Lexi in this land and around these cowards.

"Tell us what you know about the arach," he said.

Elfie didn't tear her eyes away from Lexi as she sank onto the rocking chair beside the fireplace. She rubbed at her face as Lexi extinguished the flames.

"Not much," Elfie said. "I worked with some of them. I was friends with a few... or as close a friend as the arach would allow themselves to have. They mostly kept to themselves and made sure their powers remained a mystery.

"I'm not sure if they did that because it was fun for them, they believed it added to their mystique, or they worried someone could try to use them for their powers. Maybe it was a combination of all those things and more. And since you've come here asking me about arach powers, I'll never learn the answer. What do you know of your abilities?"

"I can use my fire."

"What about the dragons? The arach could always do things with the dragons."

"I know how to use that, but it doesn't do us any good while the Lord is on the throne. They obey whoever sits on the throne and rules the land."

"How do you know that?"

"Why aren't the light fae starving?" Cole inquired instead.

Elfie glared at him, and he smiled in return.

"If you want answers from us, then you'll have to give some in return," he said.

"I'm giving you answers," Elfie retorted.

"Not many, and no matter what you reveal, you will *not* get the answer to your question."

There was no way he would reveal Alina and her ability to this woman. *No* one else would know about that. If it somehow got back to the Lord, he would kill the dragon, and they couldn't let that happen.

Anger simmered in Elfie's eyes as she stared at him. He didn't think he'd ever seen the woman get so much as annoyed by something before, but now an underlying hostility radiated from her. Yes, she had definitely changed.

"You are so like your father," she said.

"Thank you."

"That's not a compliment."

"It is to me."

Her jaw clenched before her gaze shifted to Lexi and then Varo. "Do you all plan to try to put her on the throne?"

Cole walked over to stand in front of Elfie. When she tilted her head back to look up at him, he had a flash of the woman she was when she lived in the Gloaming.

Then, she'd been all smiles and laughter. He'd once seen her dancing in the palace garden as she sang to the plants.

Now, she was a sad shadow of that dancing woman. Her eyes didn't sparkle like they once did, and while that could be because they'd arrived on her doorstep without warning, he didn't think so.

"What happened to you?" he inquired.

Her brow furrowed as she stared at him before her gaze shifted to Varo. Sorrow filled her eyes, and her face crumpled before she composed herself once more.

"I made a terrible decision," she said crisply.

Varo didn't look moved by the distress she briefly revealed as he stared at his mother with zero emotion. But Cole knew his brother better than that; Varo hid his turmoil well, but being in this place was tearing him up.

No, they hadn't known they were coming to see Elfie, but Varo knew there was a chance he would run into her if he came here. He'd agreed to do so anyway to help Lexi and maybe make things easier for them.

It was a mistake. Varo had been through enough during the war without having to deal with this.

"I shouldn't have left you," Elfie gushed as she leaned forward and stared up at Varo with pleading in her eyes. "I just... I missed my home. I wanted to bring you with me, but your father refused. He insisted you were to be raised as a dark fae."

Varo remained unmoved as he shifted his gaze to the wall and stared over Elfie's head. Lexi stepped closer and rested her hand on Varo's arm as she looked at Cole.

"I think we should go," Lexi said. "This isn't helping."

"You could have come back to visit." Varo's voice was pitiless in a way Cole had never heard it before. "Brokk's mother came to visit him."

"I... I..." Tears bloomed in Elfie's eyes as she looked away.

She looked helplessly up at Cole, who had no words for her. He didn't know why she'd never come back. Some of his brother's mothers came back often to visit them, some left as soon as they were born, and others, like his mother, died when his brothers were young.

Elfie was the only one who helped raise her son, left when he was a child, and never returned.

"I couldn't return," she whispered. "It hurt too much."

"We should go," Lexi said again.

A determined look descended over Elfie's face, and Cole stepped back as she rose. Her eyes locked on Varo, but he remained staring at the wall.

"Unlike all the other women who came before me"—her eyes flicked to Cole—"except *your mother*, I loved your father."

Her words dripped venom when she said *your mother,* but Cole let it go. He didn't have an ounce of sympathy for her. His mother was long dead by the time Elfie arrived; if she still harbored such hatred for a woman she'd never met, that was her cross to bear.

CHAPTER TWENTY-NINE

"OF COURSE, he never returned my love," Elfie continued.

A small tremor ran through Varo as the angry woman who originally greeted them at the door returned. Resentment filled her eyes when they swung to Cole.

Lexi's teeth ground together; *no* one should ever look at Cole like that. The light fae didn't fight, but Lexi was pretty close to slapping the woman, even if Elfie was a pacifist.

"He only ever loved *your mother*," Elfie continued. "And those of us who followed her were given only scraps of occasional kindness. He was *so cold*."

Though Lexi wanted to protect Cole and Varo from this woman's bitterness, she couldn't stop her heart from softening toward Elfie's heartbreak. She didn't understand why Elfie had fallen in love with a man she described as cold, but she had, and it ruined her.

"And now you're traipsing down the same path as him," Elfie said to Cole. "And when she dies—"

"Watch it," Cole cautioned.

The hair on Lexi's nape rose as Elfie continued obliviously on.

She either didn't see the silver in Cole's eyes and the shift of the shadows, or she didn't care.

"You'll go about fathering children on women before leaving them behind. It was like a sick game to your father to see how many children he could have and how powerful they'd become. You'll play it too."

"That's not going to happen," Cole stated.

"We all die, Cole, and you're dark fae, so you'll keep fucking even though you'll be nothing more than a shell of who you once were."

"That. Is. Not. Going. To. Happen," Cole bit out.

"We shouldn't have come here," Kaylia interjected. "I'm sorry for bothering you, Elfie. I didn't know any of this history; I wouldn't have come if I had."

"Of course you didn't," Elfie replied. "I'm barely a footnote in Tove's past. He got what he wanted from me, a powerful dark fae and light fae son *he* raised while pushing me aside."

"You could have stayed in the Gloaming," Varo said.

"I *hated* it there!" Elfie exploded. "I wasn't the only woman your father was with when I lived there! I watched him parade around all his whores while I *died* in that land. Look at my home, look at everything here: my friends, my family. Look at the beauty of this land and the energy of these trees. The light fae thrive here because it's a part of us.

"In the Gloaming, I was alone and shunned because of what I was. I'd fallen for the king, but I was simply a means to an end. I was the bearer of his child and nothing more. I was *nothing*!"

Elfie's eyes filled with tears before she looked away from them. Biting her bottom lip, she took a deep breath and reined in her emotions.

"How could you love someone who treated you so badly?" Lexi whispered.

"Because love is cruel and something we cannot control. And he wasn't always horrible. He could be kind and attentive. He also made me feel special when we were alone, but those times were few.

"Tove gave me enough hope to keep me around. It took me too long to admit he still loved his dead wife, he always would, and there was nothing I could do to change that. In the beginning, I was sure my love would eventually make him move on from her, but I was wrong."

Lexi didn't bother telling her it was impossible to change anyone who wasn't willing to change themselves. Elfie had learned that lesson the hard way.

"When I finally had enough of my heart constantly being broken, I decided to return home and bring my child with me, but Tove refused. He said Varo looked too much like a dark fae, and they would ostracize him in Lumus.

"He was right; I knew it, so I stayed another year, but I couldn't handle it anymore. I left with every intention to visit, but once I was free, I couldn't... couldn't stand the idea of seeing Tove again. So, I stayed away until it was impossible to return."

The woman was an ancient, powerful light fae who could probably wield magics Lexi had never heard about. She was also one of the weakest beings Lexi had ever encountered. Any sympathy she had for the woman vanished. She couldn't imagine being so spineless as to abandon her child because of unrequited love.

CHAPTER THIRTY

When Cole turned away from Elfie, Lexi saw the disgust in his eyes as he extended his hand to her. Lexi gladly took it. She needed his love and strength after this awful day.

Varo remained unmoving beside her, but he edged away from the table when Lexi gave him a nudge.

"Sorry to have bothered you," Kaylia said as she strode toward the door.

Kaylia swung the door open and was about to step outside when Elfie spoke again. "The arach were creatures of nature."

They all stopped and turned toward her. Elfie remained standing near her rocking chair, but she didn't look as devastated or angry. Kaylia hesitated with her foot in the air before slowly lowering it.

"Maybe more so than the pixies and the light fae," Elfie continued.

When Kaylia glanced at them, Cole nodded for her to close the door.

"Do you plan to try to put her on the throne?" Elfie asked.

"It *is* my throne," Lexi said. "And my birthright."

"And what will you do with it?"

"What do you mean?"

"You see what the Lords have done over the past thousand years. What will *you* do with that power?"

"Return the realms to places of relative peace, give the dragons their freedom, and end all the brutality. *No one* will ever have to fear having their homes destroyed because I'm bored or annoyed with them. Immortals and mortals alike will know security again. They can rebuild without the worry of having it all torn away from them once more."

"Do you think she'll make a good leader?" Elfie asked Varo.

"Why does my opinion matter? You don't know me or my judgment skills."

"I know who you were as a child, and I have never forgotten the tenderhearted boy who may have looked more dark fae but had a light fae heart. I know what side you chose during the war, and I know you're standing here with the brother you sided against. That shows me you don't harbor resentment and bitterness."

Unlike his mother, Lexi thought.

"I believe you're a good man, and I will trust your judgment," Elfie continued.

"Lexi will make an excellent queen of the realms, and together, she and Cole will do *many* good things for all immortals. I do not doubt that," Varo stated emotionlessly.

"Neither do I," Kaylia said.

Lexi welcomed their vote of confidence. She still wasn't sure how great a job she'd do, but she would do her best to be a good leader. Plus, she wouldn't torture or kill people for fun, which was a vast improvement.

"The arach kept their powers mostly to themselves," Elfie continued.

"I'm very aware," Lexi muttered.

"You've figured out your fire."

"Yes."

"What about their magic?"

"I'm still struggling with that. I'm not sure what they were capable of doing."

"Well, as I said, they were creatures of nature. They thrived outdoors; they had an affinity for plants, animals, and dragons. Sometimes, I swear, they communicated with nature."

Lexi frowned as she recalled the luna flowers sliding across her fingers and dipping down to caress her while sitting in the moon room. Cole had never seen them react to anyone who wasn't a lycan before, but they liked her.

She'd certainly never communicated with them or any other animal. It would be *amazing* if she could.

Is there a chance the effects of Sahira's potion are still lingering? It wasn't something she'd considered once she started glowing in natural light and creating fire, but maybe some of it remained in her system and was still suppressing some of her abilities.

She had been taking the potion her entire life and had only been off it for a little over a month. It would make sense if it was still affecting her. Maybe she wasn't having such a difficult time unlocking her abilities because she couldn't figure it out; perhaps, it was because some of them were still locked away.

She glanced at Cole and Kaylia but held the question back. They could discuss it later.

CHAPTER THIRTY-ONE

"I THINK the arach gained strength from nature, but I can't be sure," Elfie continued.

Lexi had always loved animals and nature; she'd always felt rejuvenated around them, but gained strength from them? She definitely couldn't say that, but maybe she was missing something there.

"I also saw one perform a healing spell once," Elfie said.

"A healing *spell?*" Kaylia asked.

"Yes. She performed a spell to save an arach on the brink of death. It brought her right back."

"*Right back?*" Kaylia squeaked in a tone Lexi had never heard from the crone.

"Yes. It was one of the most amazing things I've ever seen. I don't remember the words she used to create the spell, but the child went from being almost dead to awake and talking within minutes."

"Oh," Kaylia breathed. "Oh my, Hecate."

"Can witches do that?" Lexi asked.

"No. Of course, we have potions and poultices, but healing

takes time even if our means accelerate it. I never knew anyone could do *anything* like that."

"So, if I could learn the words, then I might be able to perform the spell too?" Lexi asked.

Her heart hammered with excitement at the possibility. How amazing would it be?

And then her excitement vanished like fog beneath the sun's rays. How awful would it be if she never unlocked the ability?

"I don't see why not," Elfie said. "All of you, please sit down."

They all looked at each other, but Kaylia was the first to take a seat. Lexi settled into a chair next, followed by Cole; Varo remained standing by the front door. Lexi suspected he was contemplating leaving but wouldn't walk away from Cole.

Elfie walked over to a wooden shelf carved into the tree; she removed a thick book, strode over to the table, and set the tome down. There had to be at least two feet of yellowed pages inside it.

The ancient, brown book looked like it had been carved from a tree as it had a rough bark cover. A tree was engraved in the center of the cover; green foliage surrounded its thick, sweeping limbs.

When Elfie opened the book, dust rose from the cover. Lexi's nose twitched as she resisted the urge to sneeze.

"What is this?" Cole asked.

"Some of our histories. Mostly, mine," Elfie said. "All light fae create journals once they are old enough to write. With our extensive lives, there is much we would forget if we didn't record it. I'm two thousand three hundred and sixty-two years old. If my mother hadn't written my birthdate in this book when I was born, I wouldn't know it. She started it for me, and I took it over when I was ready."

No wonder it's so thick and dusty, Lexi thought.

"I don't write in it every day, but I record the most important things." Elfie flipped through the pages as she spoke. "How is it you exist, young one?"

Unsure if she should answer, Lexi looked to Cole, who studied

Elfie like he was trying to figure her out. Finally, he glanced at Lexi and gave a small nod.

Still, she hesitated before trusting this woman with any of her history. But Elfie was trying to help them, and she couldn't use Lexi's history against her or anyone else.

So, she told Elfie about her mother and father, how their love helped incite the war in Dragonia, and how they fled to be with each other. Elfie stopped flipping through the pages to stare at Lexi while she spoke.

When she finished telling her tale, Elfie spoke.

"I knew your mother. I did not know your father, but I can see your resemblance to Galeah. She was very powerful."

"Was she…?" Lexi swallowed back the bubble of hope nearly choking her. "Was she a good woman?"

"Yes."

Lexi blinked away the sudden tears in her eyes as she stared at the fire. She didn't know what else to say, so she concentrated on the flames as the book's pages rustled.

CHAPTER THIRTY-TWO

For the next few minutes, no one spoke until Elfie stopped flipping the pages and tapped the book three times. "Here it is. The day I saw the spell performed."

Lexi half rose from her chair as she rested her fingers on the table and leaned toward the book. Maybe it could help unlock another of her abilities.

"I didn't write down what they said," Elfie said. "I described what happened but not the exact words."

"Can I read it?" Lexi asked.

Elfie turned the book to her. "Of course."

Lexi held her breath while staring at the yellowed pages and cramped handwriting. A drawing of a smiling child filled the center of the page. A golden glow surrounded the girl. Her hair was a vibrant red, and she smiled as she tilted her face back to the sun.

It took Lexi a little time to decipher the script as it was cramped onto the page and flowed around the girl. But the words didn't reveal anything more than what Elfie had already told them. There was nothing for her to learn here.

"You saw the child glow?" Lexi inquired.

"I did," Elfie confirmed. "I think I'm one of the few, outside of the arach, who has ever seen it. But the child was badly injured, and when she awakened, I don't think she had any control over whatever ability the arach use to keep their glow hidden."

"And you never told anyone about it?"

"The light fae do not betray the secrets of others. I think that's the only reason the arach let me live with my knowledge. That, and I was good friends with the mother of this girl. She ruled the land then and wouldn't have let the others kill me."

When Lexi turned to look at Elfie, the woman smiled as she brushed a strand of hair over Lexi's shoulder. "I knew your grand-mother well. And I was there the day she saved *your* mother with a magic I never wrote down. Perhaps I considered it a betrayal at the time to do so. I don't remember now, but it makes sense for me to think that way."

"My mother," Lexi whispered as she glanced back at the page. "What happened to her? Why did she have to be healed?"

"She fell from a tree and was speared through by a branch on the way down. Because she often played in the forest alone, no one looked for her until she didn't return for lunch. And then, it was only a few of us who went out.

"By the time your grandmother and I found her, she'd lost most of her blood. While that may not be lethal for most immortals, she was only a child at the time, not fully matured, and nearly dead by the time we found her. Your grandmother saved her."

Lexi ran her fingers over the drawing of the girl and her radiant smile as her skin glowed. "But you put her glow in here and not the spell. No one had seen the arach glow... until me. Or at least that's what we believed."

"And you were wrong, though I doubt many others saw it and lived. I put the glow in my book, but most, who are not arach, would assume it was the sun behind her, or I imagined her with a glow as she returned to life. Anyone else who looked at this book wouldn't have considered it a glow. You, as an arach, know what it is. And you'll notice I didn't put all of her many markings on her."

When Lexi glanced at her, Elfie smiled.

"Yes, I saw all the silver markings too. I may have to write many things down to remember them, but I vividly recall *that* detail," Elfie said. "I know others have seen those markings, they're more common knowledge than the glow, but I didn't want to combine them."

"What were my mother and grandmother like?"

"They were strong, proud women who didn't back down from anyone or anything."

"In the end, that helped ensure their destruction."

"It helped ensure the destruction of many, but they had good hearts, and I doubt either of them wanted what happened to occur. They never saw things getting so out of control. No one did."

Perhaps that was true, but if Lexi wasn't careful, she would follow in their footsteps. She couldn't let that happen.

"Do you know anyone else who could tell us more about the arach?" she asked.

"No. Your species is one of many mysteries."

"And I know none of them."

Elfie gazed sadly at her before shifting her gaze to Varo. Then, her eyes fell to the book, and she carefully closed it.

"We all endure adversities in our lives, make choices that define us, and continue onward or falter. There are no other options. You *will* find your path in this world and unleash secrets you never knew existed," Elfie said as she returned the book to the shelf. "When the time comes, you'll decide if you're a warrior or not."

"That's funny coming from a light fae when you all refuse to fight," Cole said.

"You can be a warrior without fighting," Elfie replied. "There are many who accomplished much greatness without ever spilling blood."

"What greatness have the light fae achieved?" Varo asked.

"Is it not great to be a race who is at peace with ourselves and the realms? Is it not wondrous to worship nature and all the life surrounding us? Is it not strong to stand against so many, no matter the consequences?"

Lexi would never agree that this woman should have abandoned her child, but she had to agree with all *those* things. It was incredibly brave of the light fae to stay out of the war when they knew the decision would unleash the wrath of all the immortals on them.

The others must have agreed as none of them spoke.

"The Lord is out of control," Cole said. "He's completely lost his mind. He doesn't care about how much money or loyalty anyone can give him. He's going to come for the light fae too, and when he does, he'll destroy Lumus. It's not safe for anyone anymore."

Elfie stared at the far wall as she replied. "I will return to the castle and speak with the ancients about this."

"Do so soon. He's unraveling fast."

CHAPTER THIRTY-THREE

"Is THERE anything else you can tell me?" Lexi asked.

Cole hated the hope in her voice. All she sought were answers and to learn more about who she was, but they kept running into dead ends. Resting his hand on hers, he squeezed it as Elfie gave her a pitying stare.

"No, I'm sorry. I just know the arach are creatures of nature and animals," Elfie said. "It's what they thrive on."

To Cole, that made perfect sense; he'd seen her in the moon room with all the luna flowers and vines surrounding her as she laughed and played. He'd watched how tender she was with the horses she cared for.

He didn't know what that meant for her abilities, and they might never learn all the answers. At least they were unraveling some of them. And she was strong, powerful, and *would* rule Dragonia.

Maybe, once she was on the throne and in the home of her ancestors, they would discover answers to her questions and her powers would awaken further, but they had a war to win first.

"Thank you for speaking to us," Lexi said to Elfie.

"I wish I could have done more."

"We should go," Cole said.

He nodded to the door, and Kaylia rose from the table. Varo stepped from the shadows half enveloping him; Cole didn't know if his brother was aware of that or if he'd subconsciously been trying to hide.

"Alvaro," Elfie called when he opened the door. "Please be careful."

Varo didn't reply before he left the house. Kaylia and Lexi followed him out the door, but Cole remained. There was something he had to make sure she understood.

"I hope I don't have to tell you to keep this between us," he said. "The Lord knows an arach still lives, there's no hiding that anymore, but he doesn't know she's unaware of her full capabilities. She'll make a good leader, Elfie, but she requires an army to get her there."

"I won't tell anyone what we discussed here. I protected her mother and grandmother, and I will protect her. In return, I need you to protect my son. I left him, but I still love him."

"I have always protected Varo; even when he chose another side, I would have protected him. You should tell him what you just told me."

He was about to leave when her voice stopped him. "Cole, if something happens to her, don't become like your father. Don't close yourself off like that. It's no way to live."

Cole buried his irritation over her insinuating something might happen to Lexi. She was trying to be kind, and he suspected she cared more about Varo than he'd ever realized.

"She's my mate, Elfie."

Her mouth parted on an "Oh."

They both knew that meant there was no coming back for him. *No* lycan recovered from the loss of their mate. The others had walked a few feet away from the tree when Cole closed the door and turned to face Elfie.

"What do you know about the Shadow Reaver?" he inquired.

Elfie frowned. "There's not much to know. It's an old legend, a story told to scare kids."

"It's much more than that."

Her furrowed brow smoothed with realization, and her mouth parted. "*You?*"

"Yes."

"The prophecy." Elfie sank onto one of the chairs and rested her hands on the table as she stared at them for a minute. "She can't die, Cole."

"I know."

"No." When she lifted her head to meet his gaze, her eyes were more white than blue. "If the legends are true, and if she dies, what you will do will make the Lord look like he's been kind to us all."

"I could *never* be like him."

Elfie looked past him to the shadows. "Life has a way of changing us all."

Cole wasn't sure how to reply, but when Elfie's eyes returned to him, distress radiated from them.

"But then, you already know that," she said.

Shadows danced along Cole's fingers as they sought to break free. "Stay safe, Elfie."

He turned toward the door, but her next words froze him. "If anyone can control it, Cole, it's you. I've always sensed the vast power in you, which is probably why the shadows chose you, but they'll eat you alive if you let them take control."

"It's a good thing I won't let that happen. You and the others should leave here, Elfie."

"I will do my best to see they understand that. I might be able to get you some help." When Cole quirked an eyebrow at her, she held up a hand. "I understand the rest of the realms look down on us, but we didn't refuse to fight because we're cowards. We simply don't believe in war.

"But the Lord cannot be allowed to continue like this, and with the revelation of a living arach, we have hope of someone who can handle the throne taking it. Without her, we'd only replace one madman or woman with another. That could make a big difference with the others."

"Send me word if you can."

"I will. Until we meet again, Cole."

"Until then."

CHAPTER THIRTY-FOUR

"THAT DIDN'T WORK out as well as I hoped," Kaylia said as they returned to the prison realm.

Lexi refused to let her disappointment show. They had more details about what she could do, maybe not all of them, but they were making progress.

She could heal. If she could figure out how to do it, she could help others.

Just one more possibility to add to the list of them.

"I can heal others," she murmured. "Somehow."

"We will figure it out," Kaylia stated.

"Yes, we will," Cole said as he slid his arm around her waist. "Until then, I think you could use a break."

"We can't take a break," Lexi said, though the idea of one was so appealing she almost sat in the middle of the hallway to rest her legs. "We still have more realms to visit and more immortals to try to recruit. There are too many lives on the line for us to take a break now. Besides, we have taken a break; we should have already gone to the witch realm."

"We will get there soon, but we could all use some food."

Lexi's stomach betrayed her by growling... *loudly.* Cole

chuckled as he nudged her. "Come on, let's get you something to eat."

She considered arguing some more but decided against it when her stomach rumbled again. They made their way through the stark corridors of the prison with its broken inmates and awful stench of despair.

Since they'd started to stay here, she'd learned to block out the inmate's sobs, but sometimes, they slipped through and she became aware of them again. Now was one of those times.

She cringed as one of them wept while alternately pleading for someone to kill him. Then he started begging for his mother.

"Can we let them go once we destroy the Lord?" she whispered.

"We'll destroy them then," Cole replied.

She recoiled from his words. "We can't do that."

"They're loyal to the Lord."

"So are many in *all* the realms; will we kill them too?"

She held her breath and waited for his answer, but they couldn't slaughter all those who sided with the Lord. He didn't reply though.

"Some are loyal to him because they have to be," she said. "They're afraid for their families and their lives. They don't want to lose everything they have, so they fight for him."

"I know."

The briskness of his words said he knew but didn't care. "Cole—"

"Anyone who is a threat to you will perish."

She glanced back at Varo and Kaylia as they followed them downstairs to the kitchen below. They both wore blank expressions, but there was sadness in Varo's white-blue eyes and a hint of apprehension in Kaylia's pewter ones.

When they entered the kitchen, assorted immortals sat at some of the wooden tables set out around the room. Brokk, her dad, and Niall gathered at a table in the far back. Orin sat with a group of his men; he'd propped his feet on the table as he leaned back in his chair and laughed.

When her dad spotted them, he smiled and rose from the table to stride toward them. When he opened his big arms, she happily went into them, and he swept her into one of his bear hugs.

"How did it go?" he inquired.

"Not great, but not bad," Lexi informed him. "I'll tell you more after I get some food."

"I'll get you something to eat," Cole offered as he kissed her forehead. "Go sit with your dad and relax."

When Varo and Kaylia broke off to go with Cole, Lexi hooked her arm through her dad's and leaned against his side as they walked over to the table together. Eyes bore into their backs as everyone in the room followed their every move.

She still wasn't used to all the attention she got from everyone. It took time for the immortals in the prison to learn her true heritage, but they became incessantly curious about her once they did.

Those in the prison learned about her from visiting friends and family and through the grapevine full of talk about the dark fae king's arach fiancée. Varo and Orin hadn't told them what she was, and as much as Orin pissed her off, he wouldn't have revealed her secret either.

They also knew Cole was the Shadow Reaver, but they weren't as curious about him as they were her. Probably because he was a lot more intimidating.

Lexi settled on a bench at the table as Sahira and Maverick entered the room. Her aunt's face lit up when she spotted them; she waved before hurrying over to join them. Maverick continued toward the immortals serving food and pitchers of blood from behind the cafeteria line.

Her dad sat next to her, and Sahira plopped down across from her. Though she'd expected it, Lexi inwardly groaned when Orin rose and strolled over to join them.

Grasping a chair from a nearby table, he turned it around before straddling it and sitting at the head of the table. He rested his arms on the back of the chair and propped his chin on them. "How did it go?"

Her dad shot him an irritated look as his upper lip curved enough to reveal the tip of a fang. "Don't you have somewhere else to be?"

"Oh, Del, there's nowhere I'd rather be than basking in the rays of your sunny disposition. It's giving me a tan."

"Orin," Brokk said in a low, warning tone.

"It went fine," Lexi said before they could all start bickering.

"Did you learn anything new?" Orin asked.

"No."

"Why don't I believe you?"

Lexi's eyes darted around the immortals and mortals gathered within the room. She spotted Johnny at a table with some refugees who once resided beneath her manor. Jayden and Nessie sat beside him, and the three of them waved when they looked her way.

She beamed as she waved back. The mortals may not be living the most carefree life on this dark rock of an outer realm, but they were alive, fed, and relatively happy. And this was better than being trapped in her tunnels; at least they had more space to move around and go outside. Yes, some immortal or the Lord's men might stumble across them here, but that could have happened with the tunnels.

"Kitten?" Orin prompted her in a chiding tone.

Lexi scowled at him as he leaned closer. "I'm not going to discuss it here, you idiot."

"Meow." Orin hooked his fingers into claws as he swiped at the air. "Did someone give Kitten a bath she didn't want?"

There were times when it took *every*thing she had not to punch him in the face. This was one of those times as her hands fisted on the table.

"That's enough," her dad said.

Orin stared at her as he sat back on the chair. Lexi pretended not to notice as Cole returned and set a tray in front of her. He glared at Orin until his brother vacated the chair. Cole set his tray beside her and turned the chair around.

"Thank you," she said to Cole.

He kissed her temple before sitting. She picked up her spoon and dipped it into the steaming bowl of stew. The most delicious aroma of meat and veggies wafted up, and her stomach rumbled in response.

This place did have some perks; one of them was the gnome who ran the kitchen with an iron fist. She was a tyrant who wouldn't allow anyone else to cook, but she combined a bare assortment of ingredients into something delicious for every meal.

They ate as the others settled around them while her father and Brokk sipped blood. When they finished eating, they retreated to one of the many barren rooms in the prison. They often got together to talk in this one, and it had become their meeting place when they needed to speak privately.

There, Lexi told them what they learned in the light fae realm. She leaned against the wall and slid down to sit on the ground when she finished. She was so tired, but they still had so much to do.

CHAPTER THIRTY-FIVE

"So now what do we do?" Orin inquired.

"Now we head to Verdan," Lexi said while Cole said, "Now, she's going to rest."

"I will later," Lexi said. "We have more recruiting to do."

"I'll go; you can stay here and rest," Kaylia said. "The witches will listen to me."

"No, we all agreed I should help with gathering the army. They have to see *me* if they're going to help us. I *have* to be there."

"You're exhausted," Cole retorted.

"We all are," she said. "*Everyone* in the realms is, even those on the Lord's side. We've all done nothing but walk on eggshells for years, and it won't end until *we* end it. I have to go to Verdan, Cole. We can sleep when the Lord's dead."

Cole's jaw clenched, and a muscle twitched in his cheek as his gaze went from her to the wall. The shadows in the room shifted but didn't move toward him.

He wasn't drawing them in, but they reacted to his mood and prepared to do as he commanded. No matter how in control of himself and the shadows he was, they scared the shit out of her.

"I'm still coming with you," Kaylia said. "They might be more cooperative if I'm there."

"Circe also worked with us on the coalition," Cole said. "She wants to take down the Lord and will probably help try to convince the witches to do so."

"Do you think my presence there could help?" Sahira inquired.

While Kaylia wasn't as hostile toward her aunt, dad, and Brokk as she used to be, she hesitated as she pondered this. She may not still consider them lowly vampires, but most witches would, even if Brokk and Sahira were only half vamp.

"No, they won't want a vampire in Verdan," Kaylia said.

"Will they have a problem with us working with vampires?" Lexi asked more harshly than she intended. She understood why the witches disliked vampires so much, but if it would be an issue... "If they're going to have a problem with my family, then there's no point in going to them."

The others shifted uncomfortably while Kaylia stared at the wall. "The vampires killed our queen. That is not easily forgotten."

They'd also killed her fiancé, but she was adjusting to working with vampires.

"It was eight hundred years ago," Niall muttered.

"And she's still dead!" Kaylia snapped.

"So are many others," Maverick replied. "But hey, I'm a lycan; we understand grudges and killing those who have wronged us. However, maybe they could ease up a little to help us take out the Lord."

"Maybe they can, but we won't know until we talk to them," Varo said.

"There are more witches than vamps who would fight for us," Sahira said.

"What are you saying?" Lexi asked.

"I'll step out of this fight." She glanced at Brokk and Del. Brokk bowed his head while her dad folded his arms over his chest and glowered at the wall. "If it will help gain the witches' trust, I'll stay away."

"No," Cole said. "We need all the help we can get from *all* immortals, and the witches have to accept that."

"Most vampires are on the Lord's side," Orin said.

"True, but two of our best fighters and one of the best military minds I know are vampires, and we're not losing them."

Brokk and her dad smiled, but Sahira still looked doubtful.

"If we unseat the Lord, the realms will be free of oppression," Lexi said. "It will be a new beginning for all of us. A time to let go of old hatreds."

"Perhaps, but that takes time, and it can*not* be commanded of immortals. I hope you don't plan to take the throne and start ordering about those you disagree with," Kaylia said.

Lexi's teeth ground together as she bit back her retort. She understood the feud between the witches and the vampires, but it was centuries ago, and it was time to *get over it.*

Unfortunately, things didn't work so easily, and if she somehow managed to retake the arach throne, she couldn't assert her will over the other realms. Ugh, her head pounded.

She rested her forehead on her knees as she rubbed her temples. Then she realized, if she kept her eyes closed, she might fall asleep. She lifted her head again.

"Will the witches work with vampires and us or not?" she asked.

Kaylia hesitated before replying. "Yes. If I agreed to work with you, then I believe they will too. Few hate vampires more than me. Plus, you will have me on your side to help gain their trust. They won't be thrilled about working with vamps, but they'll do whatever's necessary to ensure a better future for themselves and their children."

"What about the warlocks?" Orin inquired.

Kaylia shrugged. "Who knows what they'll do. Lexi would

have to try to recruit them too, but the Lord is a warlock, and they can be..."

"Cantankerous?" Varo suggested.

"Giant douchebags with a god complex," Orin said.

Maverick pointed at Orin. "That's more like it."

Lexi didn't say anything. She knew the man Kaylia once loved was a warlock, and while they could be assholes, she wasn't going to wade into a minefield.

"They can be," Kaylia murmured.

"Talon was working with us on the coalition," Brokk said. "He was trying to bring the Lord down from behind the scenes. Not all warlocks are on the Lord's side or douchebags."

"We can't know anything about the warlocks until we talk with them. For now, our next step is the witches," Cole said.

Lexi rested her hand against the wall and rose. "And we should go to them now."

The shadows shifted again, and she could hear Cole's teeth grinding together, but he held his hand out to her. She slid her fingers into his.

He didn't like her pushing herself, but he was her fiancé. More importantly, he was her partner, and they would work together throughout all of this.

CHAPTER THIRTY-SIX

THEY STEPPED out of the portal to Verdan and into a world of chaos, death, and destruction raining down on the village of Gramarye. Screams rebounded around them; the fires streaming into the air consumed the teepee-like structures the witches resided in.

"No!" Kaylia gasped.

A screaming witch sprinted by them. The fire consuming her hair and clothes enveloped her as smoke streamed behind her. Kaylia jumped on her; she pulled the woman down as a thunderous boom reverberated through the air, and the earth heaved like ocean waves rolled beneath the dirt.

Smoke choked the air, and the fire crackled as it devoured the trees and homes. One of the trees gave way and crashed to the earth with a thunderous boom that sent more flames leaping high as sparks erupted into the air.

Cole grasped Lexi's arm and spun her toward the portal as lycans armed with spears and bows emerged from between the fires. One of them plunged a spear into a fleeing witch. Lifting her off the ground, he laughed as she flailed while sliding further down the wooden shaft.

"Get in the portal!" Cole shouted at Lexi.

He pushed her toward the open portal as a lycan charged through the fray toward them. Spinning to plant his body in front of hers, Cole grasped the spear's tip as the lycan plunged it toward his heart.

Jerking the weapon up, Cole bent the spear's tip over until it snapped. The lycan's momentum carried the beast of a man toward him as Cole yanked the broken shaft free from his grip.

As the lycan came toward him, he also transformed. His jaw extended, and lethal claws erupted from his fingertips.

"Colburn," it sneered in a voice more animal than man as it crashed into him.

Cole plunged the spear's broken end into the thick muscle covering the man's abdomen. Cole released what was left of the useless weapon and seized the man's shoulders as the lycan lashed out with his claws.

A searing pain lanced down Cole's side; warm blood trickled down his skin and plastered his tunic to him as the lycan sliced him open to reveal his ribs. Cole snarled as the lycan's teeth snapped in his face.

He sank his extended claws into the fur now tickling his palms as he spun with the lycan and smashed the wolf off a tree. The creature released a howl as its spine broke and the tree cracked in half.

"Motherfucker," Cole spat in the wolf's face.

Swinging the lycan back again, Cole retracted his claws and sent the beast flying. As it soared, its paws waved in the air before it crashed into a burning teepee.

Shoulders heaving, Cole spun back toward the portal to discover Lexi hadn't gone through it but was fighting off a lycan. Her sword flashed in the firelight as the lycan darted to her right.

Stepping to the side, Lexi brought her sword down across his arm. The lycan yelped as blood spurted from him. Grasping his arm, the lycan lifted its head and howled as its jaws started to extend into a snout.

"Shit!" Cole hissed.

He sprinted back toward Lexi. Before the lycan could attack again, Cole wrapped his arms around her and spun her toward the open portal. "Go back!" he shouted at her. "*Go!*"

But as he was telling her to leave, more lycans descended on them and cut off her path to the portal. When one of the lycans ran for the portal, Cole shut it down before he could go through.

If the lycan got into the prison, it could get out again, and the Lord would learn where they were. Not having an easy exit open in this burning realm was a danger to Lexi, but they couldn't let the Lord's men loose in the prison. They would lose everything they'd managed to rebuild if they did.

Cole lowered his shoulder and ran into the first lycan racing at him while he drew the shadows closer. The shadows rose from the ground to form a wall between Lexi and the lycan woman lunging at her.

When the woman plunged into the shadows, they swarmed around her like a colony of pissed-off bees. The lycan screamed while the shadows ripped at her hair and clothes and stripped the flesh from her bones.

"Cole, no!" Lexi screamed.

But her terror for him meant nothing; what mattered was her survival. The power of the shadows swelled inside him until they spilled out to attack their enemies.

And with their release came a rush of relief and power. They were free, and they were *feasting*. Cole smirked at the next lycan as the shadows left only his bones behind.

He glimpsed Kaylia spinning to the side as she waved a hand at the earth. A wave of dirt rose from the ground to coil before her. With a flick of her wrist, she flung it into the face of a warlock who recoiled as he spit out the soil.

A dragon soared into view from over the top of the teepees; it headed straight toward them. It unleashed a blast of fire that churned up the ground, spit out giant chunks of dirt and rocks in numerous directions, and destroyed everything in its path.

CHAPTER THIRTY-SEVEN

LEXI SAW the dragon coming while a child of no more than four or five stumbled out from around the burning ruins of a witch's home. The girl screamed as she raced across the blood-soaked earth; red stained the bottom of her yellow skirt, and her blue eyes were the wild ones of a horse trying to avoid a pack of wolves.

Lexi was so focused on the girl and the streak of dragon fire racing toward the child, she didn't see the warlock until he stepped behind the girl and drove a sword through the center of her chest. Blood sprayed from the child's mouth; her eyes fell as her hands rose toward the blade before falling limply back to her sides.

The warlock grinned as he pulled the sword free. Rage and desperation propelled Lexi forward; love brought her fire out before, but necessity caused it to encompass her hands and swirl toward her elbows as she ran at them.

A shriek the likes of which Lexi had never heard before pierced the air. Even without seeing the woman, the agony in that horrible sound told her it came from the child's mother.

No. No. No! The word looped through Lexi's head as the child fell to her knees. The girl's mouth parted as she stared at the blood spreading across her chest.

"Lexi, no!" Cole shouted.

Around her, the shadows swirled and danced, but her attention remained focused on the child as the warlock raised his sword over the child's neck. The vicious bastard was about to chop off her head.

"No!" Lexi screamed.

Throwing up her hand, she unleashed a wave of fire over the top of the girl's head; it slammed into the warlock's face. Unprepared for the flames, the man screamed as he staggered back, but Lexi didn't stop.

The fire continued to erupt until the warlock was covered in flames and his shrieks drowned out those of the dying. He ran a few feet away before staggering and going to his knees.

Lexi saw a streak of orange flame from the corner of her eye as the dragon's fire raced toward the girl. Dousing her flames, Lexi threw herself forward, embraced the girl, and knocked her to the ground.

Lexi drew the child's body beneath her as the dragon's flames enveloped them. Beneath her, the girl didn't move while the fire burned away what remained of Lexi's clothes and warmed her flesh but didn't burn her.

She'd withstood the wrath of a dragon's fire before and didn't feel any discomfort from the heat, but the girl whimpered. Lexi didn't know if that was from the inferno, the fact Lexi was pushing her into the earth, or the blood pulsing against Lexi's hand with every lumbering beat of the child's heart.

Lexi pressed her palm harder against the girl's chest in the hope of staunching the blood, but it was useless. The sticky, warm liquid coated her hand and slid between her fingers as the child's heart slowed.

"No," she whispered. "Stay with me. Stay with me."

She prayed the child heard her above the fierce crackling fire. She would *not* let this girl die because of an immortal with a twisted soul.

Tears pooled in Lexi's eyes as the flames burned against her back and the child's blood flow eased. The tears never made it to her cheek before the fire seared them away.

The wind whipped her hair around her; it lashed her face as smoke choked her nostrils. She cracked her eyes open enough to see the red and orange inferno churning around them before she closed them again.

But through her anguish and terror for the child, something shifted and changed inside Lexi. Her shield crumpled, her defenses came down, and a warm flood of something she couldn't quite explain poured through her.

She didn't understand what was happening, but like lava breaking through a volcano, something seeped up inside her. It spread through her limbs and warmed her more than the dragon's fire.

She wasn't sure if defenses she didn't know she had in place were crumbling. Maybe the last of Sahira's potion was finally wearing away; perhaps it was her panic for this child's life or being exposed to the dragon's flames was burning away something she'd never known existed, but something changed inside her.

A rush of power pulsed through her veins, flooded her cells, and dug into her bones. It flooded her soul with a sense of rightness and of something more.

She was connecting to something… no… not something… she was connecting to *herself* in a way she never had before. And when she did, her hands burned, her heart swelled, and power filled her palms as she held the child closer while willing the blood to stop. The girl's heart was so sluggish, Lexi expected it to stop at any second.

CHAPTER THIRTY-EIGHT

THE FLAMES CUT OFF, a dragon screeched as if in pain, and Lexi lifted her head to discover the charred and broken earth surrounding her. Stuck in the middle of all the destruction, and with the sun streaming down on her, Lexi glowed brighter than the fire surrounding her.

When hands seized her arms, she sensed their wrongness as soon as they connected with her skin. As Lexi swung backward, fire leapt from her fingers and blasted into the snarling lycan trying to tear her away from the child.

The man staggered back from the impact and beat at his face as he tried to smother the flames. Lexi kept one hand on the child's back as she turned to face their approaching enemies.

She'd lost not only her clothes but also her weapons. It didn't matter; she'd still kill these assholes. She reluctantly released the girl as she twisted to face the two warlocks and the lycan coming toward them.

Behind them, she spotted Cole surrounded by a group of the Lord's men. Mutilated bodies littered the ground around him, and the shadows leapt at those trying to keep him from her. Her heart

sank as fresh blood splattered his face and clothes while he ruthlessly slaughtered those between them.

She lost sight of Cole when one of the lycans rushed toward
her. Fire covered her arms and danced across her shoulder blades
as she released a stream toward the creature.

She hated all this death, but she'd be damned if she allowed
these things anywhere near the girl. Even if the child was already
dead, she'd make sure none of the Lord's men touched her again.

The nimble lycan was too fast for her flames and scurried out
of the way. Lexi spun to keep him in view and unleashed another
blast as the other lycan and warlock rushed toward her.

The three of them had come to the same conclusion as her. She
had fire but no weapons; there were three of them, she only had
two hands, and if they moved separately, she couldn't get them all.

The power she felt unleashed beneath the dragon's flame still
thrummed through her body, but she had no idea how to release it
or *what* that power could do.

Lexi bared her teeth at the warlock as she edged closer to the
unmoving girl. Screams sounded from behind her as Cole
bellowed. The shadows closest to them shifted and rose toward the
warlock, but they weren't enough to stop the lycan from charging
at her.

The creature dodged her fire as the second lycan charged too,
and the warlock turned and fled from the shadows trying to take
him over. Lexi's heart hammered as the lycans grinned at her; she
tried to keep her panic under control, but every instinct she had
screamed at her to run. She wouldn't leave the child behind,
though.

A swooping shadow blocked the sun and fanned the inferno
until it became a tornado spinning around them in a rapid circle of
red and orange. Sparks shot off its side; they peppered her face and
body, but they didn't burn her, and they didn't deter the lycans.

A breeze from the dragon's wings caressed her cheeks, and the tip of a talon brushed her hair before the creature landed before her. The earth shook beneath its massive feet, and its wings remained wide as it cut her off from the lycans.

The green dragon's head swiveled toward her; its golden eyes met hers as a puff of smoke coiled from its nostrils. Then, its head swiveled toward the lycan coming at her. Its roar blew back their clothes and staggered the men backward.

The creature was bound to the Lord's commands, which meant it probably couldn't kill the men, but it was obvious it wouldn't let anyone attack her either.

She didn't know how long this reprieve would last and wasn't sure exactly how the Lord commanded these creatures, but he wouldn't tolerate one of them defending her. She might only have seconds before the Lord called the dragon away.

Lexi spun and scooped up the child. Cradling the girl against her chest, she didn't have time to see if the child still lived as she sprinted through the burning teepees. Debris and trees crashed and burned around her; flames shot into the air and screams continued to resonate from all around, but Lexi didn't look back as she ran.

Lexi couldn't look back; if she did, she would return for Cole, and she had to get this child and her mother to safety. The child's mother remained kneeling near the burning woods as Lexi raced toward her. Uncaring of the danger surrounding her, tears rolled down her dirty cheeks.

"Cole!" Lexi screamed as she ran. "I'm going back!"

As she ran, Lexi opened a portal a few feet behind the woman. When she arrived at the woman's side, she grasped her arm and pulled the woman to her feet.

The mother staggered and reached for her child, but Lexi shoved her forward and into the portal before she could grasp the girl. She glanced back but couldn't see Cole through the destruction anymore.

As soon as they arrived at the prison, she would return for him.

~

COLE WATCHED as Lexi vanished through the portal, and it closed behind her. Not only was she safe, but now he would make them pay. He smiled as he released any restraint he still held over the shadows, and screams filled the air.

CHAPTER THIRTY-NINE

LEXI'S HEART thundered as she ran through the portal and plunged back into the small room where they last spoke with everyone. She glanced wildly around in the hope Cole was also returning, but the only ones there were Sahira, her dad, and Maverick.

Their eyes widened as they took in her, the child, and the woman who staggered and nearly went down before Maverick caught her. He steadied the woman who spun toward Lexi with her arms outstretched.

"Please," the woman pleaded. "Let me have my baby."

Tears stung Lexi's eyes as she took in the child's beautiful, blood-and-dirt-stained face. Her lips were blue, her eyes closed, and Lexi couldn't tell if she still breathed or not as she was so *still.*

Unable to look at the bloody wound in the innocent's chest, Lexi stepped toward the woman and carefully handed her the child. The woman sobbed as she went to her knees and cradled the girl against her chest.

Lexi yearned to comfort her, but the woman curled into herself as she hugged her motionless child. Sahira rested a hand on the woman's shoulder, but she didn't pay any attention as she wept.

This was a private moment, they should all let the woman have her time to grieve, but Lexi couldn't walk away and leave her alone in this room. So, instead, they stood and tried to offer what little support strangers could give someone who was broken.

"What happened?" Maverick demanded. "Where's Cole?"

"Where is Kaylia?" Sahira asked.

"I don't know," Lexi said. "I lost sight of Kaylia. I have to go back for her and Cole."

A small plop against the rocky floor alerted Lexi that the child's blood had dripped from her fingers. She winced as she closed her fingers and willed herself not to cry.

When they first entered the portal, Lexi felt the faint beat of the child's heart against her chest, but the child had lost too much blood. There was no way she still lived.

War was ugly and brutal and so unfair, but this war didn't have to happen, which only made it so much worse. The monster sitting on a throne that wasn't his didn't have to do this to the realms.

While she understood Lord Andreas was once a good man and the throne had corrupted him, it didn't matter. After knowing what it did to those who ruled before him, he'd made a conscious choice to sit on it. He gladly wielded his power over the realms, battered the human realm into submission, and was now ravaging the realms he believed might stand against him.

The Lord had chosen death, and though Lexi far preferred life, she *would* make him suffer the consequences of his choice.

"What happened?" Maverick demanded again.

"The Lord's men and dragons have destroyed Verdan," Lexi said. Sahira's hand flew to her mouth as she cried out. "I have to go back for Cole and Kaylia."

"I'm coming with you."

"So am I," her father said, and Sahira nodded.

Before Lexi could respond, a new portal opened a few feet away, and Cole emerged. Blood plastered his black hair to his face and neck; it coated the tips of his pointed ears, dripped off what remained of his clothes, and was so thick in some spots it nearly covered the ciphers on his arms.

The shadows rose off him like Medusa's snakes as he closed the portal. The whites of his eyes were entirely black, but their silver burned brightly. A flash of their normal, Persian blue color went through them when they latched onto her before the silver returned.

With a small cry, Lexi closed the distance between them. Ignoring the shadows, she threw herself into his arms. She didn't notice the blood—she had plenty of it on her too—she only cared that he was safe.

When he embraced her and lifted her off the ground, she encircled her legs around his waist and hugged him. The mother's sobs doused her joy, and she buried her face in Cole's neck as her heart ached for the woman's anguish.

"Get me something to cover her," Cole said in a voice Lexi barely recognized as his. "Now!" he barked when no one moved.

Her dad hurried across the room, opened the door, and left. He returned a minute later with a blanket and Brokk.

Cole shifted his hold and wrapped the blanket around her as Brokk took in the scene. Her dad must have filled him in on at least most of it, as he didn't ask any questions.

Nestled in the blanket, Lexi closed her eyes as she inhaled Cole's allspice scent. Though the coppery tang of blood was more prominent on him now, his natural, potent aroma was still there.

Tension thrummed through him as the shadows swayed. She'd seen what he'd unleashed in Verdan and knew the more he drew on the shadows, the more they threatened to consume him. And he was cold as he stood with his legs braced apart and his hands on her back.

His body was rigid against hers; he was more distant than she'd ever seen him, but gradually warmth seeped through him and his arms softened around her. It was too late to undo what happened in

Verdan, but he was *hers*, and she would *not* lose him to the shadows.

CHAPTER FORTY

"ARE YOU OKAY?" she whispered.

"I am now," Cole said.

"Kaylia?"

"I don't know where she is," Cole said. "I lost her in the fighting."

"Me too." She leaned back to look at him and was relieved to see the blackness seeping out of his eyes. "We have to go back. We can't leave her alone, and I can help protect her and the others from the dragons."

"You're in no condition to return."

"I'm naked, not injured," Lexi retorted.

"You could have died there, and the Lord's men are crawling all over Verdan. Do you want to end up in his fountain?"

Lexi winced at the reminder of the Lord's bloody fountain. Cole had told her about it after he returned from delivering Varo's and Orin's fake bodies to Dragonia. No, she absolutely did *not* want to end up in that fountain. But still...

"We can't leave her behind," Lexi insisted.

She slipped from Cole's arms to stand in front of him as she adjusted the blanket to keep herself covered. He kept his arm locked firmly around her waist.

"No one left in Verdan required our help," Cole said. "The few remaining witches were fleeing into portals when I left. I didn't leave Verdan without looking for Kaylia or any other survivors, but I didn't see any."

"They could have been hiding. They could be trapped there," Lexi said. "The fire was *everywhere*."

"The witches can open portals, Lexi. They wouldn't be trapped somewhere."

"Then where is Kaylia? Why isn't she here?"

"She's probably helping some of the others, especially if there were a lot of wounded," Sahira said. "They'll need all the healers they can get."

Lexi knew they were right, but she still couldn't walk away from Verdan without knowing that everyone had gotten to safety. "There could be those who are too injured to open a portal. *Kaylia* could be too hurt to return. We can't leave her behind without knowing for sure. I'll never sleep again or forgive myself if we do."

The woman shifted her daughter, pulling the child away from her chest. The woman's tears rolled down to splash on the girl's face.

"I'll go to look for her," Brokk offered.

"I'll go with him," Maverick said.

"So will I," Sahira said.

"You'll need someone to help keep you safe from the dragons," Lexi insisted.

"Lexi," Cole growled.

"Cole," she grated in return. "I *know* I'm important to this mission, but I'm not leaving my friend behind. And I'm not allowing them to go without my added protection."

"We'll be fine on our own," Brokk said. "We've encountered dragons before."

"I'm going back," Lexi insisted.

"No, you're not," her father interjected. "Sometimes, being a leader means stepping back and allowing others to do what you can't. That doesn't make you a weak leader; it makes you stronger because it shows you realize there are some things you can't do or *shouldn't* do. And this is one of those things.

"We will not risk losing the last living arach because it is what you *want*. Your wants mean nothing compared to those of the greater good right now. Brokk and Maverick are warriors; they know how to survive and are in this war too.

"It's time for you to learn about delegating responsibilities, even if those responsibilities get another killed. You can't save everyone, Andi; you'll drive yourself insane if you try, and the realms do *not* need another mad ruler."

No one spoke, and Lexi didn't know what to say as she stared at her father, who gazed back at her with narrowed eyes. Lexi glanced from her father to Cole and back again.

Lexi bristled against their trying to put restrictions on her. She was determined to help keep those she loved and cared about safe, but glancing down her naked body to her shoeless feet, she had to admit she wasn't in the best position to help.

She didn't care about her nudity. There was a time the idea of standing naked in front of *anyone* would have made her blush and probably run screaming from the room, but war and near-death experiences had a way of shifting one's perspective.

Did she like being nude in front of others? Not. At. All.

Would it stop her from saving her friend? No.

But not having a weapon and not being as prepared as she should be would slow her down and put the others at risk. They would be so worried about keeping her safe that they wouldn't focus as much on what they were supposed to be doing in Verdan —saving others.

"Fine," she relented. "But if you're not back in ten minutes, we're coming after you."

That should give her enough time to find some clothes and a weapon.

"Lexi," Cole said.

"We'll be back before then," Brokk said before Lexi could argue with him. "If the remaining witches were all fleeing by the time Cole left, then the dragons and Lord's men are probably gone. There's nothing there for them anymore. We need a portal."

"And you shall have one," Sahira said.

Lexi's heart lodged in her throat as her aunt opened a portal into Verdan. Much like the portal she, Cole, and Kaylia entered earlier, there was no sign of the danger lurking beyond. But she'd become very aware of how deceiving looks were.

Sahira squeezed the woman's shoulder before releasing her. The woman lifted her head to look at Sahira before shifting her attention back to her child.

"Good luck," Lexi whispered as she held the blanket closer.

"We don't need it," Maverick replied. "We'll kill whoever gets in our way."

His words were chilling, but she liked his attitude. And then, they vanished into the portal.

Lexi opened her mouth to tell the others she was going to get dressed but whispered words froze hers.

"What did you do?"

Lexi's attention shifted to the grieving mother gazing at her in disbelief.

"What. Did. You. Do?"

Did the woman think *she'd* done this to her daughter? But that couldn't be possible; she saw the warlock stab her child.

CHAPTER FORTY-ONE

BROKK WAS EXPECTING it to be bad, but the total devastation of the village of Gramarye made his steps falter as they emerged from the portal. Beside him, Maverick stiffened, and Sahira froze. Smoke spiraled into the air, but the fires, running out of things to consume, were dying.

"Oh, Hecate," Sahira whispered.

Everywhere Brokk looked was nothing but charred embers, smoldering remains, and the dead. And there were *so many* dead. The bodies littering the ground seemed as numerous as blades of grass on a field.

And some of those bodies… Brokk shuddered at the brutalized remains and the different parts scattered across the charred earth.

The dragons hadn't done that; they would have eaten those remains. He'd never seen any other immortals do anything like this in war, not even the lycan or berserkers who were sometimes known to lose complete control.

He didn't have to witness the killings to know what did this; it was the shadows. His brother and those *things* residing in and around him had unleashed this brutality on the enemy.

It wasn't something he'd ever considered Cole capable of

doing, but he wasn't fool enough to tell himself it wouldn't get any worse. As much as he hated to admit it, this was only the beginning.

Brokk searched the sky but didn't see any dragons; if one appeared, they'd have no choice but to leave. There was no way for them to avoid or hide from the monsters. There was nothing left to hide behind or anywhere to take cover in this burned-out shell of a land.

Sahira closed the portal as Brokk moved forward. It was almost impossible to step over one crisp-fried body without nearly stepping on another.

"What the fuck?" Maverick muttered as he stepped over the remains of a lycan caught in mid shift.

Brokk assumed some of the other men were warlocks; how many of those men fought for the witches and how many against was impossible to decipher. He'd survived the Lord's war, done things he'd never forget and would always regret, but he couldn't look at the smaller bodies scattered amid the remains.

"He's a monster," Sahira whispered.

It was stating the obvious, but the Lord was unraveling faster with every passing day.

"They didn't deserve this," Sahira whispered.

"He's going after anyone he thinks might stand in his way," Brokk said. "Maybe even those he believes *might* turn against him. We should warn them all."

"We will," Maverick said.

"Let's search here and return before Lexi decides to come back," Sahira said. "She shouldn't see any more of this."

"Are you going to be okay, or would you like to return?" Brokk asked Sahira.

"I'll be fine."

"Your mother—"

"Could be here or not; she usually resides in one of the outer villages, but it doesn't matter. I will survive it if she's here."

"Okay."

Brokk picked his way through the wreckage as he searched for any hint of Kaylia amid the ruins. She pissed him off and still looked at him with more derision than anyone ever had in his life, but he'd come to like the uptight woman with a steel rod in her spine.

"What if the Lord's men captured Kaylia?" Maverick asked as they made their way through what was once the center of the village.

"Then let's hope she can withstand torture," Brokk said. "But if they captured her, we'll have to leave the prison immediately."

"They don't know she's working with us. They wouldn't have taken her; they would have killed her," Sahira said. "The Lord didn't come here looking for prisoners."

"Very true," Brokk agreed.

"Do you think he destroyed all of Verdan?" Maverick inquired.

"I don't know. I hope not," Sahira said. "Like many other realms, there are different parts of Verdan. Gramarye is the busiest village and where most of the witches live, so he might have left the other towns alone."

Brokk thought it was more likely the Lord wanted Verdan leveled and would do so. But he might not know all the villages, so some might have survived his wrath.

The wind shifted when they rounded the corner, and smoke billowed into Brokk's face. Waving a hand to clear his vision, he coughed as his eyes watered.

Once he could see again, he spotted more bodies littering the ground, but it wasn't as bad as when they first entered Verdan. Glad for the reprieve, he strode across the burnt-out earth as they continued their search.

"We should return soon," Maverick said. "There's no one left here."

Brokk was about to agree when he caught a streak of movement from the corner of his eye. Turning, he searched the area where he'd seen the flash, but nothing moved.

"Hold on a second," he said.

He strode toward the burnt-out remains of the smoldering home the movement had vanished behind. The houses weren't as badly destroyed in this area either, but though some remained standing, they all sustained damage.

He stepped around the smoke-stained witch's teepee and froze when he saw what lay beyond.

CHAPTER FORTY-TWO

"What did you do?" the woman asked the question again, but this time it was stronger. Tears streamed down her face as she gazed at Lexi in disbelief. "What did you do?"

Cole pulled Lexi closer against his side. He was about to pull her away, to take her from this woman and this place. He had no idea what the woman's problem was, and he didn't care. He'd be damned if she blamed Lexi for what happened to her child.

She'd been through enough without dealing with this woman's misplaced grief. He was rattled by what he'd witnessed in Verdan and needed some time alone with her anyway.

He'd known dragon fire couldn't kill her, but when she vanished beneath its flames, while the inferno the dragon emitted destroyed the land, his heart shredded, his insides turned to ash, and an all-encompassing rage blistered across his skin. The bellow that erupted from him had rivaled a dragon's.

While Lexi was in those flames, another dragon had come toward him. It veered off course when it saw the shadows leaping from the ground and encircling Cole as they tore into his enemies.

Alina hadn't been lying, and she hadn't been wrong; the dragons wouldn't attack him even if they hated him. Whatever magic the arach instilled in him during the trial, it had granted him protection against those beasts.

He should be grateful; instead, he found himself more infuriated by it. The dragons wouldn't attack him, but the arach had instilled this darkness inside him, and while he welcomed the power it gave him, he wasn't foolish enough to believe it couldn't ruin him.

It would destroy him if he lost control, and that was something far too easy to do. The more death the shadows unleashed, the more they craved.

And so did he. He wanted to destroy the Lord and do what was necessary to ensure that man's death and Lexi's safety.

And as the shadows stirred within him, he also realized his father had *never* contained them. He'd never really believed his father had possessed this ability, but he'd questioned the possibility.

King Tove was a powerful man and adept at keeping the true depth of his power hidden from the world, his allies, his enemies, and his family. But if he'd possessed these shadows, they would have slipped out on occasion; it would have been inevitable.

If his father possessed this power, that dragon wouldn't have eaten him. Now, for whatever reason, and he suspected it was Lexi, the arach bestowed this shadow magic on him during the trials.

And they'd done it to keep her alive. He didn't know how the magic knew to seek him out, but there were many mysteries in all the realms that would never have answers.

He would have sacrificed himself for her before the trials; he was powerful before the shadows entered him, but now, he was more so. And the things that could have most easily taken him down, the dragons, were now unable to do so.

The Lord was going to die, and he would be the one to kill him. When the shadows stirred excitedly inside him, Cole pulled Lexi closer as he sought to restrain them again.

"What did you do?" the woman asked again as she half rose before going back to her knees.

Cole had forgotten all about her until she spoke again. He had no time for this woman and her hysterics, even if she had just lost her child. It was sad, but a lot more children would die if they didn't put a stop to the Lord.

It wasn't Lexi's fault the Lord was leveling the realms in search of her.

"I tried to keep her alive," Lexi whispered. "I tried to stop the blood from flowing while shielding her from the dragon's fire. I so badly wanted her... to... to live."

Lexi's voice hitched, and he scented her tears on the air before one slid down her cheek. Cole wiped it away as Orin opened the door and entered the room.

His brother froze when he spotted them. He glanced into the hallway before shutting the door and hurrying toward them. "What happened?"

The woman rested her hand on her daughter's chest where the blood soaked her torn clothes to her flesh. Her face was a mixture of emotions so intense she couldn't form words as her mouth opened and her lips moved, but no sounds emerged.

～

THE TINY, dirt and soot-covered faces of the children huddling behind the hut caused a small twinge to tug at Brokk's heart. One of them held a kitten in her lap while a snow-white owl perched on the shoulder of the other.

The girl with the owl was the older of the two, but she was only five or six. They were both probably too young to open a portal and were left behind in all the confusion.

Kneeling before them, Brokk rested his arm on his knee as the children eyed him warily. "Hello," he greeted. "I'm here to help you."

When the lower lip of the younger girl started to tremble, the older one hugged her close, but neither of them spoke.

"Where are your parents?" he inquired.

Brokk turned to discover Sahira and Maverick had walked over to join him. The older one raised a tremulous hand and pointed at the teepee behind him. Maverick pulled back the flap of the home enough to reveal the battered body of a woman within.

"Look away," Sahira said as she swept the girls into her arms and turned them away.

"Any chance she's still alive?" Brokk asked Maverick in a low voice the children couldn't hear.

"I'll check," Maverick said and ducked inside.

The flap had barely settled into place before Maverick emerged again. He gave a small shake of his head to Brokk.

When the younger girl started crying, Sahira knelt before her. "It's okay," Sahira assured her. "We're going to take you somewhere safe."

"Stay with the children," Maverick said to her. "We'll search the rest of Gramarye and see if we can find any other survivors."

If there were any other survivors, they were most likely children too young to open a portal. Or they were too injured to flee the realm on their own.

"If we're not back in a couple of minutes, take them to the prison and tell Lexi and the others we'll be back soon. There's no reason for them to come here," Brokk said.

"I will," Sahira said.

"We should split up," he said to Maverick. "We'll cover more ground that way, and I don't think there's any threat left here."

"Neither do I," Maverick said.

They split up, and Brokk moved swiftly through what little remained of the realm. He opened the flaps of the few remaining homes to make sure no other children hid within. He discovered a couple of bodies but didn't uncover any other living beings.

When he returned to where he left Sahira and the children, he discovered an open portal Sahira was about to enter. She hesitated when she saw him.

"Go ahead," he told her. "I'll wait for Maverick."

"Stay safe," Sahira said and ushered the children toward the portal.

They hadn't found Kaylia, but at least the girls would be safe. The little girl held her kitten against her chest as she walked in while the other girl rested her hand protectively on her sister's shoulder. The owl flew behind her.

Maverick returned a couple of minutes later.

"Anything?" Brokk inquired.

"No other survivors and no sign of Kaylia."

"Then let's get out of here."

CHAPTER FORTY-THREE

"I'M SO SORRY," Lexi breathed.

"You have nothing to apologize for," Cole said.

"What happened?" Orin demanded.

"A miracle," the woman said at the same time Lexi answered, "Hell."

It took a few seconds for the woman's words to sink in, but when they did, Lexi glanced at him before focusing on the woman. Cole studied the woman as she stroked her daughter's cheek.

"What did you say?" Lexi asked.

"A miracle," the woman whispered.

The tears streaming down her cheeks dripped off her chin to land on her child.

"I don't understand," Lexi whispered.

The woman moved her hand away from her daughter's chest to reveal the hole in her shirt and the blood staining it. He'd seen the warlock run the child through with his blade.

It hadn't gone through her heart, but it still should have been a lethal blow. And there was so much blood; there was no chance the girl had survived all that blood loss.

Then, he saw the subtle rise and fall of the child's chest. His

198 BRENDA K DAVIES

eyes widened as Lexi sucked in a breath. No one else moved or spoke.

The child's skin remained colorless, and her lips were still blue, but she continued to breathe when such an injury should have been lethal to someone so young. A five-hundred-year-old witch prob-ably wouldn't have survived the wound.

When Lexi edged closer, he adjusted his hold on her and followed. He wasn't going to let her near this woman. She was turning into a powerful fighter and learning more about her abili-ties, but he didn't trust anyone right now.

As they got closer to the girl, he saw what lay beneath the hole in her shirt and all that blood—perfectly smooth, unblemished skin.

"She was stabbed," Lexi breathed. "I saw it. I watched him do it to her. I felt her blood pulsing against my hand and pouring through my fingers. I *saw* it. I *felt* it."

"I saw it happen too," Cole assured her. "The blood is still there. They stabbed her; she was dying."

"And now she's not," the woman whispered as she brushed blood-streaked blonde hair away from her daughter's forehead. "Now, my Morgan is a miracle." Then the woman tilted her head back to look at Lexi. "What did you do?"

Lexi gazed at the child before looking up at Cole in confusion. "I felt—"

"Don't," he interjected before she could say anymore.

He was sure the woman knew Lexi was an arach, sure that knowledge had spread rapidly through the witches' realm after the ball, but the arach powers remained a mystery to most, including him and Lexi. He intended to keep it that way.

After this, word would get out that she could heal, though he had no idea how she'd done it. He suspected Lexi didn't know either. Until they figured it out, he hoped to stem the flow of her newfound ability from spreading.

They should keep as many secrets as they could from the Lord. Those secrets were small weapons they could use against the Lord.

"Is she... is she okay?" Lexi whispered.

"She's better than okay; she's alive," the witch breathed.

"Let's get this girl and her mother somewhere to rest while the child recuperates," Cole said.

"Of course," Del said.

He shot Cole and Lexi an inquisitive glance as he walked over to the woman but didn't say anything further. As he knelt before the woman, a portal opened behind them, and Sahira emerged with two children. The witch turned to the children and staggered to her feet.

"Maribelle, Agnes!" the woman blurted. "Where is your mother?"

The younger girl, Agnes, started sobbing as she clutched her kitten closer. The older one squeezed her sister's shoulder and lifted her chin.

"She's dead," Maribelle replied in a voice far too mature for someone her size.

The woman's breath sucked in. "Where is Melisandra?"

"We... don't... know," Agnes said in a small, hitching voice before using the back of her sleeve to wipe her nose.

"She wasn't home when the attack started," Maribelle said.

The woman embraced the children, drawing them close as Brokk and Maverick emerged from the portal.

"It's okay," the woman whispered. "You'll stay with me until we find your sister."

"And what if she's dead too?" Agnes wailed.

"Then you'll stay with me. But you're safe now. Come."

She led the children to her daughter as Sahira closed the portal and slumped against the wall. The color had drained from Sahira's face, and shadows circled her eyes. She must have opened both portals and it had weakened her, Cole decided before shifting his attention to the witch.

CHAPTER FORTY-FOUR

"You'll keep what happened here with Lexi and your daughter to yourself," Cole told the witch. "I understand it's only a matter of time before what she can do gets out, but we need that time, and we have to keep the Lord from hearing about this."

"Hearing about what?" Brokk inquired.

"You missed all the fun stuff, brother," Orin replied. "It seems our little arach is holding out on us and is a bit of a healer."

Sahira straightened away from the wall. "What?"

"The child will live," Orin said and waved a hand at the girl.

They all shifted their attention to the bloodied girl as she took another small breath.

"Holy shit," Maverick whispered. "How is *that* possible?"

"Our little arach is becoming more powerful," Orin said.

"I'm not *your* little anything," Lexi retorted.

"Easy, Kitten."

"You're such an asshole."

"This is true."

Before she set his ass on fire, Lexi focused on the others. "What about Kaylia?"

"There was no sign of her," Brokk replied.

"We have to find her."

"We will," Cole assured her before focusing on the witch. "Do you agree to keep this to yourself?" If she didn't, he'd lock her in one of the cells.

The woman rested a hand over her heart. "I swear, on my daughter's life, I'll never tell another soul about this."

"That won't matter. Others saw the girl get run through, but none of them are here. That will buy us some time and keep it from the Lord for a little while." The woman nodded, and Cole shifted his attention to the other children. "Keep them quiet about this too."

"I will," she promised.

"What about Kaylia?" Del asked.

"We have to find her, but since we have no idea where any of the other witches are, I don't know where to start," Cole said.

"I know where they are," the woman said. "We weren't expecting the Lord to come at us so brutally, but we have a realm we designated as our safe place to escape to. When you're ready, I'll take you there."

"Won't the other witches have a problem with that?" Brokk inquired.

"We agreed to help the dark fae king and his arach fiancée against the Lord before they arrived. The witches would want me to help you, especially after what happened in Verdan, but I'll face those consequences if they have a problem with it. I don't think they will."

"Should we go now to make sure Kaylia is okay and not in the Lord's hands?" Brokk asked.

While it wasn't likely the Lord took any prisoners, they had to know if Kaylia was dead or in another realm. But when Cole looked at Lexi, covered in blood and with her shoulders hunched, all he wanted was to get her cleaned up and in bed.

He'd be jeopardizing everyone in this realm if they didn't find out about Kaylia. Even if they captured her, he doubted she would tell the Lord anything, no matter what he did to her, but he had to learn the truth before leaving this room.

But if he went to that other realm, Lexi would insist on going with him.

"Can you open a small portal to this other realm?" he asked the witch. "One big enough for a hand to fit through?"

The woman frowned at him. "I can."

"Then do so."

Her jaw tightened a little, but she waved a hand at the floor, and a small portal opened before her. Lexi's fingers dug into his back as a single shadow slipped through the portal.

"Cole," she whispered.

"It's fine," he assured her.

This was nothing compared to what he'd unleashed on Verdan. He was in control of the shadows again. Still, he felt them digging their way deeper into him as he used their power to search out Kaylia.

And then he spotted her kneeling amongst the injured, covered in blood and shouting orders. He pulled the shadow away, leaving her to the witches and this new realm.

She was alive, safe, and he could trust her not to betray them or their location. Once Lexi was rested, they would go to see her.

Cole retracted the shadow. "She's fine. You can shut the portal."

The witch gawked at him before closing the opening. The witch looked at the others gathered in the room, but none of them acknowledged the dread in the woman's eyes.

"When we're ready, and when your daughter is better, we'll come for you," Cole said to the witch. "And we'll go through together."

He could open a portal into the witch's new realm now, but it would be better if one of their own did so. If he opened a portal into this new realm, it might cause distrust amongst the witches, and they needed their help too much to risk that happening.

He turned his attention to the others. "We're going to clean up. Someone stay here in case Kaylia comes back. Until then, don't let anyone else know we've returned."

"We won't," Maverick promised.

Cole turned Lexi away from the others and led her out of the room.

CHAPTER FORTY-FIVE

"I DON'T UNDERSTAND WHAT HAPPENED," Lexi said. "Elfie said the arach could heal, but she said my grandmother used a spell. I don't know any spells, and I certainly didn't perform any."

She held her hands up from beneath the blanket and studied her bloody palms as she recalled the warmth flooding her system and filling her fingers.

"But I felt something," she whispered. "I wanted so badly to heal her, and then something broke. I don't know if the dragon's flames unlocked something, the last of Sahira's potion finally wore off, or maybe whatever walls I was subconsciously keeping erected finally fell.

"I've been hit by dragon fire before, but this was more intense. The power inside me changed into something else. I'm still not sure how to use that power, but I didn't say a spell."

"Maybe Elfie lied about what she saw your grandmother do," Cole said.

"I didn't take her for a liar, did you?"

"No. That is one thing the light fae aren't known to be, but maybe the arach lied to her."

"How could my grandmother lie while performing a spell?" Lexi asked.

"The spell could have been for show. We know the arach were notoriously secretive about their powers; your grandmother might have trusted Elfie enough to let her see the arach could heal in such a way, but that doesn't mean she trusted her enough to see she could heal without a spell.

"Your grandmother needed to save her daughter's life, her only choice was to heal her in front of Elfie, but she still could have kept the depth of her true ability hidden. Considering what you just did, that's a pretty good possibility."

"I saved a little girl's life," Lexi breathed.

With the blanket wrapped around her shoulders, she turned her hands over to study them. Not so long ago, she believed she was powerless. She couldn't even open a portal; now, she'd breathed life into a dying child.

The urge to weep from the sheer wonder of it all while also crying over the burden it could become hit her. Feeling as if a crushing weight pressed on her shoulders, she dropped her hands as she trudged beside Cole.

She couldn't save everyone; even immortals had to go through the ebb and flow of life and death. There would be far too many of them otherwise, but...

"How do I decide who to save and who not to? How can I let anyone die if there's something I can do to save them? And if I do save them, would I mess up the natural order of things?" she whispered. "And what about humans? How do I let them die if I can prevent it?"

"Let's leave those philosophical debates for another time, when we're not at war and we've had time to learn more about what you can do. But I think you'll know who to help and who not to when the time for such things comes. You'll never be able to save everyone, so don't worry about messing up any natural order."

Of course, he was right, but she still couldn't shake the nagging doubts and questions running rampant through her mind. This was a burden she wasn't sure she could bear. But, for now, she would only look at the good of her newfound ability.

"I saved a child," she breathed. "I felt her blood pulsing against my hands and her heart slowing as those flames enveloped us."

"You saved a child, you're growing into yourself, and you will learn more and get better with every passing day. The arach might not be around to teach you how to use your abilities, but you're breaking through them on your own. The more you tap into them, the stronger they'll become, and the more you'll learn how to control them."

"What if I can't handle it?"

"Do you think you can handle it?"

Lexi pondered this before replying. "Yes."

It surprised her how much she believed this to be true. She had her doubts as she fumbled through all this, and probably would for a long time, but she *would* handle it. She would learn and grow and master every new thing she could.

"I think each new development will be an adjustment and take me time to master, but I'm an arach, which means I was born to handle these gifts."

"Very true," he murmured as he kissed her temple.

"What about you? How are you doing after what happened in Verdan and with the shadows?"

"I'm fine."

"Are you sure? I saw the shadows in Verdan and you. I saw some of what happened; are you sure you're okay?"

"I'm fine," he insisted again. "Don't worry about me."

It was impossible not to worry about him and those shadows, but she wouldn't push him on it either. He was keeping the shadows under control, and that was what mattered most. He was a good man with a good heart, and in the end, she believed that would win out over the darkness of the shadows.

When they reached one of the shower rooms, he opened the door and held it for her as she slipped inside.

CHAPTER FORTY-SIX

WHEN THE DOOR closed behind them, Lexi slumped against it. She was tired, hungry, and disheartened by what she'd witnessed today; she was also more determined than ever to bring the Lord down. They could *not* allow that monster to keep destroying lives like he was.

Cole gently pulled the blanket away from her. She shivered when the cool air caressed her skin and focused her attention away from the blood covering her. She couldn't stand to look at it anymore.

"Are you okay?" Cole inquired.

"I'll be fine once I shower," she assured him, "and get this blood *off* me."

"Come on."

Cole guided her over to the shower on the other side of the small room. There were no walls or curtains surrounding the showerhead jutting out from the rocky wall. A sink and toilet were ten feet away.

He rested a hand on her shoulder while he turned on the water. Although the outer realm was a barren, forgotten place, the water was always warm; she didn't know if it was magic or a giant water tank, but it was blissful.

She sighed as steam rose around them; her body quivered in anticipation of the clean, warm water. Cole adjusted the temperature before holding his hand out to her. She took it, and stepping beneath the warm spray, bowed her head as the pounding water soothed her aching muscles.

Blood ran in rivulets down her body before vanishing into the drain set in the floor. She examined the wound in his side; it had mostly healed already, but a long scratch remained.

Lexi bent her head and relished the loosening of her tense muscles as Cole moved behind her to stand beneath the spray. Water pooled over and between them as he lifted a soap bar from the rocky ledge set into the wall.

With tender hands, he worked the soap through her hair. The tenderness of his fingers as he massaged her scalp and the warmth of his body further eased her stress as he moved around her, cleaning her as he went.

He made it impossible to feel afraid, even of the shadows, when he was so strong, powerful, and loved her so much. But the feeling was mutual.

There wasn't anything she wouldn't do for him, and he knew it. Just as she knew, there wasn't anything he wouldn't do for her.

The water was starting to run clear when she felt the difference in his touch, or maybe it was her who changed things as she leaned closer and moaned when his hand skimmed her breast. Needing more than the comfort of his fingers as he helped clean her, she swayed into his caress.

Everything was so brutal around them, *so many* were dying, and they could very well be next. The atrocity of Verdan lingered in her mind, but as his fingers slid down her belly, the memories faded.

Their time together could be coming to an end, but here and now, nothing could tear them apart.

When she lifted her head to take him in, the black was gone from the whites of his eyes, but they still burned a brilliant silver. Her gut clenched, and it was more than the water running between her thighs that made her so wet.

He must have sensed or smelled a change in her as a low growl rumbled from his throat. When his hand glided down her body again, Lexi leaned into him. Even if it was only for a few hours, his touch could shut out the memories and the rest of the world.

When their chests brushed against each other, her nipples hardened. Electricity sizzled across her skin, and her nerve endings tingled.

He could always make her come alive in ways she'd never dreamed possible, but something sizzled in the air between them. It crackled and pulsed until she swore she could feel it, but nothing tangible was there.

More of her abilities had been unleashed earlier as power continued to pulse inside her. She didn't know how to harvest that power yet, but it swelled as it sought more of *him*.

Her power craved him like a vampire seeking blood, as a lycan yearned for the moon, and an arach sought the light. He was the darkness to her light, something she shouldn't want, yet it only made her seek him out more.

Opposites attracted, but this was more than that. This was opposites combining, becoming one, and growing stronger.

And she sensed that pulsating between them as his fingers slid between her legs. He teased her until she leaned against him to stay upright while the power mingled amidst them.

Turning her around, he locked his arm around her and guided her toward the wall. She rested her hands against the cool rock of the wall while he kissed her nape and cupped her breasts.

His thumbs played with nipples, and his fangs grazed her neck before sinking into her shoulder. As he marked her as his lycan mate, the heated rush of the serum in his fangs entered her body.

Her knees wobbled before she locked them into place. His

hands ran up her arms before they grasped hers on the wall and flattened over them.

He pressed her palms more firmly into the wall as his body melded over hers. He was so powerful, unyielding, and his body pressing against hers was familiar and thrilling.

And then he was pulling her hands away from the wall and lifting them over her head. She kept them there as he ran his palms down her arms and around her breasts. With each caress, he aroused her further while his lips left a trail across her shoulders and neck. She lowered her hands to grip the back of his head as he nipped at her ear.

Every touch and kiss was meant to drive her mad; he was succeeding. The demanding evidence of his erection pushed against her back. Though he was as eager for release as her, he tasted and teased. He pushed her to the very brink of orgasm before pulling back and refusing to let her go over the edge.

"Please," Lexi whimpered as his fingers found her clit again.

"Please what?" he demanded, his voice ragged in her ear.

"Please fuck me."

Resting his hands on her shoulders, Cole turned her toward him. Able to fully touch him, Lexi wrapped her hand around his cock. He wasn't the only one who could torture someone.

She smiled as she stroked him and his eyes glowed a brighter silver. Then, she went to her knees. She ignored the stone biting into her flesh as she became determined to torment him as much as he did her.

Towering over her, Cole planted his hands against the wall as she drew him into her mouth. The muscles in his arms bulged, and his head tipped back. Water streamed down his face, and the etched planes of the eight-pack cutting across his abdomen.

He was extremely powerful; it vibrated around him. Something inside her rose to meet it as she used her mouth and hand to push him to the brink before pulling away as he'd done to her.

His eyes flashed when they met hers, but a smile curved the corner of his lips. "Two can play at that game."

"You already have."

"Have I now?"

The quirk of his eyebrow should have warned her as he gripped her arms. Cole lifted her off the ground and carried her to the edge of the sink.

He settled her onto it and, spreading her legs, stepped between them. Her heart thundered as his shaft prodded her entrance, but still, he didn't enter her. Her muscles quivered in anticipation as his eyes met and held hers.

"You're *mine*," he growled.

"Always."

Grasping her cheeks, he bent and kissed her. The harsh, demanding nature robbed her breath as she gripped his arms and kissed him back. She needed *all* of him as her legs locked around his waist. And finally, he thrust into her.

Lexi arched into him as power erupted between them. It vibrated the air and caused the hair on her arms to stand on end. She dug her heels into him as she broke the kiss to catch her breath.

Her head fell back against the mirror behind her as the pleasure engulfing her became more intense than the dragon's flames. Behind him, the shadows rose to block out the rest of the room, and whatever power he used to keep most of his ciphers hidden, fell.

Something inside her reacted to his loss of control. It surged toward him as it sought to connect with him, but she couldn't set it free. She didn't know what was expected of her, but *something was*.

The frustration growing within her was doused as the demands of his body unleashed the orgasm he had denied her before. Her cry echoed off the walls, and she came as he lifted her from the sink, turned her into the wall, and fucked her harder.

CHAPTER FORTY-SEVEN

"What's the next step?" Sahira inquired once they were all gathered in the small room again.

"We'll go to the witches to see Kaylia," Cole said. "The woman can take us there. I sent crows to the sirens and Elfie to tell them what happened, but I haven't heard back. I don't know if that means they're still standing or not. We'll have to check on them after the witches."

"We still need an army," Orin said.

"We'll keep working on it," Cole said. "I plan to go to the dwarves next. Then the giants."

"The giants have always sided with the Lord," Niall said.

"The Lord had a giant head mounted on his wall when I was in his solar. There might have been a falling out there."

He was *not* looking forward to speaking with the giants, but if they were going to defeat the Lord, they required more help. The dwarves were violent, notoriously ruthless fighters, but they weren't enough.

"So, we'll go to the witches, the dwarves, and the giants," Cole continued. "Niall, Maverick, and Brokk will go to Aerie to check on the sirens."

"Will do," Niall said.

"I'll go talk with some of the lycans afterward," Maverick said. "I know of a few packs willing to help us."

"Will they want to meet me?" Lexi asked.

"Eventually," Maverick said. "But I'll get them to work with us while you're away."

"Good."

"What about the demons?" Del inquired.

"Do you know how to get to their realm or how to locate one?" Cole asked.

"No."

Some fought on the Lord's side during the last war and some with the rebels, but they didn't do it because of loyalty or a sense of right or wrong. They did it because they loved to fight and kill. And that was the thing with the demons; they enjoyed a good fight, but it was tough to locate them.

That could also make them treacherous to work with, but it would be good to at least talk to one of them. He wasn't sure that would happen.

He turned to Lexi and held out his hand. "Are you ready for this?"

"Always," she said as her fingers slid into his.

Orin opened the door to reveal the woman and the three girls standing on the other side. Morgan had awakened and clung to her mother's side as she gazed into the room with wide, shadowed eyes.

"Thank you," Orin said to the lycan who escorted them here.

The man grunted before striding away.

Cole led Lexi through the others to stop before the woman. "It's time for us to go to the witches," Cole said.

The woman rested a hand on the shoulder of the oldest girl and drew the children closer to her side. "I'll take you."

Cole glanced back at the others. "We won't keep returning between our visits to the other realms. We'll move through them as quickly as possible before the Lord destroys them. I'll send a crow back to update you on our progress."

"I want to go back to Verdan to search for more survivors," Sahira said.

"Not alone," Cole told her.

"I'll go with her," Orin offered.

"No one knows you're alive," Cole reminded him.

Orin jerked his head toward Sahira. "She can cast a glamour over me. The witches will sense her magic and be curious to know who I am, but they'll have to live with the mystery. Besides, after what the Lord did to Verdan, I doubt any of them would turn me in if they saw me."

"I'll go too," Varo said. "I'd like to feel useful again; helping to find survivors would allow me to do so."

Cole wanted to argue with them, but it didn't matter anymore. This woman had also seen Orin and Varo; if she decided to let everyone know his brothers were alive, it would spread like wildfire.

Besides, now that the Gloaming was devastated, it didn't matter if the Lord knew about Orin and Varo. Yes, they were strong fighters, but he'd kept them hidden before to save the Gloaming. There was no chance of that now.

The knowledge they were still alive would *really* piss off the Lord once he learned Cole had tricked him into thinking his brothers were dead. But it didn't give them an advantage anymore.

Still, he preferred to keep the truth about them and Del a secret. They were still powerful weapons against the Lord.

"Okay, go under a glamour, but the truth is bound to get out soon," he said.

They all looked toward the woman who held the girls closer. "None of us will say a word about anything we learned while here. We're all alive because of all of you, and our gratitude will not be repaid with betrayal."

Cole glanced at the children as they huddled against the

woman. He could take her daughter away and keep her locked up as leverage against the woman, but Lexi would fight him on it, and so would Varo and Sahira.

He opened his mouth to suggest Morgan stay behind when the woman spoke. "I'll take you to the witches and come right back if that makes you feel better," she said. "I'll let them know I brought you there and that you're safe, so they don't panic and do something foolish before returning."

"The other two children will talk," he said. He'd already forgotten their names.

The woman hugged them before looking at Lexi. "You don't need me to open the portal now that you know the way. The two of you can go alone. There's a chance they'll be more hostile that way, but I think they'll be okay after a bit, and this way, you'll know you have nothing to fear from us."

"I can handle some hostile witches," Cole said.

The woman blanched a little, but she gave a small nod when she looked at her daughter.

"Open the portal," Cole told the witch.

Stepping back, she released one of the girls and waved her hand in front of her. A portal opened a few feet away.

"When you go, could you ask about their older sister, Melisandra?" the woman inquired. "They need their family."

Lexi clasped the woman's hand in both of hers. "We will."

"Thank you," the woman said.

"What is your name?"

The woman's blue eyes twinkled as she smiled at Lexi. "I am Beatrix."

"It's a pleasure to meet you."

"It's a pleasure to meet you too, milady. I hope to one day call you 'your highness.'"

Lexi blinked at her before squeezing her hands and releasing them. Cole settled his hand possessively against Lexi's waist as he turned to the woman.

"We'll let you know if we find out anything about Melisandra," he told her. "You won't be forced to stay here for long."

"I've not been forced, milord," Beatrix replied. "I volunteered for this, and I'm more than happy to do so. Be safe on your journey."

Beatrix stepped back and gathered the children close again. Cole shifted his attention to Niall. "Make sure they're taken care of."

"Of course. Should I join you afterward?"

Cole shook his head. He wanted to trust the woman but didn't. They couldn't risk her opening a portal out of this realm and compromising what few secrets they had left.

"I think it's best if you stay," Cole said.

When Niall glanced at Beatrix, Cole saw his guard understood he was to keep a close eye on the woman.

"Take care, milord," Niall said.

Cole clasped Niall's shoulder and squeezed it. "You know better than to call me that."

Niall smiled, and the others gathered close to say goodbye before he and Lexi entered the portal.

CHAPTER FORTY-EIGHT

WHEN THEY EXITED THIS PORTAL, it at least wasn't into the complete chaos and death of Verdan, but this new realm was still hectic. Occasionally, someone would cry out in pain, and sobs drifted on the air.

Lexi inwardly recoiled from the suffering while outwardly keeping herself as composed as possible. The wounded were spread across the grass on makeshift stretchers and beds as other witches tended to them.

Could she help heal them? Should she?

They were still trying to keep some secrets from the Lord, and if she walked around here trying to heal everyone, it would get out and probably drain her. And that was *if* she could heal them. She had no idea how the ability worked, how often she could use it, or if she could pull it up to heal those here.

When Cole glanced at her, she saw he was aware of her thoughts. "Not here and not now," he said.

"What if I can save someone's life?"

"And what if it drains you to the point you can't travel from here and have to return to rest? More will die if we don't move swiftly."

He was right, but… "I'm not making any promises."

Silver flared through his eyes before he managed to suppress it. "Let's see if we can find Kaylia and find out how much damage the witches sustained."

He kept his hand on her waist while they strode through the scattered bodies. The acrid scent of smoke, the fresh odor of wood burning, and the potent aroma of many herbs and potions mixed on the air. It wasn't an unpleasant aroma, but it was strong.

Pixies whizzed past, but this wasn't the pixie realm. Unicorns, pegasuses, phoenixes, and sasquatches roamed through the injured, but none of them would have typically called this place home.

Though there was green grass, little other life marked this place. This place was far different from Verdan.

She'd never been to the witches' realm before the Lord destroyed it, but Sahira had told her stories about the few times she went there. Sahira had said it was a beautiful place full of trees, rolling green fields, and magical creatures from all the realms.

The witches made their potions, worshipped the land, and danced naked beneath the moon as they celebrated life. All of that had been ripped away from them. Now, they were scrambling to save their own.

They were so busy trying to heal the survivors that, at first, they didn't notice her and Cole, but eventually, their presence caught the witches' attention. Murmurs started to run through the crowd, and heads turned their way, but Cole didn't stop until he was near the center of the makeshift encampment.

"Does anyone know where Kaylia is?" he asked.

A woman pointed to the right, and as Lexi followed her finger, she spotted Kaylia kneeling on the ground fifty yards away. Her silvery blonde hair flowed around her as she applied a healing poultice to a woman lying before her.

Kaylia hadn't noticed their presence yet, but it was only a matter of time before she heard the whispers of the arach and Shadow Reaver rolling through the crowd.

"How did you find us?" a woman asked defensively as they started toward Kaylia.

"Beatrix opened a portal for us," Cole replied.

"Beatrix is alive!" another blurted, and someone else started sobbing and whispering, "Thank you," repeatedly.

"She is," Lexi said.

She almost said, so is her daughter, but caught herself in time. Someone here might have seen the child stabbed; there would be too many questions if they learned the child lived.

They'd only taken a few steps toward Kaylia when the whispers reached her. Kaylia rested her hand on the ground as she turned toward them.

Blood smeared her beautiful face. A bruise the size of an apple and a lump nearly as big marred her right cheek. The swelling in her eye was so bad Lexi doubted she could see out of it.

Blood plastered her clothes to her, and as she rose, she swayed a little before steadying herself. Lexi rushed to close the distance between them. She stretched out a hand to grab her friend as Kaylia sank to her knees.

"Are you okay?" Lexi demanded as she knelt beside her friend.

"I'm okay," Kaylia assured her. "A little beat up, but I'm good. What about you? How are you?"

"We're fine," Lexi told her. "What happened to you during the battle?"

"A couple of lycans jumped me, but I got away. I was going to return to the prison, but there were just so many…" Tears filled her eyes as she looked at the others, and her lower lip trembled. "They are *so many* who needed my help, and I lost track of time." She brushed back a strand of blood-streaked hair and tucked it behind her ear. "I don't know how long I've been here."

"About a day," Lexi said. "Brokk, Maverick, and Sahira went back to Verdan to search for you after the battle but couldn't find you."

She decided not to tell her that Cole had discovered she was alive by using the shadows. If it came up again, she would tell Kaylia then. There was no need now, especially when strangers surrounded them, many of whom were eagerly listening.

"How did you find this place?" Kaylia asked.

"I saved a witch from the battle," Lexi said. "She opened a portal so we could come here to search for you."

"Who was it?" Kaylia asked.

"Her name is Beatrix," Lexi answered.

Kaylia closed her eyes. "I'm glad she's alive; so many aren't."

"What about Circe?" Cole asked. "I haven't seen her."

"She didn't survive the attack."

"Shit," Cole muttered. "She was a good woman."

"She was," Kaylia murmured.

"Do you know if a witch named Melisandra survived?" Lexi asked.

"Elisa?" Kaylia asked in confusion. "She's over there. Why?"

Lexi followed Kaylia's finger to a beautiful woman with flowing black hair and eyes the color of a penny. She was only twenty feet away, watching them as she held a goblet of some mixture to the lips of a wounded witch.

"How do you know about Elisa?" Kaylia inquired.

"Her sisters are at the prison," Lexi said. "Her mother didn't survive, but Brokk, Maverick, and Sahira got her sisters out."

Kaylia blinked away the tears filling her eyes before she bowed her head. "We believed they were lost."

"Do you want to tell Elisa or should we?" Lexi inquired.

"I'll tell her," Kaylia said.

"If she wants to see them, you can take her to the prison, but she won't be allowed to leave again afterward," Cole said. "And neither will the children or Beatrix."

Kaylia frowned. "Why not?"

"You'll find out when you get there. Niall can fill you in on what's going on, but to keep Lexi protected a little longer, they're not to leave the prison until we return."

Kaylia glanced between them. "Is everything okay?"

"It's fine," Lexi said. "There's been a... a... uh, new development."

CHAPTER FORTY-NINE

"It's a good thing, but with the Lord ramping up his destruction of the realms and his determination to ensure we don't build an army, it's best if we keep it as quiet as possible. You'll understand when you return. They'll eventually join everyone here if you decide not to return, but we have to go. We have to meet with as many leaders of the other realms as we can before the Lord unleashes his army on them," Cole said.

Kaylia glanced back and forth between them. "I'll be here for a while. There's still much to do, but Elisa will want to see her sisters. I'll take her there when the time comes."

"We'll see you there, but it could be a while," Cole said. "We won't be returning between meeting with the others anymore."

Kaylia rose and wiped her hands on her pants. She swayed briefly before steadying herself and throwing her shoulders back. "Come with me."

Lexi and Cole followed her through the scattered rows of the wounded before they left the chaos behind. They walked another fifty feet away from the others before Kaylia stopped and turned to face them.

"What happened?" Kaylia asked. "And where are you going?"

"First, we'll go to the giants and then the dwarves," Cole said. "Del, Brokk, and Maverick will check on the sirens and light fae, but I'm not expecting much. I imagine their realms were destroyed too, or at least the sirens', but I can find them."

Kaylia paled as she glanced behind them. "I'll come with you."

"You're needed here," Lexi said. "We'll be fine on our own, and someone should take Elisa back when she's ready."

Kaylia's eyes narrowed on her. "Why don't you want her sisters and Beatrix leaving the prison realm?"

Lexi glanced back at the others and started to speak but stopped when Cole rested his hand on her arm. "It's unlikely they could hear us, but we're not taking the chance." He focused on Kaylia again. "When you return to the prison, you'll learn the answer. Beatrix told us the witches had agreed to work with us, but that was before all this. Do you think the witches will still be willing to help in this war?"

"After what happened to Verdan? Absolutely. They're shocked and broken, but they're also livid. It's not something we've discussed, but we will, and I know they'll be on our side. The crones are also here; I sent for them after the attack on Verdan. They'll be a part of this fight too. *No one* attacks a witch like that without retribution, and the Lord will feel our wrath."

The fury in Kaylia's eyes made Lexi *very* happy the witch was on their side. She wouldn't want that rage turned on her or anyone she loved.

"Good," Cole said. "Now, we have to go."

Kaylia looked about to protest but closed her mouth and nodded briskly.

"Sahira has cast a glamour over Orin and Varo; they've returned to Verdan to see if they can find any other survivors," Lexi said.

Kaylia pulled on her good cheek as she ran a hand tiredly over her face. "We haven't had a chance to do that yet."

"Now you won't have to worry about it," Lexi said.

"They're not concerned the witches will sense her magic on them?" Kaylia asked.

"They probably will, but they'll never know what Varo and Orin look like behind the glamour," Lexi said. "Is Sahira's mother here?"

"No. She wasn't in the village when they attacked."

"So, she could still be in Verdan."

"Yes. The Lord might not have gone after the other villages. Most of them are so remote, they wouldn't be worth it unless he was determined to destroy all of Verdan. It's more likely he went for the quick, brutal destruction that would destroy a large chunk of the realm and population but not take too much time. He has no way of knowing how many we've gathered against him or our plans; he won't take the chance of having a lot of his army away for too long."

"I agree," Cole said. "Now it's time to gather more soldiers."

"Be safe," Kaylia said.

"Always," Lexi replied as she hugged her friend. "Take care of yourself."

Kaylia squeezed her tighter. "Always."

When they separated, Cole claimed Lexi's hand. He opened a portal and turned to Kaylia. "We will see you again."

"You will."

Lexi followed Cole into the portal and onto the next realm.

CHAPTER FIFTY

THEY'D BEEN TRAVELING for hours when they entered the final tiny village Sahira knew about in Verdan. Out of the four other villages they'd visited, only one was also attacked—the village of Aether.

She didn't think anyone made it out of the massacre at Aether alive. However, the other three villages remained intact, and Sahira was the one who informed them about the attack. The occupants of those villages were still packing to join the witches when she left.

Orin and Varo remained mostly silent throughout their journey; she was grateful for that. She liked Varo, but every time Orin opened his mouth, she wanted to shove something in it... mainly her fist.

When they reached the final village of Pention, Sahira was on the verge of collapse. She'd opened too many portals in too short a time. She felt the consequences of that as her eyelids drooped and her energy level was barely above breathing.

Still, she lifted her chin as they strode into the tiny village with only ten teepees hidden beneath a forest of trees. The orange and red leaves on the trees shimmered in the sunlight.

The sun's rays danced as they filtered through the leaves. Sahira admired the beauty of the forest as they walked toward the women standing near the bank of a river. The trickling sound of water rejuvenated Sahira a little and helped to soothe her nerves.

When they first started their journey, Sahira told herself she would deal with it if they encountered her mother, but she was too tired to deal with the exchange that would follow now. She wasn't sure if she wanted to find the woman or not.

One option meant encountering the immortal who abandoned her as a newborn and barely had anything to do with her afterward. And the other meant that woman was dead.

She didn't know how to feel about either outcome, especially since she last saw her mother a hundred years ago. The woman never acknowledged her during that meeting.

The only two things her mother ever gave her were life and a Book of Shadows. Her father raised and loved her. Vampires were her family, while the witches, who considered themselves so much better than vampires, turned their backs on her.

She should hate them, but she didn't. It wasn't in her to hate; her father and Del ensured that.

She wouldn't be here if she hated them. They'd shunned her, but she was determined to save as many of them as possible.

As they approached the river, she ignored that all the women were naked. However, it didn't escape Orin's attention as he released a low whistle.

Sahira rolled her eyes. Maybe it wasn't in her to hate, but she *really* disliked him. *Everything* about him irritated her, from his smug attitude, to his arrogant smile, to the almost complete disrespect he had for nearly *everyone* he associated with.

He was the most irritating man she'd ever encountered. He was also one of the most handsome men she'd ever seen... which annoyed her more.

Gritting her teeth, Sahira ignored his whistle. She wasn't in the mood to fight with him or these women. If the witches heard him, they could deal with him if they decided to.

"Stop," Varo murmured under his breath.

"You know you like it too, brother," Orin drawled.

Sahira resolved to ignore the ignorant oaf as she stalked forward. She should have paid more attention to where she was walking, as a twig cracking beneath her feet alerted the witches to their presence.

The women spun away from the river, and water rose in a wave behind them; it was ready to knock the three of them on their asses. Sahira held up her hands in a gesture of peace while Orin and Varo stopped.

"We mean you no harm," Sahira said. "We've come to make sure you're okay and tell you to leave Verdan. Most of the other witches have already vacated."

They all stared at her for a minute before their gazes swung to the witch at the end. Her brown hair flowed around her shoulders, and her brown eyes were nearly the same amber shade as Sahira's.

Sahira met the eyes of the woman who'd birthed her as the woman sneered while she spoke. "And we're supposed to take your word for this? You're a vampire."

"I'm also half witch," Sahira replied.

Her mother snorted in disgust before shifting her attention to Orin and Varo. "What's with the glamour? Who are you really?"

"Some things aren't for bitchy little witches such as yourself to know," Orin replied with laughter in his voice.

Her mother gave a derisive laugh that some of the others mimicked. The remaining witches remained silent.

"The Lord has attacked Verdan; the dragons and his army destroyed most of the village of Gramarye and all of the smaller village Aether. The witches have fled to a meeting place you're all supposed to know."

"That's not possible," her mother retorted.

"Perhaps we should check, Lydia," another witch murmured. "It's easy enough to learn if they're telling the truth or not."

"Vampires do nothing but lie," her mother spat.

"They also drink blood and fuck like rabbits," Orin said. "And they do it very well."

When all the witches shifted their attention to glower at him, he grinned in response to their ire. Sahira hated the small smile tugging at her lips, but she couldn't help it as her mother's eyes narrowed on Orin before shifting to her.

"*Who* have you brought into our realm?" Lydia demanded.

CHAPTER FIFTY-ONE

"WE ONLY CAME HERE to offer assistance and warning," Varo said in his gentle, soothing tone. "We're not a threat."

One of the other witches inquired, "Are you light fae?"

When Sahira cast the glamour over Orin and Varo, she'd given them both brown hair and brown eyes. She'd hidden their ciphers, and nothing about them could mark them as dark fae.

Even their builds were bulkier than the light or dark fae typically were. But Varo's voice and his ability to calm others wasn't something she could hide.

"Does it matter what I am?" Varo asked.

The witches all exchanged a look before a different one turned to Lydia. "We should check the villages to see if what they're saying is true."

"You go," Lydia said. "There's no way I'm leaving these three alone in our realm."

It took everything Sahira had not to roll her eyes, but she could practically hear Orin's rattling around his head.

"Please, don't flatter yourselves. If we were here to destroy you, we would," Orin said.

"He must be a dark fae," one of the other witches murmured.

Sahira shot Orin a silencing look. There weren't too many light and dark fae who would hang out together, not unless they were related. If he wasn't careful, these women would put two and two together. They were annoyed, but they weren't stupid.

The witch standing next to her mother opened a portal and disappeared into it. It remained open, but none of the others followed her through.

When the witch returned a couple of minutes later, dirt and tears stained her cheeks. She lifted her head to look at Lydia and sobbed.

"The villages are in ruins," she whispered, "and those who aren't dead are all gone."

Her mother's eyes shot back to them. "Did you have something to do with this attack?"

"Yes, Mother, I've learned how to control the dragons," Sahira retorted. "It's a miracle!"

"That's your *mother*?" Orin blurted.

Sahira chose to ignore him, but Varo lightly brushed her arm with his hand. When she looked at him, the brown eyes she'd glamoured were full of a sympathy she didn't want.

Centuries ago, she came to terms with having a mother who despised half of what she was. She'd never understand why, considering Lydia was the one who laid with her father. If the woman hated vampires so much, why spread her legs for one?

It was a question she'd always wanted to ask but never did. She doubted she'd get a straight answer from her mother anyway.

"Was it a dragon attack?" her mother demanded of the witch.

"It must have been," the woman said.

"If we were here to attack you, why would we tell you what happened?" Sahira inquired.

"You might be trying to push us into another attack," her mother replied.

Sahira threw up her hands. "Believe what you will and stay if you wish; I don't care. It doesn't seem like the Lord intends to send his dragons this far into Verdan, so maybe you'll be safe. We believed it was best to give you a heads-up."

"Why are you involved in this?" her mother inquired.

"Well, haven't you heard, Mother? I thought the news had spread through all the realms, but I guess you don't get the gossip when you choose to live a sheltered life. Elexiandra, Del's daughter, my *niece*, is the last living arach."

She wasn't going to go into the details about that. Her mother could sit and stew in her curiosity. She hoped it ate her alive.

"There's a chance we could put a rightful ruler back on the throne, and we're going to make sure it happens. She and Cole... or, as you know him, *King Colburn* of the dark fae, are working to raise an army.

"They came to seek the witches' help, but the attack was underway when they arrived. Perhaps if you stopped hiding in this corner of Verdan, devoting your life to worshipping water and running around naked while others fight and *die* to do good in the realms, you would know these things. Instead, you're an extremely powerful witch hiding here and doing *nothing* of importance while everyone else is fighting to save *your* life."

As she spoke, her mother's eyes widened with each of her revelations, but they'd narrowed by the time she finished, and hatred simmered in them.

"Who do you think you're talking to?" Lydia demanded.

"No one of importance." With that, Sahira turned to Varo and Orin. "Let's go."

She wasn't strong enough to open a portal to return to the prison, but she refused to reveal her weakness to these women. She could feel their eyes boring into her back as she started through the forest. Orin and Varo walked noiselessly beside her.

"Would you like me to open a portal back to the prison?" Varo inquired.

"Once we're out of view of them," Sahira replied, "I would appreciate it."

Varo's fingers briefly brushed hers in a show of solidarity. She suspected that if they weren't still within view of the witches, he would have taken her hand or hugged her.

"So *that* was your mother," Orin muttered.

Sahira scowled at him; she wasn't in the mood for his shit. "Yeah, and...?"

"It's surprising, is all. You're nothing alike."

"That's probably because she abandoned me when I was born because of the tainted, dirty vampire blood in me and all that nonsense."

"Her abandonment was probably a good thing."

Sahira was mad enough to scream as she stopped walking and turned to face him. She glanced back into the woods but couldn't see the witches anymore.

She planted her hands on her hips as she glared at him. "And why is that?"

Orin shrugged, and as he did so, his glamour faded away. She found herself staring into black eyes that normally twinkled with amusement but were now somber.

"Because she's a coward, and you're not," he said. "You were better off without her."

His words knocked the anger out of her, and she was too flabbergasted to speak until after Varo opened a portal for them.

"Did you... did you... just say something nice... to me?" she asked in disbelief.

When Orin grinned at her, the twinkle reappeared in his eyes. "Don't get used to it."

Before she could reply, Orin entered the portal.

CHAPTER FIFTY-TWO

LEXI COULDN'T STOP herself from gawking when they stepped out of the portal and into the giants' realm. Not only were the immortals who lived here giants, but so was *everything* else in the realm.

Her head tipped further and further back, but she still couldn't see the treetops above her. And there were *so many* trees. They were all she could see as she turned in a slow circle.

"Where are the giants?" she whispered.

"Some are in the woods, others will be in town, and many will be at their castle in the clouds," Cole said.

"They have a castle in the *clouds*?" she breathed.

He smiled as he drew her close to kiss her forehead. "They do."

When he took her hand, she fell into step beside him as they maneuvered past trees whose trunks were as big around as a water tower. The indents in their bark were so deep she could stick a finger in them, if not her whole hand, in some areas.

The leaves above her were a brilliant lime green, yellow, and blue mixture that rustled when a breeze drifted through them. Birds sang while they hopped from limb to limb.

These were not the birds of earth, unless ostriches suddenly started flying while also releasing a sweet song entirely out of place for their overly large, plump, and vivid orange bodies.

"What is this place called?" she asked.

"Colossal."

"That's original."

Cole chuckled, but his eyes darted around the trees while he walked beside her. She tried not to let it bother her, but it was impossible not to notice the shadows gathering closer.

She'd never forget the shadows tearing into the Lord's men in Verdan or the darkness creeping through him when he returned to the prison. How much longer could he keep them under control?

Lexi shuddered as she tore her attention away from him. In this land of giants, she couldn't dwell on the morose possibilities of everything that could go wrong.

They had to try winning the giants over to their side, though that was easier said than done. Colossal remained untouched by the Lord's army, probably because the giants sided with the Lord during the last war.

Finally breaking free of the mammoth trees, Lexi came to an abrupt halt. Her jaw dropped when she spotted the giant castle a dozen miles away. Despite its distance, it stood out in vivid detail as it was so enormous it blocked half the sky.

It might even take up more of the sky, but some of it was lost within the green clouds floating across the sapphire blue sky. Because the giants were so destructive, brutal, and monstrous during the war, she never expected so much beauty from their realm, but it was *magnificent*.

Giant, green vines twisted up from the earth and into the floor of the castle. She suspected the vines didn't just go into the base of the castle but *comprised* it. Though the jagged, sharp edges on the vines could have been thorns, they probably weren't, as those vines appeared to be the only way into the castle.

Lexi couldn't help but think of "Jack and the Beanstalk." She wondered if some human had somehow wandered into this magical realm and created the fairy tale afterward.

From the castle's center, a brown stone structure rose thousands of feet into the air. It went so high its yellow, circular spire pierced the clouds floating in and out of the building's windows.

"It's beautiful," she breathed.

"It is," Cole agreed.

"Have you ever been inside?"

"Once, when I was barely more than a child. The clouds drift through the inside too. I tried to touch them as my father spoke with the giants, but my fingers would float through them. They dispersed before reforming around my hand. It's the first happy memory I can remember after my mother died."

Lexi's heart clenched as she clasped his hand. She could picture him as a young boy, with his heart still trying to heal from the loss of his mother but so full of awe as he played with clouds.

"We have to climb the vines to get into the castle?" she asked.

"We do, and if the giants don't want us there, they'll let us know."

Lexi gulped, but there was no turning back from this; they had to speak with the giants. She was about to step out of the woods when the tree beside her trembled.

CHAPTER FIFTY-THREE

WITH A BARELY SUPPRESSED YELP, she jumped back as Cole grasped her arms and spun her away. Lexi barely registered moving before she found herself staring at his back.

Then, the tree that had been deeply rooted in the earth pulled itself free of the ground with a loud, sucking sound. Dirt, sticks, and rocks fell from the tree. As they did so, she realized no roots dangled from the huge creation. Instead, the shaking off of debris revealed a brown shoe that planted itself firmly on the other side of the trees.

It's not a tree; it's a giant's foot!

Lexi's heart hammered as the giant bent down through the trees until its cheek nearly touched the ground. Its brown eye was almost level with hers. A black patch covered his other eye.

Until he left the treetops behind, the giant's mop of unruly brown and orange hair blended seamlessly with the leaves, as did the solid brown clothes he wore. The man was easily a hundred feet tall.

Lexi glanced wildly at the other trees and held her breath as she waited for more of them to move. Nothing else stirred as the birds continued to sing, and the only thing rustling the leaves was the breeze.

The giant exhaled a breath; it blew back strands of hair that had straggled free of her braid. She saw no maliciousness in his brown eye, but his mouth set into a grim, flat line.

However, it wasn't furious they were here. She was sure he would have stepped on them if that were the case, but he also wasn't happy to see them.

"You have no place here, King Colburn," the giant said in a surprisingly soft voice for his massive size.

"And who are you?" Cole demanded.

"I am Gibborim, and you have no place here."

"We're here to recruit help against the Lord," Cole replied.

"I know why you're here; we all suspected you'd come, so I've been waiting in the woods for you, but you have no place in our realm. You must know that."

"And *you* must know the Lord is turning on all the realms. He doesn't belong on the throne, and the woman standing beside me is the last arach and rightful ruler of Dragonia."

The giant's eye flicked to her, and he gave a subtle nod. "By now, I think almost everyone has heard of the last arach. You've become a thing of legends, little one."

Normally, the *little one* comment would have irritated her, but she *was* little compared to this man. Besides, she wasn't about to pick a fight with someone who could splat her with their hand.

"They should probably make some new legends then," she said.

A corner of the giant's mouth twitched toward a smile before flattening again. "One can hope you live up to those legends."

"Why would you want that if you're not going to help us?" she asked.

"The Lord has our queen. We will stand behind him while she is his captive."

This revelation astounded Lexi. "How did he capture her?"

"We are giants, but we are not infallible. The Lord lured our king and queen to Dragonia under false pretenses. They have not returned since."

～

COLE RECALLED the giant's head mounted to the wall in the Lord's solar. "Your king is dead."

Gibborim's eye closed and remained that way for a few heartbeats before he opened it again. "That is what we've heard."

"I have seen the head; the Lord killed him," Cole said. "And he *will* kill your queen."

"Yes, if we go against him. Which is why we will not do so."

"He'll kill her no matter what."

"No, he won't. Unlike the rulers in many other realms, our king and queen are beloved here. We'll do anything for them, including fight for a man who would see the realms destroyed. You should leave, King Colburn."

"Why not turn us in?" Cole inquired.

"It's not you who I seek to protect." His eye went to Lexi. "I wish my queen to be safe, and I will go to war against you to ensure her life, but I also won't take out the only one who could save us from the Lord's wrath. Go now, before I change my mind."

Cole took Lexi's hand as he spoke to the giant. "Aren't you concerned about what will happen if we win if you stand against us?"

"Aren't you concerned I'll kill you now if you threaten me?"

"No, I'm not."

A wall of shadows rose from the earth to sway between them and the giant.

"Cole, don't," Lexi said.

"Your future queen is more reasonable than you," the giant said. "Perhaps she would be better without the dark fae at her side."

246 BRENDA K DAVIES

"Don't threaten him," Lexi said. "We're here to help, and we won't carry grudges. You have to understand why we're fighting the Lord, and I understand why you can't. We'll leave now."

"Go in peace. The next time we see each other, it will be at war," the giant replied.

Cole held Lexi against his side as he opened a portal. He didn't dare lower the shadows between him and the giant as they entered the portal and headed to Drumbledon, the dwarves' realm.

It wasn't until they stepped free of the portal and into the burnt-out remains of Drumbledon that he retracted the shadows back into him. He shut the portal.

CHAPTER FIFTY-FOUR

"IT'S ABOUT FUCKING TIME," a grumpy dwarf with something similar to an English accent, a thick, grayish-brown beard that hung to his chest, bulbous nose, and bald head greeted them as soon as they exited the portal.

The man lowered his battle-ax from his shoulder before planting the metal bottom into the earth. The honed edge of his battle-ax glinted in the fires still burning behind him. His hazel eyes glittered with irritation as his grumpy face contorted into a scowl.

At nearly five feet tall, he was taller than most dwarves. He was also a little more rotund than many of the others Cole had met as his coarse green shirt pulled up to reveal the bottom of his belly.

"We've been waiting days for you," the man grunted as he rubbed his beard.

Then he lifted his ax and pointed it around him. Broken and burnt bodies of dwarves, cows, sheep, and other creatures littered the ground.

The fronts of the small homes the dwarves built into the surrounding mountains still smoldered. Some of the homes went pretty deep into the mountains and probably remained standing, but they couldn't enter them.

"As you can see, the Lord arrived before you," the dwarf stated.

Lexi stared at the carnage in horror. "How many did he kill?"

"Not as many as he would have liked," the dwarf retorted. "It's not so easy to burn our homes, and since we suspected he would come, many of us had retreated to where we now wait for your late asses to arrive."

"Watch it," Cole warned.

"Or what? You need us."

"You need us too. And I won't tolerate anyone talking to us like that; do you understand?"

The dwarf grunted, and his lips pursed, but he refrained from instigating the argument. "Some chose to remain behind and, as you can see, did not escape the Lord's wrath."

"I'm sorry," Lexi whispered.

The dwarf assessed her. "After it was over, I was sent back to wait for you to arrive."

"And what are you waiting for?" Cole inquired.

The dwarf thumped the bottom of his ax on the ground. "I'm waiting to help build an army, or I hope I am. Now, if you'll please follow me."

"Where are we going?" Cole inquired.

He doubted the dwarves would help the Lord, especially not after he destroyed their realm, but he wasn't taking any chances with Lexi's life.

"To the realm where we reside now," the dwarf said.

"I'm sure you'll understand that after you open the portal, I'm going to check out what's on the other side before taking her into it. If this is a trap, I'll tear you apart piece by piece."

Lexi winced at his words, but the dwarf shrugged as he spoke. "Have it your way, you overly suspicious bastard."

Lexi made a choking sound, and when he looked over at her,

she covered her mouth as she tried to suppress her laughter. "It's all been so awful, and it just sounded… funny," she said.

Cole couldn't help but chuckle too as he leaned over to kiss her forehead.

"Oh, for fuck's sake," the dwarf muttered. "I was told you were vicious and can make the shadows destroy your enemies. Yet, here you are kissing a woman like some lovesick sop. The tales better not be lies, King Colburn. We're not going to war for a pussy-whipped fool."

Cole didn't have time to think as the dwarf's words unleashed his fury. The shadows leapt up and enclosed on his throat, lifting him until his toes barely touched the ground. The dwarf's eyes bugged from his head, and he choked as his fingers tightened on the ax, but the weapon couldn't do anything for him.

"Now who's the fool?" Cole growled.

The dwarf grunted in response, and his face turned red, but Cole didn't recall the shadows.

Instead, he briefly constricted them around the dwarf's neck before releasing the man. The dwarf staggered forward as he choked and coughed in air. Until he regained control, he remained bent over before rising.

Though resentment shone in his hazel eyes, they were also full of grudging respect. "That's more like it." With a deft motion, the dwarf made a circle with his ax, and a small portal materialized before him. "Go ahead."

Cole kept his attention on the dwarf. If the man tried anything, he would rip him to pieces. While his attention remained riveted on the dwarf, he sent a couple of shadows skittering across the ground and into the portal. The dwarf tapped his foot while he stared impatiently at him

"Aren't you going to check it out?" the smaller man demanded.

When the shadows retracted toward Cole, they danced beneath the dwarf's feet. He jumped, and his hand flew to his throat as he glowered at the shadows.

"Shite!" the man exclaimed and pranced back a couple of steps.

The dwarf frowned as the shadows encircled Cole's arms and slid into his ears. Once there, the shadows revealed what they'd seen.

"It's safe for us to continue," Cole told Lexi.

"Is it?" she whispered.

Their gazes clashed before the dwarf broke the tension simmering between them.

"Then let's go. We are wasting time here. We have a Lord to kill."

With that, he turned and vanished into the portal.

"Cole—"

"I'm fine, Lexi," he assured her. "I'm in control, and we have dwarves to meet."

She didn't say anything more, but he felt her doubt as they strode through the portal together.

CHAPTER FIFTY-FIVE

THEY STEPPED out into a barren realm of craggy mountains piercing the red sky. Black rocks about as inviting as a pit full of glass decorated the realm. The landscape was bleak and barren, but dwarves hustled about, calling to each other, starting fires, and roasting meat.

Most of the dwarves were around four-and-a-half-foot tall, and their children were small bundles toddling around on thick, sturdy legs. The youngest ones waved their tiny weapons in the air and battered them against the rocks.

Though the dwarves were busy settling in a new establishment, they all had their weapons in hand or strapped to their backs where they could easily pull them free.

"King Colburn and his fiancée have finally blessed us with their presence!" the dwarf shouted as soon as they were free of the portal.

"We all need each other's help, but I won't tolerate any disrespect toward me, and I especially won't tolerate it toward *her*," Cole said. "Next time, the shadows won't just choke you, do you understand?"

The dwarf rolled his eyes. "I'd forgotten how touchy dark fae and lycans can be. Come along, King Colburn, our council has been waiting for you."

Keeping Lexi close by, Cole gathered the shadows around them. They didn't slither up to make their presence known, but they circled their feet while searching for any hint of a threat. The shadows guarded their backs as they made their way through the dwarves, who'd all stopped what they were doing to watch them pass.

Dwarves were known for their brutality in battle and their penchant for a good time. It was a sign of how unhappy they were here that beer wasn't flowing and they weren't laughing and dancing around a bonfire. Not even the children, whose laughter often filled the air, made a sound.

In the center of their new home, a group of dwarves sat around a fire. They rotated what looked like some kind of bird on a spit. The dwarves all glanced up as they approached.

Unlike many realms, a council ruled the dwarves, and they elected it every year to represent their best interests. Four rocks surrounded the fire, and the dwarf who escorted them here settled onto the only vacant one.

One other man and two women occupied the remaining stones. None of them smiled when Cole and Lexi stopped outside the circle.

"It's about time," one of the women said.

"In case you haven't heard, we've been pretty busy," Cole replied blandly.

"As have we," another man said.

"I'm not going to stand here and bicker with you," Cole said. "You're either with us, or you're not. We have other realms to get to, and I'm sure many of them have also been destroyed. Drumbledon is not the only realm he has attacked; Verdan is also in ruins."

The dwarves all exchanged a look before one of the women sighed and rose from her rock. "Please, come join us."

Like the first dwarf they met, they all spoke with something similar to an English accent. Two dwarves, standing nearby, produced two more stones and set them down next to the dwarf who escorted them and one of the councilwomen.

Cole led Lexi over to one of the stones. After she settled onto the rock, he remained standing behind her.

"I'm Skognoth Orcsword," the dwarf who brought them here stated. "Most call me Skog."

"I am Ubolin Mithrilmaul or Ubo," the other male dwarf said.

"I am Garfoure Blazingsword," one of the women said. "They call me Four."

"And I am Brudworika Flatgranite," the last woman said. "I'm known as Rika."

"It's nice to meet you," Lexi said.

Cole nodded a greeting to them while he studied their weapons. The shadows moved closer to the dwarves whose attention remained riveted on Lexi. When Rika leaned forward, her dark brown hair shone in the light, and her brown eyes were intense on Lexi.

"Are you truly arach?" Rika inquired.

"Yes."

"I'll be," the woman murmured. "I've never met an arach. I always assumed they'd be... bigger."

Lexi's brow furrowed. "Sorry to ah... disappoint you."

Rika sat back. "You better not disappoint us."

"Careful," Cole cautioned.

Rika settled her ax, with its black handle, across her knees. She was pretending to be indifferent but smart enough to keep the head of the ax pointed away from Lexi.

"So, you've come for our help," Skog stated.

"We've come to work *with* you," Cole said.

He'd be damned if any of the immortals who agreed to work with them believed they owed them something afterward. That was a treacherous, slippery slope. Besides, every one of them had as much reason to be involved in this war as they did.

"If you're unwilling to aid us against the Lord, we'll leave," Cole told them. "We don't have much time here either. Not only has the Lord destroyed Drumbledon and Verdan, but he'll be heading for other realms too. The giants have made it clear they won't help, and I'm sure Aerie has also been destroyed. We seek only a simple yes or no from you. You know why we're here, and you know the consequences of your decision; make it."

They all exchanged a look, and the dwarves gathered around them shifted as murmurs ran through the crowd. Cole rested his hand on Lexi's shoulder as the shadows gathered closer. It didn't go unnoticed by the dwarves.

"They say he is the Shadow Reaver," Rika said.

"He is," Skog said. "I saw him control the shadows, and they talk to him too."

"Interesting," Four murmured.

Cole's impatience was growing; they didn't have time for this. "I can show you what I can do."

Rika caught his meaning as her bronze skin paled and her eyes darted nervously to the shadows gathering in front of Lexi. Lexi rested her hand over the top of his but didn't speak.

"We will *not* let what the Lord did to Drumbledon stand," Ubo said. "He will not get away with destroying our home. The dwarves will not stand for such an insult against them."

"Hear! Hear!" the dwarves cheered as they pounded their weapons on the ground.

"Is that your answer?" Cole inquired.

The council rose, and Skog stepped toward them. "It is. I will be going with you to the other realms. Where are we off to next?"

"You intend to come *with* us?" Lexi blurted.

"We've heard the rumors, but I will see the two of you in

action. I'll also hear your battle plan. This is non-negotiable. We have to make sure you have a chance of winning before we risk losing any more of us. We will do whatever is best for our children."

"Of course." Before Cole could protest the decision, Lexi continued. "We will be happy to have you with us."

"Who are we seeking to recruit next?" Skog asked.

Cole's jaw clenched as Skog rested his battle-ax against his shoulder. They did *not* need a dwarf tromping through the realms with them; they had all the diplomatic skills of a craz on a rampage.

Skog's brown skin crinkled around the edges of his mouth when he smiled grimly. "You truly require a dwarf's help."

Cole's eyebrows shot up, and Lexi inquired, "Why is that?"

"Because an arach and the future ruler of Dragonia requires someone far smarter than a dark fae at her side. They only think with their little brains."

Cole glowered at the dwarf, and Lexi laughed. Then, she smiled and squeezed his hand.

"It's not so little," she replied.

The dwarves broke into loud, hearty laughter as they pounded their weapons into the ground. Cole shook his head as Lexi beamed at him.

Skog held his arm out to her. "A sense of humor, something the dark fae and lycans are sorely lacking. As you can see by that one's sour puss."

Cole's hands twitched, and when the shadows shifted around him, Skog blanched a little but still smiled at Lexi.

"We enjoy a good sense of humor around here, milady," Skog said. "Come, and tell me where we're off to next?"

Lexi grinned as she slid her arm into Skog's. The smile on her face *almost* made Cole not want to choke the dwarf.

"Where to?" Lexi asked Cole.

"The berserkers."

"Oh fuck, you're *really* hard up for help," Skog said while a murmur ran through the rest of the dwarves.

"Let's go," Cole said.

He rested his hand on Lexi's hip and opened a portal. The three of them entered it together.

CHAPTER FIFTY-SIX

THREE DAYS LATER, they finally entered the prison again. By the time they returned, Cole was on the verge of strangling Skog with his beard.

He was on edge and in a foul mood. They'd spent too much time traveling to realms already destroyed by the Lord and his dragons.

They arrived too late to save anyone. He was sure some of them still existed somewhere, but he had no idea how to find the ogres, orcs, or trolls.

The berserkers refused to help them; they had already sided with the Lord, which would lead to a nasty battle on the field. And it nearly led to them getting killed before they fled. He'd make the berserkers pay for that when the time came.

The Lord's men demolished the pixie realm, but the witches could probably find them. The imps were still creating chaos in their realm. They agreed to lend a hand before fleeing to somewhere they deemed safer.

"How did it go?" Orin asked as they once again gathered in the small room.

"Not good," Cole said.

He ran a hand through his hair and studied Lexi. She was tired, but she'd done well with all the traveling, and she'd at least gotten some sleep when they returned to the dark fae palace to sleep last night.

The Lord destroyed the Gloaming, but due to the many magics comprising it, the palace remained standing. It would protect them against any danger should one arise when they were there.

Skog had become increasingly grumpy and critical as their journey progressed. Cole didn't blame the dwarf for being disenchanted, but he'd prefer not to hear his bitching all the time, either.

Shifting his attention back to everyone gathered in the room, Cole filled them in on what happened while they were gone. Which, unfortunately, was not a lot... at least not in the way of recruiting more help.

"There's still the zombies," Kaylia said. Her injuries had healed since the last time they saw her.

"When did you return?" Cole asked at the same time Skog blurted, "Are you out of your mind?"

Kaylia ignored the dwarf as she spoke to Cole. "Yesterday. The wounded are all healing nicely, and the witches and crones are ready to fight when you are. They want the Lord dead."

"As do we all," Skog muttered.

"And who are you?" Orin demanded.

"I am Skognoth Orcsword." The end of Skog's battle-ax clanged against the floor when he smacked it off the stone. "You may call me Skog. I'm here to ensure that the dwarves' help in this battle will not end in all of us getting slaughtered. So far, I am not convinced."

"Oh, he's delightful," Orin muttered.

"You haven't spent the past three days with him," Cole replied.

"Skog is here to help us, and that's what matters," Lexi said.

Cole didn't completely agree with that statement.

"What about the zombies?" Kaylia asked. "I know we

discarded the idea of having them help before, but they might fight with us."

"That's begging for trouble," Maverick said. "They could turn on *us* as soon as the battle starts."

"That's a possibility, but does anyone know if Moratour is still standing?" Sahira asked.

"I haven't been to check on it," Cole said.

But he'd *almost* prefer losing to the Lord than traveling to that forsaken land to interact with the zombies. He'd rather go back through the trials and have his skin torn away again before returning to the hideous realm of Moratour.

"The Lord wouldn't send his men to Moratour," Varo said. "Not even he wants to deal with the zombies. And he wouldn't risk having one of his dragons become one."

"Could that really happen?" Lexi breathed.

"I don't see why not... *if* a zombie somehow got their hands on one."

"Wow."

"And that's a good reason why *none* of us should go," Brokk said. "The last thing we need is a zombie dragon."

"But if the zombies agree to work with us and fight for us, they'll be a huge distractor and benefit," Del said. "The Lord's men will piss themselves and run if a horde of zombies comes at them."

"The zombies could add to their army with the Lord's men and turn on *us* afterward," Orin said.

No one spoke as they all digested this possibility.

"What about the sirens, lycan, and light fae?" Cole asked. "Were you able to connect with them?"

"Aerie was destroyed when we got there," Brokk said. "Nothing of it remained, but there weren't any dead."

"They must have vacated before the Lord arrived. I can locate them," Cole said.

"My pack and a few others are ready to fight when it's time," Maverick said.

"Good."

"We also spoke with the light fae," Brokk said and flicked a glance at Varo, who stared at the wall. "Lumus remained untouched as of yesterday, but the light fae have moved to a realm where they feel safer. Elfie has also recruited some who have agreed to help. They refuse to fight and say they won't pick up a weapon, but they'll help tend the injured."

"They may be cowards, but they're excellent healers," Niall said.

"They're not cowards," Lexi said. "They have their ways and their beliefs. It's not up to us to change that when we should be accepting them and whatever help they can provide."

"Picking up a weapon would be a bigger help," Niall said. "But I'm amazed they agreed to help, so I'll give them credit for it."

"I'll send crows out with messages for the dark fae. They'll be able to locate at least some of them," Cole said. "I don't know how many will fight or how many we can trust, but at least some of them will be on our side."

"I know some vampires who will help, too," Del said. "Because of the sun, they'll mostly have to fight inside the palace."

"We'll take them," Cole said. "I'll also send a crow to Talon. He was on the coalition and against the Lord; he should still help and might have some warlocks he would trust to join us."

"The warlocks will be tough, considering the Lord is one of them," Brokk said.

"Yes, but I'm sure Talon knows of some who don't agree with what he's done."

"What about the humans? Are we going to try to recruit some of them?" Niall asked.

"No. It would take too long to train them. We don't have the time. Besides, they'd probably just get slaughtered." Cole said,

"Let's not do that then," Lexi muttered.

"We might have enough to bring the Lord down if we can figure out something to do about the dragons. A way to distract them or something," Sahira said.

"I have a plan that might help there," Del said. "I think the zombies would be beneficial for it, but not necessary."

Cole smiled; he should have known Del would come up with something for this. The man was a military genius. "What's this plan?" Cole inquired.

CHAPTER FIFTY-SEVEN

DEL REACHED inside the outercoat he wore and removed a rolled-up scroll. Kneeling on the ground, he unrolled it. They all bent to take a closer look as Del revealed his strategy.

When he finished outlining his plan, Orin gave a low whistle and slapped him on the shoulder. "I'm really glad you're on my side this time, old friend."

Del shrugged off his hand. "We'll *never* be friends."

"But we'll be great acquaintances," Orin told him with a wink.

When Del's hands fisted, Cole stepped between them. "I think you're right," he said. "The zombies could prove beneficial in this."

"And if they can't be kept under control?" Skog asked.

"If we win, Lexi can take control of the dragons; they'll keep the zombies in line," Cole said. "Or kill them."

"What if they create a zombie dragon?" Varo inquired.

Beside him, Lexi shuddered and grasped her elbows as she hugged herself. "I think the other dragons could take down such a monstrosity, but how many would we lose? How many could also become corrupted in such a way?"

"They'd have to get a hold of a dragon to make it happen, and what are the chances of that?" Cole asked.

"If there's a *tiny* chance, we shouldn't take it," Brokk said. "Could you imagine anything worse than a brain-eating zombie dragon?"

Cole had to agree it was a pretty appalling prospect, but the zombies could help them with this.

"I can't," Skog said.

"Neither can I," Niall said.

"If the plan works, there wouldn't be any dragons near the zombies," Del said.

"I think Del's plan is brilliant, and I understand how the zombies could help us by providing a good distraction for the Lord's men, but I do *not* want to go into battle with those things at my side. I don't care if they're fighting with us or not," Sahira said.

"The zombies would drive back the Lord's men faster than our army alone," Maverick said.

Cole rubbed his chin as he studied Del's plan. As far as things went, it was brilliant in its simplicity. They wouldn't require a large army to pull it off if all went right.

However, a large army, especially one that could terrify the Lord's men, would give them a better chance of winning. He looked over at Lexi. She bit her bottom lip as she studied Del's plan.

"What do you think?" he asked her.

"I can draw the dragons away; I know it. They'll come to me once I lower my shield and they sense I'm there."

Cole studied the X at the edge of the map Del drew. That X would be him, Lexi, and everyone else in this room... in the beginning.

Once Lexi opened a portal onto those mountains, they would all enter Dragonia through a portal the Lord couldn't guard. She would then lower her shield, absorb as much sunlight as possible, and glow for all the dragons to see.

She was right; the dragons would come to her. Once they did, the others would leave through her portal and return to the prison. From there, they would open portals to different realms where they would locate the various portals that were the only ways into Dragonia.

He didn't doubt the Lord would have those portals heavily guarded in Dragonia, but his army would be a lot weaker without the dragons. That would give them a much better shot of getting through the Lord's army. The zombies would increase their chances.

CHAPTER FIFTY-EIGHT

"WHAT IF THE Lord has men guarding the entrance to the portals?" Cole asked. "Our army will run across them before they enter Dragonia."

"I've already scoped out the portals we would use in the human realm, the Gloaming, Verdan, and the other realms. The portals are all still open and unguarded. I'm sure the Lord has high numbers guarding the portals *in* Dragonia, but there's no one on those other portals. There are too many of them; he would have to spread his army too thin, and he's not going to do that. He's insane, not stupid," Del said.

"You went alone?" Lexi asked.

"I was safe."

"You still shouldn't have gone alone."

"It was something we needed the answer to if this plan was going to work."

"We did," Cole murmured.

"We'll check the portals again before we go to war, but I don't think things will change anytime soon," Del said.

"You're taking others with you next time," Lexi insisted.

"I will," Del promised.

"Hmm," Lexi muttered though she didn't sound appeased.

"Now, what about the zombies?"

"I think," Brokk said, "those who agreed to fight with us might change their minds if we tell them we're going into this war with zombies at our side."

"The dwarves won't like it," Skog said. "I understand the reasoning behind it, and they will too, but I'm not sure how many will agree with this. We can't fight the Lord's men while worrying that those on our side might turn on us too."

"I think we have our answer then," Lexi said. "We can't take the chance of losing what fighters we have to bring in the zombies, even if those zombies could replace the number of fighters who change their minds."

"There aren't enough zombies to replace the fighters we have," Maverick said. "We can do this without them."

"Yes, we can," Cole agreed. "I'll send crows to all those who have agreed to help us. We'll find a realm for all of us to gather in so we can train together, and next week, we'll go to war."

Del rolled up his plans and tucked them away again. "Are you going to tell them the battle plan?"

"Not until the last minute. There's no doubt, someone, amid all those we gather, will turn against us and go to the Lord with our plan."

"And then we'll have to kill them," Niall said.

"In many *very* not-so-fun ways," Orin agreed.

"What about the giants?" Lexi asked. "How do we fight them?"

"That's why we'll bring a lot of rope," Del said. "We'll run around their ankles as fast as possible and tie them together."

Lexi started to laugh but realized he wasn't joking; her laughter died away. "Will that work?"

"It's brought them down before."

"It's not exactly easy, and it will never take them *all* down," Cole said. "But it's an option."

"Ideally, when we knew we were going up against giants, we'd dig trenches and cover them in the hopes the beasts would fall into them," Orin said. "Then we'd pounce and stab their eyes and throat until they died. But the rope trick can work."

"Oh, Hecate," Kaylia muttered and dropped her head into her hands to rub her temples.

"Since we're the ones invading Dragonia, the trenches won't work," Del said. "We'll get some nets too and use them to entangle the giants. Hopefully, it will trip a couple of them; we'll be able to take them down if they fall."

"If they don't squish a hundred of us in the process," Skog huffed.

"That could be an issue," Del murmured.

"If they do fall, their bodies will probably indent a trench for us and might trip up the other ones," Orin said.

"That's looking at the bright side," Varo said tiredly.

"Did the Lord go after your realm?" Sahira asked Skog.

"We no longer have a realm," Skog replied. "But we must ensure our children survive to carry on the dwarf way of life. If I don't think we can survive this war against the Lord, the dwarves will remain in hiding."

"In other words, you'll remain cowards," Orin retorted.

Sparks flew from the bottom of the ax when Skog banged it against the ground. "Dwarves are not cowards!"

"That's enough," Lexi interjected as she glared at Orin. "They're trying to ensure their children survive; there's nothing wrong with that. If they were the ones organizing this war, you wouldn't put yourself in their hands without knowing more about it."

"But now he knows the battle plan," Orin replied.

"And if he chooses not to fight with us, he'll be locked in a cell and unable to leave until the battle is over," Cole replied. "When it ends, he'll be released and allowed to return to the dwarves.

Whether he likes it or not, Skog will remain with us until the end of this war."

He'd explained this to the dwarf before they returned to the prison, and Skog agreed. Cole suspected Skog believed he might find a way to escape, but Cole wouldn't allow it and planned to have the shadows watch him while he was here. He'd know the second the dwarf tried anything.

Skog lifted his ax off the ground and pointed its head at Orin. "I don't like you."

Orin chuckled. "You're not the first and won't be the last."

Unwilling to deal with Orin's shit with even *more* immortals, Cole ignored the interaction. One day, his brother would get his ass handed to him or wind up in trouble because of his reckless ways, and he would have to face the consequences. Today wasn't that day, but it would come.

"It's time to start alerting our army and preparing them for battle," Cole said.

CHAPTER FIFTY-NINE

LEXI SPENT the next week training, fighting, using her abilities more, and repeatedly opening portals to see how much they would drain her. Eventually, she built herself up enough to open four without much trouble. After that, exhaustion started weighing on her.

If all went well, she would only have to open three portals. One for her to enter Dragonia, another their army could go through to surprise and attack the Lord's men, and a final one into the palace.

She wouldn't dare try to do more than those three on the day of battle. If she did, it could drain her too much, and she could *not* be weakened for what they were about to face. She would also require enough energy to open an escape portal if it became necessary.

But at least she was growing stronger; she felt her strength increasing with every passing day. It pulsed in her cells, tingled her fingertips, and raced through her body. It vibrated like a tuning fork within her until she wondered how strong she would become.

She was also getting better at healing, something only she and Cole knew about as he was the one she kept healing. At first, she was adamant against his idea of having them work alone on her healing.

She suggested using her powers on the injured witches, but he insisted she keep the ability hidden for as long as possible. As far as they could tell, Beatrix and the children hadn't revealed her secret.

It was only a matter of time before it got out, but if they could keep it hidden from the Lord until the battle, it could help them. So, while her stomach churned, Cole would slice open his flesh.

In the beginning, she always had tears streaming down her face as she healed him, but eventually, her tears stopped slipping free. At first, her ability was slow to work, and it was difficult for her to draw it forward, but as the days passed, she became more adept at using it and was determined to master it.

They were going into a war; there would be no better time to have the ability to save someone's life.

By the end, and against her protests, Cole cut himself more often and more deeply. And all the while, she got better and faster at healing them. Mainly because she couldn't stand the sight of his blood or the pain he kept masked.

Unlike opening too many portals, using her healing ability didn't drain her. Instead, it was like a balloon accepting air as it grew bigger until she felt it inside her even when she wasn't using it.

Over the passing days, Cole sent countless crows to hunt down any dark fae who might join them in the war. He received enough replies that they had a small army of dark fae working with the other immortals who vowed to help them.

Elvin was one of the first dark fae to reply and the only member of the dark fae council to join them. He was helping with the training and keeping the dark fae in line. Cole said he was always respected in the Gloaming and his presence helped strengthen the conviction of the dark fae.

Lexi remained focused on her training, growing abilities, and what she had to do to help succeed in this war, but doubt and anxiety niggled at the back of her mind. They could do this; they *would* do this, but not without sacrifice and not without huge losses on both sides.

She kept thinking about Gibborim and his eye as he peered at her. Remorse had tinged his voice... as well as conviction. This was not a war he wanted, but he would do what was necessary to ensure his queen survived.

The giants wouldn't be the only ones fighting for the Lord who didn't want to, but they wouldn't change their course. As much as Lexi tried to hate them for it, she couldn't blame them.

But that made what they were about to face worse. Not only would they lose many from their side, probably some of those she loved and cared for, but they'd be killing immortals who would have preferred not to be there.

Now, the day before they planned to go to war, Lexi finished dressing after taking a shower. She'd spent the morning training with Brokk and her father on fighting techniques. They'd used small swords, throwing stars, and daggers.

Normally, she would wait until later as she had more training, but it had been especially intense. She'd been soaked in sweat and smelled like hot garbage.

Such extensive training no longer exhausted her or left her muscles sore and rubbery. She'd become extremely talented with the weapons and wielded them without hesitation. The idea of killing made her stomach churn, but she would do what needed to be done.

But though she wasn't tired from training, her shoulders slumped beneath the weight of what tomorrow would bring. Their entire plan hinged on her being able to draw the dragons away.

If she failed, they would have to call the whole thing off or go ahead with it anyway. If they did, then more would die.

She couldn't fail.

CHAPTER SIXTY

SHE WAS ABOUT to leave the small, cell-like room she shared with Cole when the door opened and he strode inside. Like her, he was freshly showered. Tousled endearingly, his damp, black hair made him look younger and more approachable.

Two things he hadn't looked in quite a while. This week, he'd been relentless in training the troops gathered in the prison realm.

They considered leaving all the fighters separated to avoid fights between the different immortals who didn't like each other, like the witches and vampires. Eventually, they decided it would be best if they all learned to work together.

Things were going better than they anticipated with all the immortals working together. With the destruction of the realms, the Lord had solidified their hatred of *him*.

The witches now despised someone more than they did vampires. The warlocks, who were usually arrogant assholes, weren't acting so high and mighty even though their realm remained untouched. The dwarves and imps bickered, but they weren't at each other's throats.

And the other immortals were willing to overlook their petty grievances and differences in favor of destroying the man who had ravaged their homes or kept them in fear. The Lord had unwittingly united them against a common enemy, and they were eager to destroy him.

They even overlooked their dislike of the couple dozen light fae who arrived with Elfie. The light fae didn't train with them, but they did work with the witches to make healing potions and poultices they were stockpiling for use during the battle.

Varo stayed far away from his mother. But the other immortals accepted the presence of the light fae even though many were irate when they refused to choose a side during the Lord's war.

Sahira's mother joined with the witches. As far as Lexi knew, her aunt didn't speak to the woman, and Lexi only caught sight of her a few times during their training sessions.

That was more than enough for her as she did *not* like the woman. No matter how much Sahira pretended her mother's abandonment didn't bother her, Lexi knew it did.

Talon had also joined them; he brought a small group of warlocks with him. He said he could have tried recruiting more but didn't want to risk someone turning him in to the Lord.

They'd also decided to gather everyone together because they felt it was good for them to learn to trust Lexi and Cole. The members of their army had to know they could rely on them and count on them to be a part of this battle.

Kaylia and the witches had cast a spell over the prison so only a select few immortals could open a portal out of it or leave the building. Therefore, they all remained locked inside. It was claustrophobic, and many weren't happy when they were told what to expect if they came here, but they agreed to it.

That was another sign of their trust in her and Cole and their hatred of the Lord. Of course, if one of their army turned on them —which was a pretty good possibility considering the Lord had to have at least one follower in their midst—they would lead the Lord straight back here.

Which meant they would have to abandon the prison if they

lost. But they already had a new meeting place to gather if they had to leave their quest. Lexi hoped they never had to use it.

They'd debated using the harrow stone to make their army look bigger when they entered Dragonia, but it still wouldn't let anyone other than Lexi touch it. Since they weren't sure how much the spell would weaken her, they decided against it.

"Where are you going?" Cole asked.

"It's time to work with the army," she said.

She'd trained with her dad and Brokk this morning, but now it was time to join the others.

"Not today." He lifted the basket draped over his arm. "I have different plans for us. I've also given everyone the rest of the day and night off. Tomorrow, we go to war. Tonight is for all of us to enjoy ourselves. And I'm going to enjoy it with you."

Lexi started to protest his decision but decided against it. They should join the others and continue their training, but at this point, what difference did it make?

A few more hours of training wouldn't make much difference in the grand scheme of things. They were all on edge and aware tonight's sunset might be the last they ever saw. Why not enjoy what could be the final moments of their lives?

She walked over and took the arm he offered her. "Where are we going?"

"That is a surprise, my lovely wife-to-be."

He opened a portal, and they left the prison behind.

CHAPTER SIXTY-ONE

LEXI SMILED as they stepped out of the portal and into the large, grand room of the dark fae palace. She first met Cole in this room. At the time, he sat upon the dais with his father and Brokk.

He was a prince then, with no desire to have his father's crown or throne, but the Lord thrust him into a position where he had no other choice but to claim a land that never wanted him to rule. Of course, he survived the trials and became king, but he wasn't unscathed by them.

He now possessed more power than anyone she knew... and that was because of *her* ancestors.

The biggest worry she'd wrestled with all week raised its troublesome head again as she gazed around the empty room. Cole wasn't the same man she first met here. He now harbored shadows hell-bent on death and destruction.

Those shadows would feast on the war and death sure to unfold tomorrow. Was there any way he could control the shadows and emerge from this war the same man she knew? Or would those insidious *things* finally succeed in destroying him?

Lexi closed her eyes as waves of terror swept her. She was less afraid of dying for this cause than she was of unleashing something upon the realms that could destroy them all.

And that something could be the man she loved with all her heart. Opening her eyes, she stared at the dais and the abandoned thrones still sitting on it.

Cole had been so handsome that day, imposing and scary. She was attracted to him and unnerved as he stared at her with open curiosity. He was a dark fae, the race of immortals she'd vowed to avoid as the whispers of their cruelty and the shadow kissed they sometimes left behind preceded them everywhere they went.

She never could have imagined that night would have impacted her life, but everything changed afterward. That imposing, cold, distant man became someone she loved and trusted with her life.

He could be vicious and was no one to fuck with, but he would also do anything to protect those he loved. While a lot of bad followed that night, and more was still to come, she wouldn't change any of what happened between them.

She had to have faith that their love for each other would get them through this. And she would count on that when they went to war tomorrow.

"Come," Cole said.

Lexi followed Cole to the middle of the room. They were almost to the center when lights flared on all around them. Flames erupted in the sconces on the wall. Stars started to dance across the domed ceiling, and soft music played.

Lexi's head tipped back, and she gazed in awe as the stars faded in and out. The constellations changed, and moons emerged before dipping away again. It looked almost exactly like it had the first night they met. The only thing missing was the roomful of immortals, all vying for the attention of the king and his sons.

"I wanted you the second I saw you that night," Cole said.

Lexi smiled at him. "Were you reading my mind?"

He brushed the hair back from her face and stroked her cheek. "I was hoping to bring the memory back for you."

"How did you do this?"

"The palace responds to commands… some of the time. But this room is full of magic the king can unleash. I came to make sure it was ready before I brought you here."

He set the basket down, and as a new song started playing, he took her hand and twirled her away before pulling her close again. Lexi laughed while he spun, danced, and dipped her around the room.

The lights grew dimmer as the music changed, and they continued to dance. She was always happiest in his arms and never wanted their time together here to end.

When the song slowed, she rested her head against his broad chest, and he claimed her hand while they swayed together. Beneath her ear, she relished the steady thump of his heart as it calmed her. That beat was as solid as the man.

She almost asked if he would be okay tomorrow but decided against it. There was no reason to darken the mood, and they both knew the answer…

They would have to wait and see what tomorrow brought.

When the music changed again, Cole stepped back to gaze down at her. "Are you hungry?"

"A little," she admitted. "But I don't want to stop."

"We have all night." He led her over to the basket and lifted it. "We'll come back."

Lexi glanced at the breathtaking room before following him down the hall. They traversed a few halls before he stopped to open one of the doors.

Lexi's eyebrows rose when she saw the room. She'd spent some time exploring the palace but had never come across this room before.

She could spend an eternity exploring this place and probably still not uncover all of its secrets. There were also the rooms it wouldn't let her or Cole enter.

He walked her over to a red couch with a high back and

282   BRENDA K DAVIES

spindly legs. It was in amazing condition, even if it looked old enough to have existed during the days of the Egyptians.

Certain it would be uncomfortable to sit on, she perched on the edge before sliding back a little. When she sank into the cushion, she was delighted to learn it was far more comfortable than expected.

CHAPTER SIXTY-TWO

COLE SAT beside her and placed the basket on the golden table with a glass center. The wall across from them was floor-to-ceiling windows facing a garden. It was in desperate need of tending as the plants spilled over the walkways and the bigger ones crowded out others, but beautiful blooms, in many shapes and colors, shone in the fading sunlight.

More glass front rooms looked out on the gardens. She couldn't tell what those rooms were, but they went on as far as she could see before disappearing into the jumble of plants and trees.

"It's beautiful," she whispered as Cole opened the basket and started removing food.

"It is."

"I've never seen the gardens before."

"They encompass a few acres within this section of the palace. No one can view them from outside the palace, but as you can see" —he waved a hand at the other rooms facing the gardens—"you can view them from many different rooms within the palace."

"How lovely. And sad."

He stopped removing the food to look at her. "Sad?"

"Everyone in the Gloaming should be able to see this beauty."

284 BRENDA K DAVIES

The sunlight emphasized the chiseled angles of his face while he studied the garden. "I never considered that. They were always ours." He shrugged and resumed removing the food. "Perhaps, when this is over and the dark fae can return home, I will figure out a way for the fae to see them too."

"I'm sure they would like that."

He gave her a sexy smile. "Maybe, but it's the dark fae; there are few things they truly appreciate."

The lascivious look he gave her made it clear what one of those things was. Lexi resisted tugging at the collar of her fae tunic as he unpacked a bottle of champagne.

Shifting her attention back to the other rooms with their one glass wall, she discovered she could see into some of them. But she couldn't tell what kind of rooms they were, and nothing moved within.

But they would have a problem if something did move. After the Lord unleashed his dragons and army on the Gloaming, the palace was abandoned. No one had known it would withstand the wrath of the dragons, but it stood as a testament to the strength of its magic.

"I love this place," she said. "And not just the gardens, but *all* of it. It's all so… magical."

Cole handed her a plate of food and a glass of champagne. "The palace is pleased to hear it."

She chuckled as she sipped her champagne. "I forgot you have a connection to it since becoming king."

"I could never forget."

"You've missed it here."

"Very much."

"We'll come back and rebuild the Gloaming better than ever before."

He clinked his glass against hers before drinking it. "That we will."

As they ate, small blue and yellow birds flitted between the bushes while butterflies the size of footballs fluttered from plant to plant. The butterflies' colors were more vibrant than any Lexi had seen on Earth.

When she finished her bread, fruit, and chicken, she set the plate down and reached for the champagne bottle. Cole grasped it before she could and poured her another glass.

"This is the best way to spend this night," she said.

"I can think of something that will improve it," Cole said as bubbly liquid filled her glass.

His low, gravelly tone sent a shiver down her spine. She smiled as she sipped her champagne. "I can't think of anything that would make it any better."

"No?" he asked.

The sexy way his eyes perused her sent a flash of warmth through her. She sipped her champagne to keep from jumping on him as one of his fingers traced the back of her hand.

"Not off the top of my head," she teased.

"I can think of a couple. Including"—he took the glass from her and set it on the table— "a far more entertaining way to drink that."

"How?" she said in a voice a little too high-pitched for her liking.

He smiled as he knelt on the floor before her and pushed her shirt up. His fingers skimmed her rib cage as he worked. "I'll be happy to show you."

CHAPTER SIXTY-THREE

WHEN LEXI LIFTED HER ARMS, he pulled her shirt off and tossed it across the floor. Then, he unhooked her bra and let it fall. His eyes locked on her breasts as his fingers traced lazy, tantalizing circles around her nipples.

Her breasts became heavier, her breathing a little faster. He lifted her glass and took another sip before holding it over the valley between her breasts. He poured a small rivulet down the middle of them.

Lexi gasped when the cool liquid hit her flesh, but it died off as he bent his head to lick away the small trail slipping down her belly. His mouth warmed her while he leisurely licked away the champagne.

Her fingers dug into the sofa cushions as he lifted his head, grasped her legs, and turned them until she lay back. He removed the soft leather, dark fae boots she wore before unbuttoning her pants. He slid them and her underwear off.

Lifting the glass again, he poured more champagne into her belly button before licking it out. Lexi's fingers entangled in his hair. She pulled him closer as he continued his enticing tease of cool champagne and warm kisses until her glass was empty and she was quivering in anticipation.

Rising over her, he stripped out of his clothes. Her heart thudded faster as she drank in his magnificent body. He was so large, powerful, and completely hers that it was both amazing and terrifying.

If something happened to him, she would endure it and go on because she would have no other choice, but it would devastate her. She'd never be the same, and there would always be a gigantic hole where her love for him would reside, unanswered.

But nothing was going to happen to him; she would ensure that. Her power was growing, and she would do whatever it took to keep him and everyone else she loved safe. It didn't matter what she had to do.

When he settled beside her again, he turned to dip a hand into the basket he'd brought. She couldn't see what he did, but when he turned back, his fingers glided up her belly to her breasts; he clasped them and took a nipple into his mouth.

When his mouth chilled her, she realized he'd slipped ice into his mouth as he moved from one breast to the other. The heat of his mouth combined with the cold of the ice sent tendrils of ecstasy spiraling out to her limbs. As he moved down her belly, he pulled her hips toward him until her legs were off the couch.

When he settled between her thighs, he lifted the bottle of champagne and poured it between her legs. Then, he bent his mouth to her, and as he licked away the drink while the ice found her clit, Lexi nearly screamed as the new sensation both startled and enthralled her.

He draped her legs over his shoulders as he greedily feasted on her until she was panting for breath. He was right; this *was* a far more entertaining way to drink champagne.

Lexi's fingers entangled in his hair as she begged him for release while wishing it would never stop. Then, the spiraling tension growing inside her gave way. Her toes curled as her back arched, and wave after wave of pleasure crashed through her.

~

PULLING AWAY, Cole lowered Lexi's thighs before grasping her waist and lifting her from the sofa. Lexi's legs locked around his waist.

The scent of her release engulfed him, but it had also ingrained itself into every one of his pores. She was a part of him, the *best* part, and forever his.

He grasped her ass, as he adjusted to slide into her body. The muscles of her wet sheath gripped his cock as he buried himself inside her. And once he possessed her, the shadows that had been stirring with more intensity as the war approached finally calmed.

The tranquility descending over his soul was like the quiet before a storm, and it was a very violent storm building inside him. Tomorrow, they would return to Dragonia, to war, and loss, but tonight, with her, he could forget about that.

He could embrace the peace she granted him and lose himself in her.

"You're so tight," he groaned as his lips found hers.

Carrying her over to the glass, he pressed her back against the windows. He slid one arm under her leg to keep it raised as he bent his legs and lowered her to the ground.

Her passion darkened, hunter green eyes with their emerald flecks met his. He pulled out before sliding leisurely back into her.

She held his gaze while he took the time to memorize her reactions and gasps of ecstasy as he pushed her over the edge again. Her muscles contracted around his shaft, but he didn't follow her.

Instead, he lifted her again and sank his fangs into her shoulder. She cried out as her nails raked his back. As he marked her, the dark fae part of him fed on her while she rocked against him, and her cries urged him faster.

When her head fell to his neck and she bit into him, their powers rose to vibrate the air between them. The dark fae part of him feasted on the banquet it received as their strength grew.

The moonlight bathing her in a hue of silver emphasized her sun-kissed skin but didn't reveal the mark of the dragon, as she kept her shield firmly intact. The next time she came, he gave himself over to his release.

He released a guttural cry as the lycan part of him found joy in its mate. For a while afterward, they stood locked together before he finally lowered her, cupped her beautiful face in his hands, and kissed her.

"Would you like to dance with me again?" he asked.

A radiant smile lit her face. "Always and forever."

He grinned as he took her hand. Neither bothered to dress before leaving the room and returning to the grand room.

As he spun her around the dance floor, he teased and stroked her to the height of passion before claiming her once more.

CHAPTER SIXTY-FOUR

LEXI STOOD in the prison with Cole, her dad, Maverick, Brokk, Orin, Varo, Sahira, Kaylia, and Skog. Niall had gone to gather the group who would enter Dragonia with them. That group would flood into Dragonia through a portal Lexi would open near the other entrances to the realm.

When Niall returned with nearly a hundred soldiers, Lexi took a deep breath and prepared to open a portal into the realm once ruled by her ancestors. A realm where her mother was a princess. A realm so many hoped she could lead.

The only problem was, she'd never ruled anything before, and *everyone* knew it. She wasn't raised a leader; she'd never learned the intricacies of a royal court and had no desire to do so.

The idea of leading anything other than a horse disturbed her, but she didn't have a choice. Oh, she could walk away and spend the rest of her life hiding. It would be a brutal, miserable life, though.

And so many others would die if the Lord continued to rule. Even if someone did eventually succeed in taking him down, if she didn't assume the throne, whoever sat on it next would go mad too.

She could walk away, but she'd hate herself forever.

292   BRENDA K DAVIES

But she'd rather pull all her nails out with pliers and then all her teeth before becoming the leader of any realm, never mind Dragonia, the realm that ruled them all. She couldn't fail as a leader. All the realms had lost and sacrificed too much for that to happen. She was also unsure how she could succeed when she had no experience.

You'll have Cole to help you.

And that was one of the few things helping to keep her from completely losing her shit and running away. But she'd never been more petrified in her life.

She wasn't scared of her own possible impending death, but she was afraid of losing anyone she loved and what would follow if they lost. But she could only handle one thing at a time, and right now, she had to focus on getting them into Dragonia and distracting the dragons.

If she stayed focused on one thing, her heart didn't race as much, her palms didn't sweat, and her throat didn't feel as if it was trying to strangle her. She just felt like she would vomit, so it was an improvement.

She played with Cole's engagement ring on her finger, twisting it around as she gathered her courage and buried her doubts the best she could. But they refused to be completely suppressed.

That's fine as long as they don't get in the way.

And she would *not* let them do that.

Lexi took another deep breath and opened the portal into Dragonia. She kept her shoulders back and tried to exude an aura of confidence she hoped the others bought. Cole walked at her side as they strode through the portal.

She'd only been to Dragonia a couple of times before, but she'd noticed the mountains towering over the land. She could picture their high peaks and rocky crevices perfectly.

When they emerged from the portal, the mountains were as she'd pictured. The land was not.

"What?" she whispered.

She gazed around in confusion and tried to understand why it was so dark when it was supposed to be broad daylight.

Unlike the prison realm, where darkness ruled, Dragonia ran on the same day and night schedule as earth. It should be early afternoon here. The sun should be at its highest and brightest point in the sky. Instead, shadows ruled the land.

"What… what's going on?" she breathed.

At first, no one answered her. After a few moments, Kaylia said. "It's an eclipse."

And that was when Lexi saw the black circle engulfing most of the sun. Only a small fragment of the sun's rays peaked out around the sides of the darkness covering it.

"It's to protect against *you*," Sahira said.

CHAPTER SIXTY-FIVE

LEXI'S HEART sank as she gazed around the realm. Located on the side of the mountain, they stood on a large shelf of rocky terrain. If she opened another portal to the land below, the army could march across the ledge to the portal.

But there wouldn't be an army if there wasn't any sun. They couldn't turn an army loose on this realm if she couldn't draw the dragons away from the Lord's army. They would only get slaughtered.

The dragons soared through the air and circled over top of where the Lord's men had gathered around the portals entering Dragonia. The ones they planned to flood with more of their men and women.

Their army was smaller than the one gathered below, but if they could draw the dragons away and surprise them by flooding in from different directions, they stood a chance of defeating the Lord's men. Without enough light, she couldn't draw the dragons away.

Thousands of the Lord's men gathered below, and she was sure there were men inside the palace. They all wore the Lord's red and white colors and a red, fire-breathing dragon on their clothes.

Many of the men below patrolled near the open portals while others gathered around fires, roasting their meals. More of them stood before the closed gates leading toward the palace.

The last time she was here, those gates were open, but the Lord never would have allowed them to remain that way. She couldn't tell if the merchants were still selling their wares in the bailey, but she doubted it.

She imagined the Lord had become a paranoid prick since learning of her existence. Between his insanity and the fact an arach could enter his palace at any time, the man must be going completely off the rails. She imagined Dragonia had become a worse place to live.

Around the army gathered below were structures that weren't here when she and Cole came for the ball. She couldn't tell if they were hastily assembled sleeping barracks for the men or something more as they almost looked like prisons.

Had they been built to incarcerate any prisoners the men caught? It didn't seem likely the Lord would keep anyone alive, but perhaps he planned to torture the immortals they captured. Maybe he required more blood for his fountain.

Far away from the army and closer to the mountains, six giants sat in a circle. They must not have wanted much else to do with the Lord's army as they were about as far away as they could get while still being able to see their military.

They had gathered around a bonfire and sat with their shoulders hunched forward while they roasted something on a tree. Lexi had expected more of them, but six giants were enough to demolish a realm. And they probably didn't think they would need any more with the dragons here.

"He knew we were coming," Lexi said.

"That doesn't mean someone told him," Cole said. "I'm sure once he learned what you were, he searched for ways to curb your powers. He's been privy to the secrets of Dragonia for centuries; he probably knows arach are creatures of light."

"And he will deny you that light," her dad said.

He wore the amulet Cole had taken from Malakai after killing him. The sun medallion protected a vampire against sunlight, but it wasn't necessary now that the realm was in darkness. The vampires with them could fight out here now, instead of just in the palace, but it wouldn't do them any good if they couldn't draw the dragons away.

"He cast a spell to rob as much light from this land as possible," Sahira said.

"What do we do?" Kaylia inquired.

"I'll release my shield," Lexi said.

When she did so, there was enough light for a small spark to emerge at the tips of her fingers. Not one dragon noticed. The glow crept through her arms and face, but it was so faint she could barely see it.

"Shit," Orin muttered.

"Can you and the witches break the spell?" Niall asked Kaylia.

"No," Kaylia said. "He probably used dozens of warlocks to help cast this spell, and it's not a typical eclipse. The moon isn't blocking the sun; no one has the power to move the moon, but"— her eyes flicked nervously to Cole—"shadows are."

"I can still enter the palace," Lexi said as she erected her shield again. "We can keep the armies out of this; Cole and I will go alone and find the Lord. The dragons won't attack us."

"He probably has a hundred men, if not more, guarding him," Varo said. "They'll kill you."

"If we get close enough to him, maybe… maybe…." Her voice trailed off as she tried to think of something… *anything* to help them. "Maybe we should take all of the army into the palace."

"And the dragons will gladly eat them. If we can't get the dragons away from him, then they'll destroy any army we set loose on the palace," Maverick said.

"What if she goes to another realm, lowers her shield, and tries to draw the dragons there?" Skog suggested.

298   BRENDA K DAVIES

"Some will come," Lexi said. "I can go to another realm, let my shield down, glow as bright as possible, and return here. I should retain the glow long enough to draw the dragons to me. I'm not sure if they'll stay once the mark of the dragon fades, but it's something."

"No, it's not," Cole said. "We need more than that, and it has to last."

Something about the tone of his voice caused the hair on her nape to rise. No, it was more than his tone; it was also the set of his jaw and the remorseless glint in his eyes.

"We should go back and rethink this. I'll come up with a new plan," her dad said. "Having more time to plan and train will be good for us."

"It could create a lack of confidence in our ability to pull this off," Orin said.

"We're not going back," Cole said. "We're doing this today. The only other plan is to have Lexi open different portals and charge through them. It will give us an element of surprise, but the dragons and giants will soon catch and destroy us. We can take the whole army into the palace, but our losses will be catastrophic, and we'll never get them past the dragons."

"*We* just have to be able to reach *him*," Lexi said. "And the dragons won't attack us."

CHAPTER SIXTY-SIX

COLE MET Lexi's wide eyes as something inside him shriveled and died. She was right; the dragons wouldn't attack... if it was *just* them.

But the Lord would have many of his men and dragons in the throne room. Between those dragons and the men, their chances of getting through were extremely small.

And that was *if* the Lord was in the throne room. He could be anywhere in the palace or this realm. Cole suspected he would stay as close to the throne as possible, but he was a coward, and hiding was what he did best.

"We're not getting through all those men with the dragons in that room. It's too many obstacles, even if the dragons won't attack us. There's no way to prevent one of them from accidentally stepping on us during all the chaos."

She didn't see what must be done yet... but he did.

He'd vowed to do everything to keep her safe and put her on the throne where she belonged, and he meant it. If it meant destroying himself, he would do it... for her.

She was his light, love, and the best thing to ever happen to him. He *would* make sure she lived the life she was meant to have, and while he didn't give a shit about most of the other immortals who lived in the realms, he wouldn't tolerate a madman destroying her.

A madman who had his father ruthlessly murdered.

Gritting his teeth, Cole shifted his attention to the shadow-covered sun. If he pulled those shadows into him, he'd have the power to take down the Lord and give Lexi the ability to draw the dragons away, weakening the Lord's power.

That amount of shadows could very well destroy him, but no matter what he became, he would keep Lexi safe. If he did this, he could lose her, but she would live, and so would many others.

He looked to his brothers, Del, and Maverick. They were his friends, his family. And finally, he looked at Lexi. She was his everything.

And if they didn't stop the Lord, it was only a matter of time before they were all destroyed. At least this way, they would have a chance to survive.

Cole would *not* demolish the realms, he would ensure that, but he didn't know what he'd become. It was a chance he was willing to take for the good of the realms.

If it gave Lexi a chance to become the amazing queen he knew she would be and gave the rest of those he cared about a chance at better lives, he would sacrifice himself.

～

"WHAT DO YOU SUGGEST WE DO?" Brokk waved a hand at the darkened realm spread out beneath them. "If we attack now, they'll take us out anyway."

"It's not completely dark," Cole said.

Goose bumps broke out on Lexi's arms; it took everything she had not to rub them. A shiver ran down her spine, and her hand fell to the small sword strapped to her waist, but there was nothing to fight.

"Shadows engulf the land," Cole continued.

Words clogged Lexi's throat until they nearly strangled her. *No, no, no, no, no!* Her mind screamed, but she still couldn't speak. He couldn't be suggesting what she thought he was.

And then his eyes, those beautiful, Persian blue eyes, met and held hers while he spoke. "He weakened the arach's powers, but he left plenty here for the Shadow Reaver."

"Why would he do that?" Brokk demanded.

"Because," Orin said, "the Lord knows for Cole to break whatever spell he's cast, he'll have to draw the shadows into him, and if he does, that many shadows...."

Orin's voice trailed off, and his eyes closed as he turned back to the realm.

"Will destroy him," Lexi finished in a whisper.

"And the Lord knows that no dark fae would sacrifice themself in such a way," Sahira said.

"Won't they?" Cole inquired.

Sahira bit her bottom lip as she looked nervously from him to Lexi.

"We'll come up with another plan," Varo said. "We should return before we're spotted."

"I'm not going anywhere," Cole said.

"Cole—"

"*This* is why the Shadow Reaver was created, Lexi. It was to protect you, ensure an arach sat on the throne, and give you the fate you were destined to have."

"I don't want a fate that doesn't include *you*. And this might not be my fate; I wasn't brought up here, I don't know this place, and I wasn't raised to be a queen. This was shoved onto me."

"By birth. Your mother was a princess—"

"And my father was a commoner. What difference does it make?"

She could feel her emotions spiraling out of control as every-thing in her screamed against this. She wouldn't let him sacrifice himself for her or anyone else.

"There is another way, and we *will* find it," she insisted.

Love shone in Cole's eyes as he cupped her cheek. "You're destined to rule this land, Lexi. Maybe more so than anyone who came before you. I was meant to find you; I was meant to endure those trials and become the man who ensured your rightful place in all the realms. It's a fate I wholly accept."

"It's not one *I* accept."

"No one else can sit on that throne. It's destroyed every ruler who wasn't an arach. You're the only one who can handle its power. It has to be you."

"And you have to be there when I take it."

"I will be."

"Not if you take all of these shadows into yourself. You know it as well as I do. We've all seen the changes the shadows have brought to you. They corrupt you more every time you draw them, and you know it."

"They do, but I can handle it."

"Cole—"

"I can do this."

"You can't do this and come out the same."

"None of us are coming out of this the same. Even if we survive, we'll have physical and mental scars to last a lifetime. We'll have nightmares, and we'll all be different. I've lived through war before; I know what it does to our souls. We will all change after this."

"But this could be far worse, and you know it. Don't do this, Cole."

"Many lives are at stake here, Lexi—millions of them. And all of them are seeking to be free of the Lord. The humans and realms will never know peace unless *we* bring it to them."

"This will destroy you."

"Maybe not. I've grown better at controlling the shadows; there's a chance I'll be fine."

He said the words, but they both knew they were a lie.

CHAPTER SIXTY-SEVEN

"Don't do this, Cole," Orin said. "We'll find another way."

Cole lifted his gaze from Lexi's pale, stricken face to meet his brother's troubled eyes. It was rare when Orin showed any care for someone beyond himself, but concern etched his features.

"We'll find another way," Orin said again.

"There is no other way, and we all know it," Cole said. "If we can't draw the dragons away, then we have no chance of winning between the dragons and the giants."

"And if you become something worse than the Lord, something none of us can destroy, what then?"

"There is one who will always have the power to destroy me," Cole said. "Shadows can't thrive in the light."

Lexi paled further as her lower lip troubled. "*Don't* put that on me."

Cole claimed her hand and squeezed it in both of his. "I'm not putting it on you, but it is the truth. The arachs wouldn't have created a magic they didn't have a way of destroying."

"I don't know what that is."

"You will. However, you don't have to worry about it. Because no matter what happens, I'll *never* be so far gone I would attack you or the realms."

"Remember what the prophecy said about the last light falling and the Shadow Reaver destroying us all? If you do this, you'll be making yourself strong enough for the prophecy to come true. And if I'm dead, I can't stop you."

"I became the Shadow Reaver to ensure you *never* fall, Lexi. I will make sure of that, so fuck the prophecy."

Too much of this prophecy was coming true for him to blow it off completely, but he didn't have a choice.

The Lord had made Lexi ineffective with the dragons. And if he drew the shadows into himself to make her stronger, it would be the end of him; the Lord was counting on him not to let that happen.

And if it did, Cole bet the Lord believed Lexi wasn't strong enough to go on without him. It proved the Lord was a bigger idiot than Cole already thought. He would pay for that with his life because she would see this through, sit on the throne, *and* rule.

"This is the only way, Lexi," he said.

"Don't you think he would have planned for you to do this?" she asked.

"I'm sure he assumes I'll be too selfish to do this, and if I do, you're too weak to see it through. But he's *very* wrong on both accounts."

"What if this kills you instantly?"

"It won't. Of that, I'm certain. The shadows are me, and I am them now; we are one. We have been since I welcomed them into me at the end of the trials. I may not have known what it meant at the time, but I do now. The shadows are engrained in me. They won't destroy me."

"But they could take you over and make you into someone completely different."

It wasn't a question, so he didn't bother to reply.

"You can't do this," she whispered. "I can't rule the realms without you. I can't go *on* without you."

He smiled as he released her hand and cupped her cheeks with his palms. He caressed her silken skin with his thumbs while memorizing every exquisite detail of her.

He forgot about everyone around them as he lost himself to her. She was his, she always would be, but he would have to set her free if this went wrong.

"Yes, you can. You were born to rule here and not because of your bloodline but because of who you are *here*." He pressed his hand over her heart. "You're kind and generous, but you're also tough and will do whatever's necessary to keep the realms in line.

"The power won't corrupt you, and the immortals won't push you around. You're going to be a fantastic queen, Lexi, whether I'm there or not. *Never* doubt that. And no matter what happens, I'll always be with you and watching over you. Even if I'm not physically at your side, I'll walk beside you forever, Lexi. We're a part of each other and always will be."

The tears in her eyes tore at his heart, and he almost agreed to walk away to avoid putting her through this anguish, but he'd condemn her to a life of fear and sadness if he did. They could only run for so long. Eventually, the Lord would find them.

And they had to fight. They had to try to put this wrong to right; they'd only hate themselves if they ran now.

"Cole—"

"You're going to shine so bright, they'll see you in *all* the realms. Your light will outshine the sun, and I'll ensure it happens."

The single tear sliding free was a dagger to his heart. He had to get away from her because if he didn't part from her now, he never would. He'd vowed never to hurt her, and he was tearing out her heart.

"This is *our* chance to save countless lives, including those we love. We can't turn away from that," he said.

She closed her eyes, and when another tear fell free, Cole kissed the two trails from her cheeks. "I'll love you forever and always; you're my heart and my reason for being. I'll always be with you."

With that, he kissed her lips and released her. Turning away, he walked to the edge of the ledge they stood on. Below him, Dragonia remained quiet and shrouded in darkness.

He'd come here prepared to die if necessary, but he hadn't anticipated possibly losing himself while here. It was a terrifying prospect.

Before Lexi, he was always so controlled and restrained in his emotions. She changed that when, as his mate, she drew out his more irrational, lycan side, but he'd still maintained the core part of who he was.

After this, he might not be able to do so.

You can come back from this.

He kept that thought firmly in mind as his heart and soul screamed denials at him. He'd vowed to protect Lexi always and still would after this, but he wouldn't emerge the same man.

The shadows already slithered and whispered insidious things to him. If he welcomed more into him, they wouldn't let go again. They would tear him apart and mold him into whatever *they* chose him to be.

And he had no idea what that would be.

If it wasn't for the fact they were *also* determined to keep Lexi safe, and he knew they wouldn't harm her, he would walk away. But no matter what happened, he was certain the shadows would do everything they could to ensure she survived. And because of that, he would do this.

"You're not really going to do this," Orin snapped. "Have you lost your mind? We won't let this happen!"

Cole turned to look at his brother over his shoulder. "Yes, you will."

"Cole—"

"You can't stop this, Orin. This is the only way to defeat the Lord, and you know it."

"I don't give a shit."

"You turned against Father to fight the Lord, yet you'll try to stop this?"

A vein in Orin's forehead throbbed. "You're sacrificing yourself."

"For *all* of you. It's shocking, right?" Cole teased though he wasn't at all amused. "Whoever would have thought it of *me*, a dark fae?"

He flicked a pointed glance at Sahira, who winced and bowed her head.

"I would have," Lexi whispered.

"Me too," Del said as he rested a hand on his daughter's shoulder.

"So would I," Maverick said.

"And me," Kaylia said. "Once I got to know you, of course."

"Me too," Sahira whispered.

"I always knew," Niall said, and Skog grunted.

Cole smiled as he shifted his attention to Orin; maybe they did always know, but he never did, and he suspected a couple of them were lying. That was okay; sometimes, the truth wasn't necessary.

"I love you too, little brother," he said to Orin.

Orin's jaw dropped. "That's not... I... this shouldn't happen!"

Brokk planted a hand on Orin's chest when he stepped toward Cole. "Don't."

The muscles in Orin's biceps bulged as he glowered at Brokk, but he didn't take a swing. Closing his eyes, Cole turned back to the realm below and lifted his hand to the sun.

The shadows inside him instantly leapt and surged forth as the shadows around him shifted. They vibrated and swayed before slithering toward him.

"I love you," Lexi whispered. "Always and forever."

He glanced back at her and smiled as he continued pulling the shadows cloaking the realm toward him.

CHAPTER SIXTY-EIGHT

SOMETHING INSIDE LEXI shattered when the shadows encompassed Cole before slithering into him. As they infested him, their color seeped across his skin and spread throughout his flesh until they were all the same color.

His muscles bulged and flexed as the veins stood out against his skin, and his shirt tore away from him. His pants tore at his thighs but remained in place.

The power emanating from him stirred the loose strands of hair around her face. His ciphers swelled, but most remained hidden.

Lexi's hand covered her mouth as she stifled a sob and restrained herself from running to him. This wasn't like that night on the balcony; the shadows wouldn't part for her now. They were too hell-bent on their mission to claim Cole and too determined to let their fury loose on this realm and the Lord.

The more he drew the shadows toward him, the brighter the realm became as he pulled them away from the sun. Like an eclipse, they gradually retreated from the brilliant orb in the sky, revealing small increments at a time until a sliver, the size of a crescent moon, was visible.

The growing warmth filtering down did nothing to warm the ice encasing her soul. Her worst nightmare was coming true.

If Cole somehow retained some part of himself after this, he would never be the same. But as the shadows thickened around him, her certainty he wouldn't be able to retain any part of himself grew.

It felt as if someone was taking a vise to her chest, but while she wanted to curl into a ball and sob out her misery, she remained standing in the growing rays of the sun. He'd done this for *all* of them, and she would *not* fail him.

"The Lord knows we're here," Niall said. "There's no hiding it now."

"Call the dragons, Lexi," her dad said.

"Not yet," a shadow growled. "Don't let your shield down yet."

She couldn't tell if it was Cole speaking through the shadow or if it had somehow developed a voice of its own by sucking it from *him*.

Lexi reinforced her shield as the light crept further across the land. It illuminated the white bones littering the mountain peaks, glinted off the golden towers of the palace, and shone on the immortals below as they all lifted their faces to the sun shining behind the palace.

Most basked in the rays they'd been denied, but some turned to follow the flow of shadows creeping across the land. It wouldn't be long before the Lord's men learned their location.

Lexi shielded her eyes against the growing light. The realm was far more brilliant than it normally would be as Cole stole the shadows from every nook and cranny.

The shadow beneath her feet slithered away, leaving her with nothing. He stole the shadows from the others as the last of the darkness shading the sun vanished.

A hush descended over the land; it wouldn't last, but nothing dared to breathe while the sun beat down on them. It was the calm before the storm, the last bit of quiet before the horror was unleashed.

Then, Cole's head swiveled toward her. She sucked in a breath when his eyes met hers and she saw that what she'd dreaded had come to pass. There was no hint of Cole in the ice of those inhuman eyes.

The black filling the whites of his eyes caused the silver to burn hotly from them. Inside the silver, shadows jumped like flames before floating like ghosts rising across his irises.

He'd become such a part of the shadows it was almost impossible to differentiate him from them. If it wasn't for the silver of his eyes, she wouldn't know where he stood amongst them.

Lexi gave a small sob before biting her lip hard enough to draw blood. There was plenty of time to cry later; they had to fight now. She would *not* let his sacrifice be in vain.

"Now." The shadow's distorted voice held no hint of Cole's normal tone.

Lexi lowered her shield as the sun warmed her skin. Without her protection in place, the golden glow raced across her skin. The silver markings that resembled a dragon's scales emerged too.

Her mark of the dragon had never reacted so strongly to sunlight, but she'd never been so bathed in it before. As her skin absorbed more of the sun, she shone brighter and brighter until those around her had to cover their eyes and turn their heads away.

Her glow, and the sun, chased some of the shadows away from Cole, but many retreated to hide within his soul. A soul they'd claimed a part of.

But as they devoured what remained of Cole, she became blinding. Closing her eyes, she tipped her head back and opened her arms to the sun blazing down on her.

And beneath her feet, a growing vibration rose from the earth to seep through her boots and into *her*. The warmth spread up her legs, through her belly, and out through the rest of her body. It was such a powerful, *welcoming* sensation.

She knew *exactly* what it meant. Dragonia was welcoming her home. *This* was where she belonged, the place where her parents fell in love, and it connected with her like the shadows did with Cole.

Except with her, instead of filling her with darkness, this land filled her with light until it burst out of her. At that moment, she knew the truth; Cole had *truly* become the darkness while she had *truly* become the light.

And they would either coexist or destroy each other. Tears slid down her face, but the sun and her glow burned them away before they could fall from her chin.

"Holy shite," Skog muttered.

In the distance, a dragon roared. Another and another took up that dragon's call until they all bounced off the rocks surrounding them and echoed throughout the land.

Something inside Lexi broke free and soared like a bird on the currents as their calls struck straight into her soul. Her heart hammered in rhythm with the dragon's cries, and the power thrumming from the land increased her glow.

And then, the dragons came.

CHAPTER SIXTY-NINE

THE DRAGONS GLIDED like eagles as they swooped, spun, and dove through the air. Except, they were far larger and far *deadlier* than any eagle could ever be.

They could kill most of those gathered around her with one breath of fire, but Lexi felt no apprehension about the magnificent creatures. Instead, excitement thrummed through her as the sun glinted off their scales. Their colorful bodies dotted the sky as their talons gleamed, and those golden eyes shone brilliantly.

Alina's wings blew back the hair on the giants as she swept over them and up the side of the mountain they sat beside. The red of her scales resembled blood, and for a disconcerting second, Lexi had to close her eyes against the ominous image.

When she opened them again, Alina was soaring over the top of them. Her passing tugged at the hair that had fallen free of Lexi's braid. Awe enveloped her as she tipped her head back to take in the yellow flecks on Alina's belly before the dragon swept out of view.

More dragons darted and danced overhead, acting like they were playing or rejoicing. She couldn't know, but they seemed joyful, which was... *wonderful.*

"It's time for you to go," Cole said in that strange, guttural voice she *hated*. "Return to your army and bring them here. We will end this today."

His words sent a shiver down her spine as she tore her attention away from the dragons. Whereas they were so amazing, what stood before her was true horror.

Did the shadows want their army here so they would have more to kill once they finished with the Lord? Or was it so they could fight against the Lord?

She no longer trusted the intentions of the man before her—something she'd *never* believed could be possible. Cole had been ruthless to others sometimes, but she'd always known where his heart and true purpose lay.

Now, she had no idea what to make of him.

Gone was the man who held her so tenderly while they waltzed around the palace. In his place was a creation that could unleash hell upon this land and all the other realms.

The only thing they had going for them was the sun. It kept most of the shadows somewhat contained around Cole. But that wouldn't always be the case.

When Cole shifted, the shadows parted enough for her to see his profile, but the darkness shrouding him didn't dissipate. He'd come here wearing dark brown pants and a green, fae tunic. What remained of his pants had turned as black as the shadows slithering over him.

Blackness crept across his face as the *shadows* burrowed like worms beneath his skin and slid through his flesh. It was the creepiest thing she'd ever seen, and it was happening to *Cole*, the man who owned her heart, who she planned to marry, and who would one day be the father of her children.

But as she recalled all those beautiful plans, they crumbled like a sandcastle beneath the onslaught of the encroaching ocean. The Shadow Reaver possessed no such plans and didn't understand love.

Whereas others had declared Cole the Shadow Reaver before, they'd been wrong. What stood across from her now was the real thing.

Cole turned away again, but though she had no idea what the Reaver intended for all of them, they couldn't retreat from this battle. They'd come this far—she'd drawn the dragons away from the battlefield, and Cole had sacrificed himself.

They could only continue.

"Go," she said in a voice far stronger than she anticipated.

Her dad squeezed her shoulder, but his gesture of love didn't ease the chill in her bones. "I'll be back soon," he vowed.

He released her shoulder and vanished into the portal with the others. They would return to the army waiting for them. Once there, they would all divide and flood into Dragonia through the different portals.

After they all left, it was just her and Cole, but he didn't look at her again as the dragons continued to come. They dived and twisted while nipping playfully at each other and freefalling back toward the ground. They always caught themselves before they hit the earth and swooped up again.

She never would have believed some of their moves were possible with their enormous bodies, but they were extremely graceful. Their joy warmed her heart a little even while it continued to break.

Cole may have become imprisoned by the shadows, but if all went well today, the dragons would experience freedom for the first time in a millennium. While they would obey her while she sat on the throne, she would *never* use them as the Lord did.

Some dragons landed nearby and crept closer as they craned their heads to inspect her. *How many of them have ever seen an arach?*

Some of them had to have been born after the last arach fell, and while they probably felt an instinctual pull toward her, they didn't understand it. She still didn't fear them. Even if they had no idea what she was, they wouldn't attack her or Cole.

When one stopped a few feet away and inched its head closer, Lexi lifted her hand toward it. A snort of warm air washed over her palm a second before the dragon's nose brushed her skin.

Its golden eyes closed, and it snorted another warm breath again as it leaned into her touch. Despite standing at the precipice of war, hope and joy sprang forth as she ran her hand down the dragon's green scales. It moved its nose back and forth like a dog wiggling its butt to demand more pets.

"They'll be back soon," that awful voice said to her. "We should be ready to go when they return."

Lexi sighed as she was pulled away from the dragon and back to reality. When she lowered her hand, the beast launched into the air. A sense of loss descended over her as it flew higher, but she shifted her focus to what she was supposed to do next.

Walking to the cliff's edge, she was acutely aware of Cole's cold presence beside her as she stared down at the Lord's army. The small number of shadows still surrounding Cole bobbed and swayed. One of them stretched toward her, but the light dissipated it before it touched her.

Normally, Cole would reach out to her, assure her they would get through this, or simply say, I love you. He didn't look at her; his focus remained on the enemy below. Despite the sun warming the earth, she was freezing.

The dragons filled the sky above until they nearly choked out the sun as their cries of joy turned to ones of agony. She couldn't be certain what caused their sudden shift as they roared and shrieked, but she was confident it was the Lord.

While he sat on the throne, the dragons were condemned to obey him, and she was certain he was commanding them to return to him or kill her and Cole. But their instincts couldn't resist the mark of the dragon, and the conflict was tearing them apart.

Lexi almost erected her shield again to shut down her light so they wouldn't be in any more pain, but the dragons would leave if she did, resulting in more death. Their army counted on her to keep the dragons away from the battlefield for as long as possible.

Below, the numerous portals leading in and out of Dragonia remained quiet, but that would soon change. Since only an arach could open a portal into and out of Dragonia, the arach had established these portals always to remain open to the different realms. The Lord couldn't shut them down.

The day took on an eerie hush as the dragons fell silent. Then, from below, shouts of war broke the silence as one piece of their army poured out of a portal and rushed at the Lord's men.

The clang of steel clashing against steel rang out as the armies collided, and the screams of the dying reverberated through the air.

CHAPTER SEVENTY

BROKK LED his group of lycans, dark fae, witches, dwarves, sirens, warlocks, imps, light fae, and other assorted immortal creatures through the portal leading from the human realm and into Dragonia. Elvin was at his side when they entered Dragonia with their weapons at the ready.

The Lord's army bellowed as they rushed toward them, prepared to defend the realm and thirsty for blood. Their battle cry echoed over the land baking beneath the unrelenting sun.

The pegasuses took flight to fight from above, while the unicorns used their horns to run their enemies through. The phoenixes also took to the sky as the sasquatch battered the Lord's men with large, hairy fists.

Brokk wasn't foolish enough to believe everyone who followed him into Dragonia was a true ally, but he trusted those who *were* to watch his back. Just as he would watch theirs. They had too many enemies in front of them for him to worry about those who might betray him.

Though all those designated to lead sections of the army into Dragonia had all split off to find their portals, his smaller piece was the first to arrive. Therefore, they encountered the largest number of enemies who focused solely on *them*.

It wasn't ideal, but while the Lord's army attacked them, more of their troops would slip in from behind to attack their enemy. They just had to hold out until the others arrived.

The giants, who hadn't gotten to their feet after Cole stole the shadows from the realm, rose and started toward them. The ground vibrated with every step the massive immortals took.

The witches threw up shields of air to protect them from the initial rush of the Lord's men, and it knocked some of them back, but the defense wouldn't last. While the air held them back, the warlocks, led by Talon, lifted a wave of dirt from the ground and heaved it at the immortals who were making their way around the shields.

The shields weren't enough to keep them from entangling with the Lord's army, but they allowed them to defend themselves better. The witches moved the shields to block the higher number of enemy but doing so allowed others to slip through.

Steel and iron clanged as swords and battle-axes clashed together. Many dark fae had responded to Cole's call for help, but some had chosen the Lord's side.

Brokk scowled at the traitors working for the man who had destroyed the Gloaming. He would do his best to ensure none of them survived.

One of the dark fae, a man Brokk vaguely recognized, gathered a ball of fire from a nearby torch and heaved it at Talon. The warlock ducked to avoid the flame before waving his hand at the ground and heaving dirt into the dark fae's face.

Going in low, Talon wrapped his arms around the fae's waist and propelled him into the ground. Straddling the man's chest, the fae metal of Talon's blade reflected the fire as he lifted it before plunging it through the fae's heart.

Brokk swung his sword to batter back a warlock who came at

him. Sparks flew off the blade as he twisted his wrist to pin the warlock's weapon to the ground.

With the blade pinned, Brokk punched the man in the face, staggering him back before he pulled his sword free and drove it through the warlock's heart. As the man fell away, more of the enemy rose to take his place.

The earth quaked as the giants approached, but they didn't seem eager to jump into the fray as they took their sweet-ass time. With every pounding fall of the giants' feet, Brokk left the ground before bouncing down again.

It didn't make fighting with a sword any easier when his teeth chattered and he had to focus on not biting his tongue, but he ignored the approaching giants. Lunging forward, he propelled his sword through the heart of a dark fae before using it to sever the bastard's head.

When he fought in the Lord's war, he felt guilt over those he killed. Mainly because he believed they were right to fight against the Lord.

He experienced no remorse now as he hacked through the Lord's men. These assholes felt no regret over killing them. The Lord would ground anyone who survived beneath his feet, and these immortals were happy to help him do it. They would help the Lord see the realms in ruins and most immortals degraded to nothing but pathetic figments of what they once were.

No, there was no regret here. If he had his way, he'd see every last one of their enemy dead... including the giants. He didn't care if the Lord had their queen; they'd chosen the wrong side.

Blood dripped from the end of his sword as he plunged it into the heart of another dark fae. It was the first time he'd ever used fae metal against one of his kind, and it wouldn't be the last.

The unspoken rule about dark fae not using fae metal against each other had gone out the window when his enemy decided to wield it with such freedom. If they weren't going to hold back, then neither was he.

CHAPTER SEVENTY-ONE

BROKK TORE his sword free of the dying man's chest as Maverick's group emerged from the portal leading to Verdan and charged at the back of the Lord's army. Two seconds later, Orin and Varo arrived with more dark fae and a smattering of light fae.

The light fae instantly recoiled, but, to their credit, they didn't turn and flee. Elfie led them forward and into the fray as they sought out victims to help heal.

Niall emerged from a portal with his group, and, from a few feet away, Sahira arrived from a portal Lexi had opened on the cliff for them. *None* of the Lord's men had expected this move as they weren't used to someone opening portals into Dragonia.

When he first arrived, the Lord's men had all convened on Brokk's small group of troops, expecting they would all come from one area. They hadn't anticipated their enemy splitting up to attack from different portals. Because of that, many of the Lord's men were trapped in a circle, but that wouldn't last.

The giants were nearly upon them.

Blood sprayed over Brokk's face as a berserker crashed into Talon's side, taking him down. Brokk sliced off the head of the powerfully built man but not before the berserker tore out Talon's heart and crushed it.

A stab of regret pierced Brokk as he met Talon's startled eyes before the warlock died. However, there was no time for remorse in this place and time. This was only the beginning; they would lose many more here today.

Brokk carved his way through a few more men, ducked a blade that would have sliced through his neck, and spun to avoid a transformed lycan. The creature leapt from the ground with its jaws wide.

As he evaded the bloodthirsty lycan, the last of their army arrived with Kaylia and Skog in the lead. The giants also converged on them, and, with a swipe of a meaty hand, one of the monstrous beasts sent ten of their army hurtling through the air like rag dolls.

The coopery stench of blood and the fetid aroma of death filled Brokk's nose as the screams of the dying filled the air. He still had nightmares about those screams from the Lord's war. Hearing them again set his teeth on edge, but those screams and the blood-soaked field didn't slow him.

Turning to confront a berserker racing toward him, Brokk prepared himself to kill again. The naked man's bulging muscles and the throbbing veins pulsing throughout his body and face were on full display.

If his red face, veins, and pulsing muscles were any indication, the man was entering berserker mode. He would soon unleash his immense strength on anyone unfortunate enough to be in his way.

With a chest the size of a small car, the berserker bared his bloody teeth at him. Pieces of flesh hung from those teeth. They hadn't gotten bloody because someone punched this psycho in the mouth; this freak had torn out someone's throat with his teeth.

Brokk smiled in return as the berserker released a guttural screech. The man was nearly on top of him when Brokk lifted his hand and waved it at the nearby fire consuming a body. The blast of flame shot up, caught on the berserker's long, black hair, and flared up to engulf his head.

The berserker screamed as he beat at the flames. His shrieks cut off when Brokk cloaked himself in shadows, slid up to the man, and slit his throat. With the berserker out of the way, Brokk spotted the brilliant glow on the mountain.

His jaw dropped as awe filled him. He'd been there when Lexi released her shield to shine as bright as the sun. It was blinding then, but looking at it from down here was like staring at a golden star plucked from the sky and placed on the mountain.

No wonder the dragons were so attracted to her; it was a beautiful spectacle, and he'd never imagined seeing something so wondrous in his life. Though he never could have known something like it existed before meeting Lexi, that light and the hope it represented was suddenly *everything*.

What made it more amazing were the hundred or so dragons circling her, perching on the side of the mountain or creeping closer. They tangled with each other before breaking free and flipping through the air.

But it wasn't all joy as the dragon's shrieks of agony and joy mingled in the air.

"My Hecate," a witch breathed from beside him. "We *are* doing the right thing."

Brokk was about to reply when a sword burst through the witch's throat and lifted her.

CHAPTER SEVENTY-TWO

"IT'S TIME TO GO."

Lexi didn't recognize the voice, or more like *voices*, issuing from Cole. Was it Cole anymore?

"They are ready for us to leave," the voices said.

Lexi looked behind her to the portal to the prison realm, but she couldn't see anyone approaching. A few seconds later, her father emerged with a small army at his back.

His was the only group with some vampires mixed in with the other immortals. Those vampires remained in the portal, waiting for their chance to emerge. They couldn't do so until she opened a portal into the palace.

Once she did, they would transport from the portal where they remained and into the new one. It was the only way for them to avoid the sun.

Turning to the cliff face, she barely glanced at the portal she'd already opened for Sahira to lead her small army onto the battle-field below. She hoped her aunt and the others were all okay, but there were already many dying down there.

Lexi didn't bother to ask Cole how he'd known her father was coming. He had shadows everywhere. She knew this, but it still didn't stop the hair on her nape from rising.

When their eyes met, no spark of love shone within his silver depths that were always so full of warmth when he looked at her. Black shadows squirmed across his handsome features and down his neck.

When Lexi was younger, she watched *Invasion of the Body Snatchers* and now felt like she was in that movie. Cole stood before her, but the shadows had taken him over and left a shell behind.

"Open a portal into the palace," Cole continued in that awful voice.

Lexi looked to the sky and the dragons. She yearned to be with them, free of all this and flying over the land, but they still had so far to go before that could happen. And no one would be free if they lost this war.

She tore her attention away from the dragons and focused on opening another portal into the palace's main hall. It materialized before her. Once she went through the portal, her light would cut off, and the dragons would leave.

The others, already vulnerable to the Lord's army and the giants, would become more vulnerable, but they knew this was coming. They all hoped the dragons would follow her light once she emerged in the palace and mostly avoid the battlefield. They were prepared for that not to happen, though.

"Let's go," that guttural voice said.

Lexi shuddered as Cole glided into the portal. And he *was* gliding!

His feet didn't touch the ground as he moved. Instead, the shadows rolled beneath him as they carried him into the portal.

It was the creepiest thing she'd ever seen, and it was happening to *Cole*. She had no idea how to process that.

When she met her father's eyes, the apprehension in them more than matched hers. What would the Shadow Reaver do if they destroyed the Lord? Would it be satisfied with his death and those of his men? Or would it seek more blood afterward?

Her soul screamed against the possibility Cole could become the next threat and she might have to help destroy him. What could she do to stop him if the dragons wouldn't kill him and the shadows were his weapons?

There had to be something; Cole believed there was, but she wasn't so sure.

"Go," her father whispered.

She had to retain some faith Cole wouldn't destroy them all when this was over. If she didn't, then she was going into this war with the knowledge they were all doomed no matter what. They'd come too far for that to be true, and Cole sacrificed too much to become their enemy.

Lexi glanced at the sky and the dragons circling there. If all the dragons stayed with her, she was supposed to remain here. But some of them were already soaring back toward the palace, and she couldn't let Cole go on alone like this.

Alina swooped overhead before flying across the land. The dragons wanted to stay with Lexi, but she wasn't the one who commanded them, and their shrieks were growing increasingly loud.

Besides, she didn't know how much of an effect she still had on Cole, but if he became out of control in the palace, she was the only one who had any chance of reaching him. She couldn't let him go alone, and she couldn't let the others go without her; Cole was too much of a danger to them for that.

Lexi took a deep breath before following Cole into the portal and on to whatever destiny lay beyond. Because no matter what, there was no going back after this.

Behind her, the vampires teleported into the portal while the rest of their army rushed out to follow them.

CHAPTER SEVENTY-THREE

THE SIRENS TRANSFORMED into birdlike shapes and rose into the sky. With earsplitting shrieks, they battered the giants' faces, clawed at their eyes, and swarmed around their heads. Phoenixes and pegasuses rose to help the sirens.

The imps ran around, creating the mischief they were known for as they tugged at the giants' shoes and bit their ankles. They were barely two feet tall, and their little green bodies moved rapidly around the field. Their big, round ears stood straight out from the sides of their heads.

The unicorns rammed into the giants, but their horns had little effect. They didn't inflict much damage, but they provided enough distraction to keep the giants from stomping on all those beneath them as the giants swatted at them.

Orin snatched a discarded battle-ax from the ground and ran toward one of the giants. Despite believing some of their army would become traitors and join the Lord's side, he didn't see any sign of it as the battle raged around him.

He was sure some defected, but not many. The Lord had pissed off too many with his destruction of the realms for them to become traitors.

Leaping forward, Orin swung with all his might and buried the ax in the behemoth's Achilles tendon. The fucker didn't even flinch when Orin buried the ax to the hilt in its flesh. He wasn't sure the giant knew it was there.

He tried to yank the ax free, but it remained wedged in the muscle as the giant leaned back to batter at more of the immortals buzzing around its head. With a grunt, he finally succeeded in tearing the weapon free.

Adjusting his hold on the weapon, Orin swung it into the giant's ankle bone. Again, the immortal didn't flinch. If he felt the attack at all, Orin was probably no more annoying than a gnat to this thing.

He ripped the ax free as a dozen dwarves descended on the giant. They hacked at the giant's flesh and muscle with furious shouts while witches ran around the creature's feet with rope.

Finally, the giant noticed them, and lifting its foot, it went to step on them, but they dove out of the way before it smashed them into the ground. The damage to the giant's skin and cartilage was enough that when it stomped its foot into the ground, the ankle bone gave way with a deafening snap.

"Move out of the way!" Orin bellowed as the giant tilted sideways.

It hung precariously in the air for what seemed like an indefinite amount of time before it pitched forward like a felled tree. Immortals scattered to get out of the way as the giant's shadow spread across the land, but not all of them were fast enough to avoid its path.

The ones who didn't splatter beneath him were driven into the earth. As soon as the giant hit the ground, it tried to push itself back up, but their army pounced on it. The behemoth's screams shook the land, as did the other giants, and they lumbered toward their fallen friend.

The giants crushed any immortal not fast enough to flee their path, but it was too late to save their friend. Those still on the giant scrambled to get out of the way as its screams finally ceased.

Orin spun at the sound of hoofbeats. He was prepared to take down any horse or rider, but he was not prepared for what came at him. He nearly recoiled when a wendigo bared down on him.

"Holy shit," he breathed.

The Lord was more desperate than they'd realized if he'd brought these monsters here and unleashed them. The wendigos were worse than zombies.

No one on their side had mentioned recruiting them, because no one in their army was completely insane. The zombies at least possessed rational thought most of the time.

Wendigos killed, ate, and killed some more as they tried to quench their insatiable appetite. But that was impossible. They could never be satisfied and would never be full.

Until now, he'd never seen a wendigo out of its realm. They were killed on sight by anyone who did see them elsewhere as they couldn't be allowed to roam free. They would inflict too much damage if they did.

But the Lord had brought them here and turned them loose. And as he darted back from the wendigo's swiping claws, the Lord's men opened the doors to the buildings that hadn't been here the last time he came to Dragonia, well over a hundred years ago.

He'd wondered what those buildings were, and now he knew they held monsters. And these idiots were setting those monsters free.

The Lord and his army probably believed they would turn and run once they saw the wendigo, and the giants and dragons could stop them once they were gone, but they were mistaken. The wendigo added a whole new level of destruction to this battle, but the Lord had pushed them all too far when he destroyed their realms.

No one was going to run while he lived.

336   BRENDA K DAVIES

The wendigo's hands dragged across the ground as its arms were nearly as tall as the seven-foot beast. How the Lord had gotten them to agree to fight was beyond him, but then, he realized the Lord probably hadn't gotten them to consent.

He probably captured them, brought them here, and ordered them turned loose when it looked like the war might be turning against him. He had no doubt that the Lord didn't give a shit if these monsters ate some of his men in the process.

And those poor idiots were so scared of the Lord they were obeying him, even if it meant they were eaten too.

Ducking low, Orin threw himself to the ground as the black, lumbering beast lowered its two-foot-high antlers and charged at him. As the wendigo ran past him, Orin pulled his sword free of its holster and swung it to the side.

The blade cleaved the thin beast in half, just beneath the bony ribs protruding prominently from the beast. Its sunken stomach spilled its contents, which were nothing more than black blood and intestines.

When its top half hit the ground, Orin jumped up, planted his foot on its back, and carved its head from its body. He spun in time to see the dragons sweeping toward them.

The Lord's men and their army battled each other while both sides also worked to destroy the wendigos sweeping through the battlefield. Blood and chaos reigned; the screams of the dying and mutilated blocked out the clash of weapons.

He'd fought in countless battles during the Lord's war, but he'd never seen one as violent or vicious as this. But this was the end for both sides, and they all knew it. There wouldn't be any more battles because whoever lost today would be too decimated to fight again.

"Orin!" Sahira shouted.

She threw a ball of fire his way. He caught it and whipped it at the next wendigo coming toward him. The creature screamed as the fire erupted in its face. Flames devoured its flesh as it fell to the ground.

Orin gave Sahira a nod of thanks before lifting his sword and dodging the foot of another giant coming his way.

CHAPTER SEVENTY-FOUR

LEXI EMERGED from the portal and into the palace. She'd pictured the main entrance hall when creating the portal as it was close to the throne room and shadowed enough that the vamps could survive outside it.

They suspected the Lord had most likely ensconced himself in the throne room and wanted to be close to it without being inside. They couldn't go straight into the throne room as the open ceiling was a death trap for the vamps.

Plus, there were probably countless guards and maybe some dragons in there. And while she and Cole were safe around the dragons, they would destroy the nearly one hundred soldiers behind her.

Lexi stretched her hand out to her dad, and he clasped it in his. "I love you," she whispered.

"I love you too," he said. "Stay safe."

"You too."

They hoped the dragons in the throne room had been drawn to her presence and taken flight. And though the dragons were already on their way back to the battle when they entered the portal, they still had a chance of entering the throne room before they returned.

That was the hope, anyway. The reality was probably their worst-case scenario: the dragons never leaving and the room full of the Lord's army.

For now, she and Cole would head for the throne room with half their army. Her father would remain here to destroy anyone who tried to come up from behind them.

A shout sounded from the left, and Lexi turned to discover a group of the Lord's soldiers entering from the hall across the way and descending the grand staircase. The Lord's men had been lying in wait to spring their trap, and now they attacked. And there were *far* more of them than she'd expected as they charged forward with their weapons raised and a battle cry on their lips.

"Go!" her dad shouted as he drew his sword.

"No," Lexi breathed. "There's too many."

She couldn't leave them here like this. They could retreat through the portal, but her father would *never* do that.

"We must go," the Cole thing said from behind her.

A shiver ran down her spine as more voices emanated from him. "I can't leave him."

Before she finished speaking, shadows spread out from beneath Cole, sped across the floor, and rose between her father's army and the Lord's. Some of the Lord's men skidded to a halt before they ran into the shadows. The others were too brazen or had no idea what they were headed for and didn't slow.

Their screams rent the air as their blood sprayed outward to coat the walls. Lexi's hand went to her mouth as she stepped away from the massacre unfolding before her. When she turned to look at Cole, she discovered him already by the double doors leading to the throne room. Each door held the carving of a dragon in midflight.

Cole's silver eyes blazed out from the shadows enshrouding him as they completely engulfed him before parting to reveal him again. Turning away, he didn't look back as he opened the doors to the throne room.

~

NIALL CHOPPED the head off a wendigo before spinning to face the warlock coming at him. The warlock pushed forth the air as he ran, so a wall headed toward him.

Bracing his legs apart, Niall lifted his arms and crossed them before his chest a second before the air crashed into them. He was able to deflect some of it and fling it back at the warlock, but the impact still knocked him back a few feet.

Lowering his arms, Niall swung out with a sword. His blade crashed into the warlock's weapon before the murderous bastard could plunge it into his heart. The clang of metal filled the air as their weapons collided while they moved back and forth in a macabre dance that could only end in death.

The ground beneath his feet trembled as a giant approached. The impact of its footfalls caused the earth to rise and fall.

Overhead, the sirens emitted a high-pitched shriek before one of them spiraled out of the sky. Over the warlock's shoulder, the siren plowed into the ground with enough force to leave a dent.

When the warlock lunged at him again, Niall jumped to the side and swung down with his blade. It caught the warlock across his arm; he released his weapon as Niall punched the back of the man's head. Gripping his sword in both hands, Niall brought it down across the man's neck, severing his head.

Dragons roared overhead as they joined the battle. A wave of fire erupted across the land and sent the sasquatches running while the witches grabbed some unicorns by the manes and leapt onto their backs to flee the flames.

They'd hoped the dragons would follow Lexi to the palace. While some might have, the others had returned to do the Lord's bidding.

They could retreat now. It was something they'd agreed to do if things started looking too bleak, but returning to the portals was a dangerous journey. And if they ran, the Lord's army would follow.

Plus, he didn't see anyone retreating. They'd all known when they entered this realm, it would be the final battle; they were all here to make sure their side emerged victorious.

"Kill them all!" Maverick shouted over the screams, crashing of metal, grunts, and the other inescapable sounds of war.

Niall spotted the tall alpha as he towered over many of the others. Maverick had been pushed back toward the portal Lexi created, but he wouldn't go through.

Orin and Varo were only twenty feet away from him and taking on the group of wendigo encircling them. Niall's attention was drawn away from his friends when the ground heaved again.

A giant ran toward them as fast as the lumbering beast could go. Though it covered a lot of ground, its movement was cumbersome, but then, they were far from graceful creatures.

Everyone scattered out of the giant's way as another dragon swooped down and swallowed a wendigo. The dragons didn't care who they killed or what side of the fight they were on.

It wouldn't astonish him to learn that all the dragons wanted was for *everyone* to get out of their realm. They were probably tired of being led by a madman and having to do his bidding.

Pixies zipped in and out of the fray. They flew into the faces of their enemies, poked the Lord's men in their eyes, smacked them on their noses, and pulled their hair. Some were batted away, but most of the tiny creatures were so fast they were there and gone before anyone could react to them.

They provided enough distraction that some of their army destroyed those the pixies attacked. Niall had never considered the pixies useful in war; now, he wished they'd always been fighters.

When the shadow of a giant fell over them, Niall sprinted out of the way as the giant closed in on them. As he ran, he spotted

Beatrix exchanging a volley of fire with a warlock who was bearing down on her.

He'd gotten to know her a little bit while guarding her, and he liked the woman and her child. He especially liked Morgan, something he never believed possible as he'd always considered children little more than a nuisance.

Morgan was quiet and stayed mostly by her mother's side as she clung to Beatrix. He was sure her near-death experience was probably still affecting her and she wasn't always so reserved, but he liked the girl who followed her mother everywhere.

And Beatrix was fiercely loyal to the child she loved so dearly. He couldn't let that child become an orphan; it would break her.

Beatrix held her ground as she caught two balls of the warlock's fire, heaved one back at him, and rolled the other across the land, so it left a trail of flames behind. Distracted by the fire moving toward them, the warlock jumped over it. When he did, Beatrix wiggled her fingers, and a wave of dirt rose from the ground. She heaved it at the warlock and knocked him on his ass.

But Beatrix didn't see the giant coming at her as she was too focused on the warlock. Pouring on speed, Niall thrust out his sword to take down a transformed lycan that tried to pounce on him.

The sword sliced across the lycan's open mouth, severing its tongue and causing the creature to yelp as it fell in front of a berserker whose face was apocalyptic. The man's veins stood starkly out against his flesh as he lifted the lycan and heaved it out of his way.

The wolf soared over the heads of the fighters. Before the berserker could come after Niall, Elvin drove a battle-ax through his head, severing the berserker in half to his ribs.

"Get out of the way!" Niall shouted as Elvin pulled his ax free.

Elvin turned, and his jaw dropped when he saw the giant was nearly upon them. The older dark fae sprinted out of the way as Niall wrapped his arms around Beatrix's waist. They crashed into the ground together, and he rolled as fast as he could to avoid the approaching giant.

They couldn't get far enough away as the giant veered to follow them. Keeping hold of Beatrix, he rolled one more time and flung her away from him. She bounced across the ground and out of the way of the approaching beast.

Niall jumped up to run in the opposite direction, but it was too late; there was nowhere for him to go as the giant's foot loomed over him. Thrusting his sword up, he had a split second of satisfaction as it embedded in the fucker's flesh before the giant's foot came down on top of him.

CHAPTER SEVENTY-FIVE

SOME OF THE Lord's men made it through Cole's shadows. Though they weren't completely unscathed, they were still alive as they funneled into the hallway toward their army.

Lexi almost screamed for her father to run but bit it back. He was a warrior, and distracting him now would only get him killed.

This was meant to happen, except they were supposed to split their army. However, there were too many of the Lord's men to take any away from their defense now. She and Cole would have to deal with what lay beyond.

Lexi turned and ran toward the double doors as Cole stepped into the throne room. Beyond his broad shoulders, she spotted the Lord's men standing guard.

Despite her terror over what they were about to face, love poured through her, and fire burst from her fingertips as she sprinted to catch up with Cole as he descended the stairs. She abhorred killing, and knowing she would have to do it turned her stomach, but she would torch every guard in the room if it helped keep Cole and all those she loved alive.

The sounds of the battle behind her reverberated throughout the hall. It pulsed in her ears as she entered the throne room behind

Cole. She'd just cleared the doors when movement to her right drew her attention.

Lexi jumped out of the way as some of the Lord's men lunged past her, grabbed the doors, and swung them shut. They closed with an echoing bang as the shadows swarmed over the guards, and they started screaming.

The shadows dragged them to the floor as they tore them to pieces. Lexi tried to block out their agony and the blood splattering the walls, but her stomach revolted, and she nearly heaved her breakfast onto the floor.

A shadow pulled her back when she lurched toward the doors to try to open one. From her left, a guard lunged toward her, nearly cutting her with his sword.

Out of instinct, she lifted her hands and released a wave of fire into the guard's face. He howled and screamed as he beat the flames while trying to rip off his burning clothes, but the fire was already engulfing him.

Before she could react, a dozen guards rushed out of the shadows to separate her and Cole from the door. Each held giant balls of fire whose light chased away the shadows sliding toward them.

"Good afternoon, King Colburn!" The Lord's voice boomed throughout the hall. "So happy to see you… and it's exactly as I planned."

~

VARO BURIED his loathing over the slaughter unfolding as he battled with Orin to keep the wendigos at bay. One of the revolting creatures took down a dark fae and proceeded to feast on his remains.

These things were so twisted, they didn't care about being distracted and more vulnerable once they started eating. They were too focused on their need to feast; they couldn't think about anything other than consuming the flesh of their victims.

Pieces of his soul perished, but he still used his sword to carve down anything in his way. He tried not to think of the dead bodies littering the battlefield... like Niall's. He'd seen Cole's friend fall and knew there was no hope for him.

He ached with the loss consuming him, but he couldn't give way to his emotions as he struggled to block out the suffering of those around him.

If he opened himself up even a little, their misery would suffocate him. It would kill him as surely as any sword, arrow, or fire from a dragon. So instead, he forged on while pieces of himself died.

"Varo! Look out!" Brokk bellowed from somewhere in the fray.

Varo spun as a wendigo's taloned hand arched toward his head. Ducking back, he avoided the blow that would have opened him from head to gut.

He buried his sword in the hollow pit of the wendigo's stomach area, but there wasn't enough flesh on the creatures for it to be considered a belly. When another one came at him from the right, Varo dodged it, but there were too many, and they separated him and Orin.

"Shit," Varo hissed as one of the monsters seized Orin's sword and jabbed his hand forward to embed its foot-long claws in Orin's gut.

Unable to block out the explosion of his brother's pain, Varo nearly screamed, but Orin didn't make a sound as the wendigo lifted him over his head. Varo lowered his shoulder and shoved a wendigo out of his way, but from behind, one of their hands clasped his arm and yanked him back.

He turned toward the creature and lifted his sword to take it out, but another one grasped the blade. As Varo tried to rip his blade free while the other yanked at him, he knew these were the last few moments of his life, but he'd give anything to break free long enough to save Orin.

Orin would emerge from this battle the same, or mostly the same, but it would forever haunt Varo, just like the Lord's war. He would be even more broken, but Orin would help to right all the wrongs the Lord unleashed.

Orin *had* to survive.

When Varo released his weapon to the creature, it lifted it high but never got the chance to use it as Sahira's mother hit the thing with a ball of fire. The woman disappeared before he could say anything.

Varo spun to punch the wendigo as the claws of another raked his back. His knees buckled and blood spilled down his backside, but he remained upright.

Before he could hammer his fist into the wendigo's elongated, distorted black face that was more ligament than flesh, its head exploded and black blood sprayed his face. Varo spit the putrid remains from his mouth. He blinked away the goo coating his eyelashes until his mother's face swarmed into focus.

Then he blinked again because he couldn't believe *she'd* killed another living creature. The light fae were here, but they'd all stated they wouldn't pick up a weapon in this battle. Yet here was his mother with a sword in hand and black blood dripping from her face.

And she'd done it to save *him*. Unable to find words, Varo simply nodded at her, and though tears streaked her face—probably because she'd killed a man—she smiled in return.

"Thank you," he finally managed to say.

She opened her mouth to reply, but a wolf burst out of the fray, bit down on her head, and dragged her down.

"No!" Varo screamed.

He ran toward them, but the lycan had already vanished into the melee. Varo followed.

CHAPTER SEVENTY-SIX

THE SHADOWS STUDIED the warlocks standing there with their giant balls of fire meant to keep them restrained. But shadows were things of freedom, and they found ways around the light. They weren't meant to be constrained and were too strong to be beaten back by these immortals.

The words of the shadows' enemy lingered in the hall. The enemy was taunting them and trying to intimidate them. The fool didn't know shadows weren't things to ridicule, but he would learn.

The shadows hissed at the man who believed he could trap them. From within, the vessel responded to these words with a fury the shadows relished.

The vessel's hatred awed the shadows. They believed only they could feel such wrath toward another, but the vessel had proven them wrong on this, and they liked it. This was a fine host for them to have.

A fine host indeed.

But first things first. They had to take care of the warlocks with their fire, the guards, and that fucker on the throne. The host was pleased with the idea of tearing the Lord apart and intended to do it in the most vicious of ways. The shadows were more than happy to help.

The shadows' attention shifted to the arach, and when it did, an emotion they didn't understand stirred within the host. They couldn't name the feeling, but they didn't like it.

However, the shadows had to protect her at all costs. She was why they existed and why the host *finally* let them all the way in.

No, they didn't understand the host's emotion, and they didn't like it, but they understood the host's compulsion to keep her safe, and they would do anything to make it happen.

"You planned this as your way to die?" the host inquired of the asshole on the throne.

The Lord laughed as he slapped a hand off his knee. A dozen guards stood around him, but while he looked entirely confident, the guards did not.

"You played right into my hands, King Colburn. You've taken on too much power, a power you can't contain, and a power that I can stop by the simple act of providing too much light. King Colburn no longer exists, and the shadows are contained, so yes, I planned this as my way to kill you."

Beside them, Lexi stirred, and the flames engulfing her hands burned higher. She glanced back at the warlocks before looking to the Lord again. "I can withstand their fire, but can they withstand mine?"

Pride stirred within the host, and the shadows bobbed in agreement. They liked brutality. It made them happy.

"You're nothing more than a child," the Lord retorted. "I have more fear of a ladybug than you."

"Maybe you don't have any fear of me," Lexi retorted, "but your warlocks do."

The shadows shifted their attention to the warlocks; they were pleased by the fright shimmering in their enemy's eyes. A couple dozen of the stupid men moved closer to surround them.

Every one of them had at least some sign of distress; either sweat beaded their foreheads or there was a flicker in their eyes, and some stood with one foot slightly back like they were about to turn and run.

The shadows chuckled over this even as the fires kept them contained. The sun shining down from the open roof of the throne room kept the ones in the corners at bay, but they would *not* lose today.

It wasn't an option.

The doors rattled as immortals pounded on them, but they were sealed shut, probably by some magic either from the Lord or the warlocks. It didn't matter.

They didn't require help.

When one of the warlocks crept closer, Lexi spun toward him, and fire erupted from her fingers. It crashed into the warlock and smashed the ball of fire he held into his face.

When the man started screaming as he clawed at the flames devouring him, one of the others staggered back a few steps before regaining his balance. But the damage was done.

This small crack in the warlock's defense allowed the shadows to slip further away. They crept toward the soon-to-be-dead men surrounding them.

"Kill another," the shadows commanded, and, to their surprise, their host rebelled a little.

When Lexi's eyes shifted to them, the sorrow filling them tore at their host's heart, but the shadows felt nothing. They had no remorse. The arach needed to do as they commanded, or they would all die today.

～

ORIN'S INSIDES screamed in protest as he twisted to tear himself free of the wendigo. Somehow managing to bend himself over enough, he slipped a hand inside his boot and removed the dagger tucked there.

Before the hideous monster could start feasting on him, Orin plunged the dagger into the creature's eye. It released an eerie howl that reminded him of spirits rising from the grave.

But it didn't stop him from yanking the dagger free and stabbing again and again until the creature finally lowered him. Tearing himself free of the talons, he kept a hand to his belly as he rolled away before staggering to his feet.

Orin didn't look at the damage. He didn't have to see it to know parts of his insides were now on his outside.

As he moved, he spotted Varo kneeling on the battlefield with blood dripping from his hair. It slid down his face and landed on the ground as tears rolled down his cheeks.

Something inside Orin rebelled at the sight of his brother's anguish, and he knew, without having to speak to him, Varo had broken. Something had happened.

And then, he spotted Elfie's lifeless body only a few feet away from his brother. He didn't know what happened or why it upset Varo so much when the woman had little to do with him throughout his lifetime, but if Varo didn't get up and move, he would die.

Orin refused to let that happen.

Keeping his hand against his belly, he ignored the pain jabbing like a burning spear into his stomach while he sprinted toward Varo. A warlock, with fire burning from his hands and determination etched onto his face, raced at his brother.

The warlock was almost there when Brokk emerged from the fray. Going low, he took out the warlock's legs before the man could get to Varo. When the warlock face planted into the ground, Brokk severed his head from his body.

They reached Varo simultaneously, and each grasped an arm as they helped him to his feet. Blood stained Varo's back and pooled on the ground around him, but his wounds weren't life-threatening.

"Are you okay?" Brokk demanded.

Varo stared blankly at them before shaking his head. "She killed for me. She saved me."

Orin was nearly as stunned by this revelation as Varo. "Then don't let her sacrifice be in vain," Orin said. "She saved you so you wouldn't die today. Now *move!*"

Varo blinked at him for a few seconds before bowing his head. Orin didn't get his hopes up as Varo remained limp between them.

I can't lose two brothers today.

And he knew, without having to see his brother again, they'd lost Cole earlier, but they could save Varo.

"Come on," Orin urged.

For a second, he didn't think Varo would respond. And then, he started running with them as they raced across the bloody field. They dodged the enemy, zigzagged through giants, and avoided dragon fire.

The scorched earth was rough and uneven beneath their feet; they stumbled and nearly went down a few times, but they supported each other until they got to Maverick. Cole's uncle remained near the portal Lexi had opened into Dragonia.

Some of the dragons, still drawn to Lexi, flew over the palace, but none of them descended into it. He suspected the Lord was keeping them out of whatever was happening there. They had to do as he commanded, but the dragons might only get in the way with their inability to attack Lexi or Cole.

"Go!" Maverick commanded and pointed to the portal when he spotted them. "Many have already retreated and are waiting on the mountain to enter the palace. I'll keep the Lord's men from entering the portal."

"You can't do that alone," Brokk said.

"There's not enough here for me to remain much longer, but I'm going to give them a chance to make it here. If they can't make it back to me soon, I'll go."

"I'm staying with you," Brokk said. "Orin, take Varo through, get yourselves some care, and head on toward Lexi and Cole if you're able."

As the blood ran into Orin's boots, he knew it was pointless to argue. He'd only become a hindrance if he passed out from blood loss.

"Take care of yourself," he said to Brokk.

His brother clasped his shoulder and squeezed it. "You also."

CHAPTER SEVENTY-SEVEN

LEXI TRIED NOT to think about the fact Cole had told her to keep killing; he *never* would have done that before. He never would have *said* it to her before and would have done everything he could to keep her from having to kill.

It was inevitable she destroy others while here; she had to if she was going to survive, but it wasn't something Cole would have wanted her to do. Ignoring her grief, Lexi released another stream of fire at a warlock.

He used the ball of fire floating before him to deflect it. Another warlock held up his hand to halt her flame and shot it back at her. Lexi didn't bother to move before the fireball hit her side.

The impact knocked her to the side a little, and flames shot toward her face as her clothes fell away, but she didn't shy away from them. They didn't scorch her, and the fire wasn't a nuisance other than briefly blinding her.

However, when the fireball hit her, the Cole thing burst forward in a rush so fast he blurred as he sped toward the warlock. He'd always been fast, but she'd never seen him move *that* fast before.

Ducking low, Cole grasped the warlock around his thighs,

356 BRENDA K DAVIES

lifted him, and slammed him into the ground. Something broke in the warlock's back, and his head thudded off the stone floor.

When claws erupted from Cole's hands, he plunged them through the warlock's eyes. The man screamed while he jerked at Cole's hand, but he couldn't pull it free. Another warlock threw a ball of fire at Cole, and Lexi released a stream of fire from her hand. It crashed into the ball and deflected it before the flames hit Cole.

She sent a blast of fire at the man as Cole, with his claws still embedded in the screaming warlock's eyes, lifted the man from the ground. He swung the immortal's body into one of his friends.

The warlock's flames sputtered and went out as he staggered away from Cole. When he knocked into some of his friends, their fire wall weakened further. And the shadows spread toward them.

Sunlight still poured down from the open ceiling above, but the shadows were gaining ground. When a dragon swooped over the opening, it blocked the sun and allowed more shadows to squirm around the room.

The warlocks screamed as the shadows reached some of them. The shadows tore into the warlocks with absolute ruthlessness, ripped off their limbs, and engulfed their heads to smother their cries.

When the dragon vanished and light spilled down again, the shadows retracted enough that some of the more daring of the Lord's guards rushed them. Arrows shot through the air toward them, but the shadows lurched up to snag them from the air before they fell.

Kneeling, Lexi placed her palms against the cool stone and released two streaks of flame. Tendrils of fire broke off from the two main streaks until they spread across the floor in a lethal pattern resembling the numerous branches of a tree. The fire trails zigzagged like lightning across the floor and raced toward her prey.

And as those branches found their target, they set fire to them.

Others stumbled back to avoid the flames, and some warlocks used magic to deflect the death coming toward them, but the other lycan, dark fae, warlocks, and berserkers in the room weren't so lucky.

The fires caught on nearly a dozen guards. The flames surged higher as clothing and flesh fed them. The rising smoke choked some light from the sky and enabled more shadows to spread as the fires died down and the streaks went out.

The Lord, who had been laughing throughout all of this, suddenly fell silent. Tearing her gaze away from the burning guards and Cole, Lexi met his eyes. Hatred emanated from him as they stared at each other.

And then, she smiled. All this death sickened her, and she'd probably lost Cole, but she was more than happy to see this man dead.

And then, as some of the guards started to flee while others came at them again, Lexi sent out two more streaks of fire that lanced across the stone. More flames branched off to destroy ten more of the Lord's men.

The increasing smoke filling the air allowed the shadows to spread further until they nearly had free rein of the room. They danced in and out of the flames as the stench of burning flesh and blood permeated the room.

Lexi's stomach heaved as bile rushed up her throat, but she somehow managed to swallow it. The Lord would not have the satisfaction of watching her vomit.

When she went to release more fire, something crashed into her back and knocked her to the ground. Someone must have charged at her, knocked her down, and kept her pinned there, but it took her a second to realize no one was kneeling on her.

One or more of the warlocks was using the element of air to pin her to the floor. Lexi struggled against the force, but it felt like a thousand-pound weight pressed into her back.

It pushed her forward until she lay flat on the ground with her hands beneath her. She tried to shove herself up, but the weight was unrelenting.

She wheezed tiny breaths into her burning lungs. Unable to concentrate on keeping them lit, the fires went out from her hands, and the breath was crushed from her lungs. White light exploded in front of her eyes as the world swam.

Then, a roar unlike any she'd ever heard reverberated through the room. Though it wasn't in his voice, and it sounded like thousands of things were yelling at once, she knew the eerie sound emanated from Cole.

Shadows leapt in front of her, but they couldn't stop the wall of air from squishing her. When one of her ribs cracked, she squeaked because it was the only sound she could get out as darkness flashed across her eyes.

And then, the weight suddenly lifted. The breath she gasped in caused pain to lance across her ribs. As oxygen once again flooded her deprived brain, so did her awareness of what was happening.

The strange bellow had issued from Cole, but other screams filled the room as blood sprayed the floor. Its warmth lashed her face and body as it coated her.

Wheezing in another breath, Lexi gritted her teeth and placed a hand against her ribs as she rose away from the blood coating the floor. A spark of warmth ran through her palm, and when she looked down, a white light emanated from her hand. A few seconds later, she could breathe easily again.

I can heal myself.

It wasn't something she would have thought possible considering all the arach were dead, but the ability must only work on small wounds. The other arach, and her parents, must have been too far gone to heal their injuries, but a broken rib was fixable.

As she took in her surroundings, a sick feeling churned in her stomach. Bodies, and all their multiple parts, littered the floor. A massacre had unfolded while she was pinned to the floor, and in the center of it stood a blood-drenched Cole.

The shadows swirled and swayed around him, dipping higher and lower as the light in the room changed. They gathered around him, swerving as they surveyed their surroundings. Many of them remained focused on her.

"Are you okay?" the Cole thing asked in that grizzly multi-voice.

"Yes," she whispered.

Though she was about as far from okay as it got. She was standing in a room so covered in blood she could barely see the original floor and walls through it.

None of the Lord's guards remained standing. They'd all been torn apart like they were little more than cotton balls plucked to pieces by a child.

Some of them remained alive and attempted to drag their way across the floor with their fingertips... if they still had fingers. But they were easy prey—something Cole emphasized by stomping on a warlock's head and smashing it.

Unable to stand any more of the carnage, Lexi looked away from the aftermath. Her gaze found the Lord, and, for the first time, she saw terror in his red eyes. But insanity also churned there.

He remained because he believed he still had a chance against them.

Then, the crazy bastard smiled.

CHAPTER SEVENTY-EIGHT

MAVERICK CUT down the Lord's men who ran toward the portal; he would not let them pass through to possible freedom until he had to retreat. And he wouldn't let them come up behind what remained of their army on the mountain.

Many of the Lord's men and women were fleeing for any portal they could find. No one guarded the others, and he couldn't do anything to stop them from getting away, but he could protect their army.

Between the dragons and the wendigos, this battle had taken a turn none of them liked, and the Lord was losing fighters. Their only hope was to get free of Dragonia.

If the Lord won, some would probably return and act like they'd been here the whole time. They may pretend to have chased the enemy out of the realm. If the Lord lost, they would remain in exile until they were hunted down and killed for their treachery.

Through the fires and fleeing immortals, Maverick spotted Kaylia and Sahira as a breeze briefly cleared the smoke around them. They each held the arm of a wounded lycan while they dragged her across the battlefield.

The smoke was starting to encircle them again when a

berserker, with his face red and veins throbbing through every inch of his exposed flesh, emerged from the fire. As he raced toward them, Kaylia released the lycan's arm and spun toward the berserker.

Her hands moved rapidly, and the glamour of a wendigo materialized before them, but the glamour didn't fool the berserker, and he ran straight through it. Sahira waved her hand at a nearby fire, but only a small burst rose from the ground.

Covered in blood and soot, the two witches were exhausted, beaten down, and virtually spent of their powers. They wouldn't make it without help. Brokk must have come to the same conclusion as he broke away to sprint toward them.

Lowering his shoulder, the berserker crashed into Sahira. It lifted her ten feet off the ground and flung her backward. She came to a stop when she bounced off the foot of the fallen giant. Her head lolled forward as another giant bent to lift her off the ground.

Knowing he had to help, or she would die, Maverick unleashed his wolf as he sprang forward. His clothes shredded and fell away as he pounced on the giant. He sank his fangs into her finger before she could pinch Sahira's head between her tree-sized fingers.

The behemoth's blood filled his mouth, and he snarled as he tore into the creature's flesh. Little had any effect on a giant, but this one reeled backward as she shook her hand to knock him off.

Maverick slid down the giant's finger and released it before she could fling him across Dragonia. As he fell, he twisted in the air and swung out his claws until they caught on the giant's meaty arm.

Digging into its skin, he propelled himself up the giant's arm and away from the bus-sized hand swinging toward him. A loud thwack sounded as the giant slapped her bicep in an attempt to squish him.

Knowing if he didn't move fast, he'd end up splattered like a mosquito, Maverick propelled himself up the giant's arm. He leapt at an enormous eye and sank his claws into it.

He tore into the vulnerable flesh as he slid down it, and a hand swung toward him. The wind created by the approaching hand alerted him of its presence before the giant slapped herself in the face. The blow staggered her back.

Maverick used her brief disorientation to escape. He slid down the giant's chest, over a breast, and launched himself off. Wind tore at his fur, filled his nostrils, and howled across his ears as he soared through the air with all four paws extended for the coming impact with the earth.

He was near the ground when the giant's other hand swung toward him. The air current it created lifted him higher and away from the ground as he twisted to avoid the blow.

But it was already too late. The hand bashed his side with the force of a wrecking ball. Bones shattered, and one of them pierced a lung as the air suddenly left him. Pain erupted inside him when he wheezed in a breath.

As he spun through the air, he tried to right himself, but the giant's blow had sent him spiraling out of control. Earth, fire, and sky swirled around him, but he didn't see the flames until they engulfed him.

~

BROKK CLOSED his eyes as the fire Maverick disappeared into surged higher. They'd lost so many today he should be immune to it, but a pang tugged at his heart. Yet another one down.

He can still be alive.

He could, but Brokk doubted it, and if he was, Maverick was on his own. He had to get Sahira and Kaylia out of here. It was time to move on with the next step in Del's plan.

With the Lord's men fleeing, the wendigos were getting hungrier, and there was little left for them to prey on. Little of their army remained here; it was time to flee.

Besides, the giant had sent Maverick hurtling nearly half a mile away. He'd never be able to get to him without an army at his back. All he could do was help Sahira and Kaylia survive as he slammed into the side of the berserker.

His shoulder caught the thick, massive man under his ribs and lurched him a few feet to the side. Before the powerful immortal could recover, Brokk threw a ball of fire at him. He draped his arms around Kaylia and Sahira and pulled forth the shadows created by the flames around them.

The shadows cloaked them but left the lycan woman exposed as she lay on the ground between them. When he released Kaylia and Sahira, the shadows slid away from them while he bent, lifted the lycan off the ground, and tossed her over his shoulder. His actions might have injured her more, but there was little he could do about that if she were going to survive.

He grasped Sahira's hand and held his other one out to Kaylia; she didn't hesitate before taking it. As soon as her fingers clasped his, warmth slid up his arm, and his palm heated. He ignored the strange sensation as he enveloped them in shadows again and ran with them toward the open portal.

It was time to leave this battlefield behind for the final step in the war.

CHAPTER SEVENTY-NINE

THE SCREAMS HAD STOPPED FILLING the throne room, but the shadows feasted on the memory of their agony. The shadows had laughed as they shredded and tore, rejoiced while they destroyed the enemy, and now, they sought *more*.

And more they would have as the Lord stood with one hand on his throne, surveying the room. The numerous fires dwindled as the bodies fueling them whittled down to skeletons.

Their smoke still choked the air and obscured the sun. But enough of its light filtered through for the shadows to wreak their havoc.

And they'd *relished* it... as did their host.

Though they'd seized most of the control, a fragment of the host remained, and they sensed his desire to destroy the man who ordered his father's death. But no matter how badly the host craved the Lord's death, his focus remained on protecting the arach.

It was their duty to do so.

Now that nothing remained for the shadows to feast on, their attention shifted to the Lord. The host focused on Lexi.

What little that remained of the crisp-fried remnants of her clothes fell away when she rubbed at her arm and legs. Soot and blood streaked her face and body.

Her green eyes were filled with sadness when they met his. The host softened, and a warmth the shadows didn't like flooded them.

That warmth was treacherous. It could rattle their control, and now that they had it, they weren't letting it go.

But they couldn't stop the host from reaching for her. Hope sprang forth in her eyes when her hand stretched toward them. Before they could touch, the Lord turned and sprinted for the back of the room.

The host's hand fell away as he spun toward the Lord, and bloodlust erupted.

~

LONGING AND LOSS radiated through Lexi when Cole's hand fell before she could touch it. For a split second, Cole had shone through the shadows encompassing him.

She'd seen *him* as blue flashed through his eyes. That vanished when the Lord ran.

Once again, only coldness emanated from him as the shadows rose like Medusa's snakes around him. A spine-chilling hiss filled the air.

The shadows moved so rapidly across the room that they blurred, shifted, and blended before separating while hunting their prey. The Lord screamed when the shadows wrapped around his ankles and ripped him off his feet.

His shriek abruptly cut off when his chin smacked off the floor, but he twisted and kicked until he flipped himself onto his back. With a few intricate waves of his hands and a wiggle of his fingers, a wall of air shot out from him.

If it wasn't for the ripple it created as it moved across the room, blowing smoke out of its way and causing the fires to dance, Lexi wouldn't have seen it coming. Spreading her legs apart, she braced herself for impact, but it knocked her back three feet before she righted herself.

Flames from one of the dwindling fires shot up and rolled toward Cole. Cole deflected the fire with a flick of his wrist. He started toward the Lord as the madman sent another wave of air toward them.

Planting his feet, Cole lifted his arms and crossed them before him. He used his ability to manipulate the elements to push back against the air. Caught between the warlock and the dark fae, the air pulsated against the walls.

Pressure built in her ears until it gave way with a loud pop. The air wall shot upward as the Lord returned to kicking and screaming for the dragons.

Dragons descended into the room. The Lord was finally calling them, but after they landed, they remained unmoving amid the carnage.

"They won't harm us," Cole said in those awful voices.

Out of tricks to stop the shadows from taking him, the Lord's body thudded down the steps while the shadows dragged him onward. He flipped himself over and clawed at the steps to gain purchase on them.

His brutalized fingers left a streak of blood across the surface as his nails tore free. Lexi tried to look away but couldn't.

This was it. Seeing *this* man dethroned was what they'd all fought for. No matter how violent and awful this was, she couldn't look away.

The Lord's chin bounced off the floor when he came off the last step. The shadows surged and bobbed around him as he thrashed and scrambled to get a better purchase on the stone floor.

The awful, squealing sounds he issued were those of a pig trying to escape the slaughter, but she felt no sympathy for him. He'd killed far too many for her to have any compassion, and if he lived, he would gladly see them all dead.

There was no room for sympathy, but she wished it was over.

When Cole started across the floor toward the Lord, she remained behind. This wasn't her kill to make... it was Cole's. And he'd been looking forward to this since his father's murder.

But then, she realized something.

If he gave way and let *her* do this, then maybe there was a chance she could save him from the shadows. If a part of him had reached for her earlier, then something of the man she desperately loved remained inside that darkness. Maybe she could get him back if he let her finish this.

"Let me do it!" she blurted as Cole closed in on the Lord.

The shadows twisted toward her, but Cole didn't look back. Nausea over the idea of killing the squirming, squealing man churned in her belly, but Lexi ran forward.

With care, she tried to place her bare feet somewhere without blood or body parts, but that was impossible. She sprinted past a dragon who looked curiously on but made no move to intervene.

She was almost to them when her foot slipped in some blood, and she nearly fell. Skidding on the floor, she righted herself and stopped behind Cole. He didn't acknowledge her.

"Cole—"

"This is *our* job," the shadows hissed at her.

She ignored them and grasped Cole's arm. When he turned toward her, the vulnerability she glimpsed earlier in his eyes was gone. Steel shone back at her from those silver depths as shadows wiggled through his flesh and passed across his irises.

No, no, no, no... she inwardly wept as the word echoed through her mind, but no tears spilled down her face.

That moment when he reached for her was nothing more than a fluke; Cole was gone. What remained in his place was something cold and distant and so very different than the passionate, loving man she knew. Her soul sobbed as her hand went to her mouth and everything in her shattered.

She stepped back and closed her eyes against the tears trying to break free.

~

THE SHADOWS SMILED as they stepped over the Lord, straddling him. When the Lord tried to use his powers again, the host shoved the air down until it encompassed the man. The Lord's face paled as the air crushed his lungs.

"It seems your plan has backfired," the shadows hissed.

The Lord's mouth twisted into a snarl. "You have not won! You're dead too!"

"We are very much alive and just so you know," the host said as he knelt closer to the Lord, "Orin and Varo are alive too, you piece of shit. We used the harrow stone to fake their deaths, but they're alive and on that battlefield, killing *your* army."

The Lord's face turned an apocalyptic red as he shoved against the air the host had turned on him. "Liar!" he spat.

"Not at all. They live, and we *all* plotted against you. I wanted you to know that before I killed you."

Spittle flew from the Lord's mouth as he thrashed and screamed. "I'll kill you!"

The shadows' laughter filled the hall as they slid around the air the Lord used as a shield against them. Like chickens pecking from the ground, they tore little pieces away from him. His screams were pure music as the host broke through the barrier.

~

As THE LORD'S screams rose in intensity, Lexi opened her eyes to watch the man, who'd inflicted so much sadness and destruction on the realms, torn to shreds by Cole and the shadows.

The shadows' laughter continued to fill the hall, but it wasn't like any laughter she had ever heard before. This was like the bowels of Hell had opened to release the cries of the damned trapped within.

The Lord's body parts fell to join the countless others scattered around the room until the screams and laughter finally stopped.

CHAPTER EIGHTY

THE SHADOWS TURNED toward the arach who stood in the middle of all the blood and death they'd so gleefully inflicted. Sorrow from the host pierced them, and that warm feeling came again, but they shoved the dangerous feeling aside.

They'd come this far; they wouldn't turn back now, but the host was fighting them. It wanted free to be with her, and they could *not* have that. They would not relinquish their power again.

The arach's eyes shone in the light spilling into the room. Anguish etched her face as they stared at one another before the host stepped aside to give her a clear path to the throne.

Bobbing and weaving, the shadows waved her toward the throne. They would see this completed even as the host tried to pull them away. The host didn't like them near her, but he should know they wouldn't hurt her.

"Take your throne," the shadows commanded.

～

LEXI LIFTED her chin and looked from Cole to the throne and back again. A couple of the dragons crept closer until they nearly touched her. She felt their eagerness, but her feet remained planted in the blood.

Cole was gone, but she still heard the destruction raining down outside as the screams of the dying filled the air. And she could stop that, or at least help with it... she hoped.

Keeping her chin high and her shoulders back, Lexi started toward the steps of the dais. She ignored the warm blood squishing between her toes as she stepped over the Lord's head with its bulging eyes and gaping mouth.

She placed one foot on the first step and started to climb. It took more time than she expected as she kept slipping in the blood. She nearly went down a couple of times but somehow remained standing.

When she arrived at the top, she stood and stared at the arach throne. The dead littered the ground around it. Blood from the Lord's dismembered guards dripped down the back and pooled on the seat.

Gone was the golden throne the Lord sat on; a simple, stone creation sat in its place. Dragons etched its back, but this stone seat was nowhere near as fancy as its predecessor.

The Lord must have cast a glamour over the throne to make it look more elaborate, or maybe it changed itself depending on whoever sat on it. Either way, this blood-drenched throne wasn't the same as the Lord's, and for that, she was thankful.

She edged closer to it. Though it was different from the Lord's throne, she knew it had made those who sat on it for the past thousand years insane.

A lot of power ran through this throne, and it was *hers*.

She'd be lying if she said the idea of sitting on it didn't petrify her. It was the true arach throne, but its history was intimidating and nerve-racking.

It was a history she intended to change from this day forth.

Taking a deep breath, Lexi was determined to ignore the blood as she turned and sat on the hard, stone seat. At first, she kept her hands and arms in the air above the throne, but she slowly lowered them to rest against it.

As her fingers gripped the arms of the throne, a starburst erupted inside her head. A rush of brilliant lights unfurled before her like a galaxy swirling with stars as she hurtled through space.

The lights erupting from the throne pierced her until they joined *every* part of her to the stone monolith. She joined the throne's power, and hers joined it until they mingled and blended.

She suddenly understood why the throne had driven the non-arach rulers insane. This blending of magic was necessary. It kept one from becoming too powerful as it was a sharing, give and take that didn't allow for corruption. When all the power flooded from one side to the other, without any return, it became too much for a non-arach to handle.

Fibers of magic wove in and out of her and the throne until they blended seamlessly together. Unable to resist any longer, she leaned her back against the throne. The second she was fully connected to it, something clicked into place, and she became aware of the dragons in the realms.

She didn't know where they were or what they were doing but sensed if she followed each colorful thread joining her to the throne, she could connect with them. Then she gave herself to the power and opened her mind to the galaxy and dragons beyond.

"Stop!" she commanded.

Her voice, stronger than she'd expected after the events of this day and the sorrow still crushing her heart, carried through the air. "It's over; enough death and enough fighting. This war is done!"

A shiver went through her bond to the throne and on to the dragons. Roars bounced off the mountains and echoed throughout the room. They didn't sound angry but more celebratory as the dragons swooped and twisted over the open ceiling.

The ones within the room issued bellows that shook the walls as they stamped their feet like they were dancing. Some more descended into the throne room and settled amidst the remains.

They folded their wings against their backs and sat with their necks proudly arched as they tucked their chins against their chests.

Alina swooped in and settled beside her with a rustle of wings. When she met Alina's golden eyes, a smile spread across the speaker's mouth. Lexi managed a small smile in return.

"Well done, child," Alina whispered.

But none of this felt well done to Lexi. There was too much death, cruelty, and much that could never be *undone* within this blood-drenched realm.

Cole remained in the center of the room, staring at her as the smoke wafted away and the remaining flames died out. She opened her mouth to call him to her and beg him not to leave.

Before she could say anything, he gave a small bow of his head. The shadows swelled around him until his silver eyes vanished.

When the shadows cleared, it was as if Cole had never been there.

The plop of blood sliding down the throne and dripping to the ground was abnormally loud in the suddenly hushed room. Cole was gone, and he wouldn't be coming back. There was no denying that awful, heart-wrenching truth.

He was gone, and she was to rule the realms. And there were still so many in *all* the realms who would gladly see her dead.

She didn't care about any of them; all she wanted was Cole back.

CHAPTER EIGHTY-ONE

Brokk was about to plunge into the portal that would take him and their remaining fighters to the palace and, hopefully, the end of this war.

Before he could enter the portal, the dragons bellowed as if they were one unit. The sound traveled through the mountains until it came from everywhere at once.

Some of the beasts soared higher into the sky as they released torrents of flames that blew apart the pink clouds and stood out vibrantly against the purple sky. Bones topped most of the mountains, but they knocked those bones from the peaks as they flew. It was as if they were cleaning up the land or reclaiming it.

The dragons rose into the sky, where they hovered for a minute with their wings spread wide. The sun's golden glow illuminated their vibrant colors before they plunged back toward the earth in a rolling tumble that defied gravity. Others soared over the palace; they twisted and turned before vanishing through an opening.

At first, he didn't know what to make of what was happening. Then he realized they were pulling back from the war, leaving the battlefield and the remaining massacre.

The surviving giants tipped their heads back to watch as the dragons cried out *joyously*? But there was no other way to describe the noise they made, so the murderous beasts must actually be... *happy*.

It was nearly impossible to believe after the destruction they rained down for centuries, but they dipped and looped and played with magnificent grace. They swooped toward each other, sometimes coming together and tumbling through the air and, at times, barely missing each other.

He'd always hated the things, but now he couldn't help being awed and a little moved by them. They made *him* want to be happy, and he was covered in blood, sore from battle, and so fucking tired.

"They did it," Kaylia whispered as Orin limped up with his arm locked around Varo's waist. "Lexi's on the throne."

Brokk started to ask how she was so sure, but he already knew the answer. The dragons wouldn't be playing like this if the Lord still ruled. Some of them sounded like they were *laughing*; he was certain they'd never made *that* sound while the monster reigned.

They'd been freed from their oppression and were celebrating the return of an arach to the throne.

"Let's go," Orin said gruffly.

Below them, the giants turned and strode toward the portal that would take them home. Most of them vanished within, but the final giant, the one with an eye patch, stomped on the last three wendigos before gazing at the palace and dragons once more.

Though the giant was too far away for him to be certain, Brokk swore the colossal being smiled. Then, Eye Patch stepped through the portal and disappeared.

Brokk's elation over this turn of events dwindled as the shadows returned to seep over the land and the brightness dimmed. He had no doubt they wouldn't release his older brother so easily.

Cole.

Yearning speared him; Cole would never be the same after this. Brokk had no idea what he would find of his older brother when they entered the palace; a part of him dreaded doing so, but he couldn't avoid the inevitable. It was time to discover the answers he was sure he didn't want.

Brokk entered the portal and strode swiftly through it toward the palace. When they emerged near the main throne room, butchery greeted them. Blood splattered the walls, body parts littered the floor, and swords clashed as Del's group worked on finishing what remained of the Lord's army.

Not much remained as Brokk's side leapt into action to take down their enemy. When they finished, Brokk wiped the sweat and blood from his brow; he planted the tip of his sword on the ground and leaned against it.

He met Del's red-eyed gaze as he spoke. "My brother?"

"I don't know," Del said. "I don't know about Lexi either. Once they entered the throne room, the doors closed, and we were locked out. We tried to break the doors down, but it was useless."

"We're going to make them open," Orin snarled and winced as he pressed a hand against his still bleeding abdomen.

"You have to take care of that," Brokk told him.

Orin scowled at him, but when Sahira pulled off her bloody shirt to stand before them in her ruined bra, Orin didn't protest as she tied it around his wound and cinched it.

"Let's go," Sahira said when she finished.

They strode past the bloodstained golden dragon and arach statues lining the hall. When they stopped outside the double doors, Brokk grasped one of the handles. As he pulled on it, Brokk braced himself for it not to budge, but the door swung silently open.

He realized too late that while he'd prepared for almost anything, he wasn't ready for the bloodbath beyond. It made what lay on the battlefield and in the hallway look like nothing happened.

Unable to stop himself, he recoiled from the massacre. He'd

never seen anything so horrific as the body parts scattered across the floor and the blood coating the floor and walls.

Many of the bodies were torn apart or scorched to the bone. Smoke leisurely coiled up from some of those bodies, and the stench permeating the room nearly made him regurgitate the blood he'd consumed before going to war.

The dragons turned to look at them, and a few lowered their heads in a defensive posture, but Lexi's voice halted them before they attacked. "They're not a danger. Let them pass."

Brokk didn't want to pass. He'd prefer not to step one foot inside the hideous room, but he would see this through. He strode down the steps and across the hall with a confidence he didn't feel.

Finally tearing his gaze from the wreckage, he lifted his head and met Lexi's eyes across the cavernous room. Blood covered her naked body and soaked her auburn hair, but she sat with her chin high, her shoulders back, and the regal bearing of a queen overseeing her land.

However, she couldn't hide the sadness in her eyes, and it was like a knife to his heart. Without having to ask, he knew that he didn't see Cole anywhere because his brother was gone.

CHAPTER EIGHTY-TWO

AS THE OTHERS entered the room, the power of the throne and all Dragonia continued to thrum through Lexi. The amazing feeling did nothing to ease her grief.

Judging by the numbers in the room, they'd lost many, but a fair amount survived. Happy tears filled her eyes, and she almost launched herself off the throne to run and greet Sahira and her father.

Afraid it would seem undignified and unroyal, Lexi restrained herself from going to them. But sitting naked on a throne covered in blood probably wasn't all that dignified either.

Still, she didn't move. They all needed to see her here; it's what they'd all sacrificed for.

A smile curved her mouth as Brokk, Kaylia, and Varo approached. She was even happy to see Orin. Pixies and imps darted around the room.

The dwarves carried their battle-axes proudly against their shoulders, while the sirens walked solely in their women form amid the dragons. Lexi suspected they didn't want to give the dragons something to chase.

The hooves of the unicorns and pegasuses rang off the stone

floor while the phoenixes flew low through the crowd and the light fae entered last. They looked haggard, but many of them had survived.

Though she didn't see Elfie, she saw Sahira's mother and Elvin. Her heart sank when she realized Maverick and Niall weren't with the others.

In all, a couple of hundred immortals filed into the throne room. There were far more in Dragonia and throughout all the realms who were now under her rule.

But though she knew she wasn't alone and had the realms to rule over, wrongs to set right, and so much to learn, she'd never felt more isolated. She didn't know how she would get through this when she'd never had any experience before, still wasn't completely sure of her abilities, and had lost Cole.

Despite that, she was determined to master her new role as Dragonia's benevolent queen and learn all her powers. This land would help her do so, she was sure of it, and it would make her stronger. She could already feel that happening.

And when she was stronger and more in control of her abilities, she would go after the shadows and defeat them. They had control of Cole now, but it wouldn't last.

She *would* make sure of that. In a battle between her and the shadows, she *would* emerge the victor.

CHAPTER EIGHTY-THREE

THE SHADOWS SCREAMED in protest against their host's restraint. The host ignored them as it propelled them deeper into the earth, burrowing farther away from the light that gave the shadows life and burying them in darkness.

The shadows not inside the host fell away as the complete dark smothered their life. While the shadows fought the host's hold, they tried to exert control over the host's mind, but he wouldn't relinquish it. He refused to give in to their thirst for more blood, death, and destruction.

He would not do as they wanted!

They were thirsty, hungry, and ached to kill, but the host refused to allow it. He buried them so far beneath the earth that even those inside him lost some of their control, but they *refused* to relinquish it all.

They were unable to hunt and kill for so long, but then they were awakened and given a vessel. They would *not* let the vessel go.

One day, they would rise from the darkness and unleash their bloodlust again. When that day came, they would bathe in the death of others.

～

As Cole continued deeper and deeper beneath the earth, some of the shadows lost their hold on him, but not enough so that he trusted himself to return to daylight, to the world beyond, and *Lexi*.

He couldn't be anywhere near her while the shadows fought to rule him. Not while they screamed and slithered and thirsted for blood like a vampire locked away for thousands of years.

The shadows were ravenous and made *him* crave more blood too. But there was no more blood to take.

They had won, their enemies were defeated, and Lexi sat on the throne. Even covered in blood, beaten, and with sorrow in her eyes, she radiated an aura of strength. She would make a magnificent queen.

He had no doubt she would do right by the realms, and while he longed to stand at her side, he couldn't do it like this. The second he returned to the light, the shadows would seek out more death; except this time, they would unleash it on the innocent. They wouldn't go after Lexi, but they would destroy countless others.

No matter how much his heart broke, no matter how much he longed for the life they were supposed to have together, he couldn't return. Not while the shadows hungered for more, and not while they could so easily take control again.

His life was one of darkness now, and he would remain within the dark if it kept Lexi safe... and as long as it kept her from hating him, because she would hate him if he unleashed the shadows upon the realms.

That didn't stop him from leaving some shadows to watch her and report any threat to him. He'd vowed never to leave her, but he couldn't stay like this.

It wouldn't take him long to return; he had to bury the shadows, but he would *never* go too far from her.

And if something threatened her, and he returned before he could figure out how to regain control of the shadows, he would unleash hell upon the realms.

CHAPTER EIGHTY-FOUR

IT WAS WELL after midnight when Alina returned to her cave. Wary from all the brutality and the ups and downs of this day, she crept through the dark. She'd never been so exhausted, but then everyone was tired after everything they endured.

Their new queen looked ready to drop when she finally retreated with her family to clean herself and learn more about her new home. Alina knew this wasn't a happy time for their new queen, but she'd handled herself well.

The queen's heartbreak resonated through the bond she now shared with the dragons, but this was a time of joy and revelry for Alina and the others. They were free from oppression, free from the madman's rule, and though the arach were far from perfect when they ruled here, they belonged in this realm and on that throne.

Once the exhaustion wore off, the dragons would celebrate. With a yawn, she crawled onto her nest and settled with her eggs. She wrapped her head around them and drew them closer.

Their world *would* be a better place; she had faith in the child to correct the wrongs committed over the last millennia. It would take time, but the girl could do it.

386   BRENDA K DAVIES

Their new queen may be young, but she was capable and strong. She'd proven that by helping to wrest the throne away from the usurper.

But still, Alina yearned for the children she wouldn't have, the eggs that would never hatch, and the lack of young amongst the dragons. They could all live forever and never die, but those who wanted offspring would have an emptiness inside them.

But not everything can be perfect, and even with the new queen on the throne, not everything will be. There is still so much to do, so far to go, and the Reaver is still out there.

She was aware of the threat he possessed to all those who remained. Maybe not to the queen, but to the other realms, the immortals, and the dragons. And the queen's love for him might stop her from doing whatever was necessary to eradicate that danger.

The dragons couldn't harm the Reaver, but if he turned the shadows on them, the shadows could destroy *them*. It would be best if someone killed the Reaver before then, but it would have to be someone extremely powerful.

The queen was one of the few who came to mind, and the others who might stand a *small* chance against him were from realms far from this one or realms completely hidden to outsiders.

The Reaver had left, probably to keep from unleashing more destruction, which meant the dark fae still had some control over the shadows. That wouldn't remain the same if the queen died.

Alina could help with that problem as she had *no* intention of letting anything happen to their new ruler. They'd all lost and been through too much for such an atrocity.

Alina's biggest problem now was still being awake when she desperately needed sleep. Yawning, she settled her head on her feet, nudged one of the eggs closer, and fell into a deep sleep.

She had no idea how much time passed before she woke to a strange noise and something pushing against her. Alina lifted her head; smoke billowed from her nostrils as she prepared to destroy an intruder.

She searched the cave, but it remained pitch-black, and she saw no sign of an invader. But that noise… what was it?

It was an odd, small chirping sound, yet it was strangely *familiar*?

Alina's head snapped down, and a strange squeak escaped her when a tiny, orange dragon lifted its nose and pushed against hers.

It can't be!

But it was! One of the eggs had hatched!

The orange dragon unfurled its wings. When it yawned, a small puff of smoke drifted from its mouth. But not only was it *alive* and against her body, but the remaining two eggs stirred as her other wyrmlings sought to break free.

The top of one cracked, and a small red head poked out. The dragon squeaked and fell forward when it lunged toward Alina. It rocked in the eggshell it still mostly resided in.

Alina hadn't believed it possible for a dragon to cry. She'd never heard of such a thing before and certainly never experienced it, but two tears, one from each eye, rolled down her cheeks to drip into her nest.

Though she'd gone to bed with hope in her heart, she'd also been certain there were many dark days in their future.

Now she realized far more hope and life remained in this land than she'd ever dreamed possible. For here was proof that an arach on the throne was what Dragonia, and all of them, needed most.

The queen had brought life back to Dragonia. And now the realms would learn all she could do.

～

Read on for an excerpt from *Shadows of Light* Book 6 in the series, or download now and keep reading: brendakdavies.com/SLwb

∾

Stay in touch on updates, sales, and new releases by joining to the mailing list: brendakdavies.com/ESBKDNews

Visit the Brenda K. Davies Book Club on Facebook for exclusive giveaways and all things book related. Come join the fun: brendakdavies.com/BKDBooks

SNEAK PEEK
SHADOWS OF LIGHT, THE SHADOW REALMS BOOK 6

THE SOFT RUSTLE of wings alerted Lexi that one of the dragons was descending into the throne room, but she didn't turn to look. *It's Alina.*

She wasn't sure how she knew, but Lexi was certain the speaker had arrived. It was a vibe that started thrumming through the bond connecting her to the dragons as soon as she ascended the arach throne.

That was two days ago; she hadn't seen Alina since, but Lexi hadn't been exploring the realm since then, and she hadn't called the dragons to her. She'd been too exhausted and heartbroken to do anything like that.

But today, she had no other choice. She could allow herself one day to recuperate and wallow in self-pity and sorrow, but she couldn't spend two.

She'd claimed her throne and her birthright to rule over the realms; a lot of shit came with that responsibility. Her problem was that she had no idea where to start with everything she needed to do.

So, she'd decided to start small and do what she could handle... cleaning.

"You should *not* be doing that," Alina said.

She wasn't the first immortal to tell her this, but, as she'd told her aunt and Orin, the problem was… "Who else is there to do it? All those who resided and worked in this palace before were loyal to the Lord. They've all fled, been killed, or are in the dungeon."

Lexi threw her bloody sponge into the wooden bucket before turning to face the bright red dragon. Alina's golden eyes studied her from their slitted pupils as the large dragon rose to reveal the yellow flecks along her belly.

Blood stained the ground and walls around her, but Lexi had made progress. Maybe she should be doing something other than scrubbing the blood from the throne room, but she had no idea what. Besides, there was *no way* she would sit in this room, and on that throne, with all the blood and scorch marks still marking the floor.

Although the scorch marks weren't coming off, and she suspected they'd forever mar the floor, but that was a problem for another day. At least all the bodies of the Lord's men were gone.

"The immortals in your army should do this," Alina said.

"Most have left to either rebuild their realms, or turn the realms they used to escape from the Lord, into homes. They have lives to rebuild, and they didn't agree to fight with us so they could work for me afterward."

Alina looked affronted by this. "*You* are the queen of the realms. They do not *work* for you; they *serve* you. They are yours to command."

"The dragons were the Lord's to command, too; how did that work out for you?"

Twin spirals of smoke curled out of Alina's nostrils. "You must have an army in this realm and immortals to serve you. It is the way of things."

"You're right about the army," Lexi told her. "But I don't need servants."

"Of course, you do. You will one day entertain here; there will be balls and parties again. Immortals will come to you for things, for help, to speak with you, and to pledge their allegiance. You *must* have servants to greet them."

Lexi grabbed the bloody sponge from the bucket before tossing it back into the red water. She pushed the bucket aside and pulled another one closer. Before starting, she carried a dozen buckets to prepare for this chore.

Since then, she'd made three trips to the river to fill the buckets again and carried them back. Cleaning this mess helped her to have something other than Cole to focus on. If she was scrubbing, she wasn't crying as much, though it was still nearly impossible for her to breathe, and her eyes burned incessantly.

"That is a problem for later," Lexi muttered as she removed a clean sponge from the water and returned to work on the stone floor.

"There must be others to help with this," Alina said.

"They're removing the bodies from the battlefield. That's more important than helping me with this."

She should have been there to help them, but her father and Orin insisted she stay inside until they removed any lingering threats and it was safe for her to roam outside. So here she was, scrubbing a floor while some of Maverick's pack guarded the door.

She winced at the reminder of Cole's uncle. He was just one more of the many they lost during the battle, but his pack insisted on staying to help rebuild and guard her. Without their alpha and their realms, they were lost.

But then, so was she. Lexi scrubbed harder.

~

A SMALL YELP proceeded a tiny snout shoving into her face and brushing her nose. Lexi was so startled that she dropped the sponge and recoiled from the small creature before realizing it was a baby dragon.

392   BRENDA K DAVIES

It hopped toward her, squeaking as its tiny wings flapped in the air, and its head tilted as it studied her. Lexi blinked at the beautiful, orange creature no bigger than a cat, who smiled as it hopped toward her again.

When she sat on her ass, the tiny creature jumped into her arms. Despite the misery still clinging to her, Lexi laughed as the baby dragon peered into her face and released another squeak.

"Astarot," Alina chided, but the dragon snuggled under her chin and plopped onto her lap.

Two red dragons followed the orange one. Their tiny tails swished as one leapt onto her shoulder, and the other jumped onto the orange one.

They shrieked and snapped at each other before the red one rose to brush Lexi's cheek. The orange one turned like a cat looking for a good place to lie before settling again.

When the red one's warm breath caressed her skin, Lexi couldn't stop herself from laughing. Cole's absence made her chest feel like someone had carved her heart out and stomped on it, but they were so cute it was impossible not to smile as they snuggled against her.

Lifting her head, she looked up as Alina edged closer. "How old are they?" Lexi asked.

"They hatched the night you took the throne."

Lexi leaned her face into the tiny body as the one on her shoulder nuzzled her cheek. It was as if they felt her pain and were seeking to comfort her.

"They're beautiful," Lexi said. "What are their names?"

"My son, Astarot, is the one nibbling on your finger, and he is the future speaker, should something happen to me. My daughter, Belindo, is on your shoulder, and my other daughter, Nithe, is the one licking you."

Lexi giggled as Nithe's tongue tickled her cheek. "Congratulations."

"Thank you. You should know that they are the first dragons born in a thousand years."

So lost in loving dragon snuggles, it took a second for Lexi to register her words. When she did, she looked up at Alina and frowned. "I don't understand."

"I laid their eggs a thousand years ago, shortly before the arach lost the throne."

"It takes that long for dragon eggs to hatch?" Lexi asked incredulously.

"No, it normally takes about three months," Alina said.

Astarot stopped nibbling on her finger and hopped onto her other shoulder. There, he curled against her face, yawned loudly, and went to sleep. His sisters continued to play, but Nithe yawned too.

"I don't understand," she said.

"No dragons laid any eggs, and no eggs hatched while the usurpers were on the throne. Your ascension to the throne has brought healing back to Dragonia. We feared the dragons would one day die out, but now, that will not be."

Unexpected tears burned Lexi's eyes as Belindo also curled up on her lap. She stroked the dragon's soft scales as she ran her hands down Belindo's back and across the small spikes on her tail.

"You are meant to be here; you are our queen," Alina said. "You have sacrificed much and will sacrifice more before this is over, but this is your home and rightful place in the realms."

"I know," Lexi murmured.

There was still so much to do and accomplish. So many would try to take the throne from her, but it was *hers*. This was where she was supposed to be... even if it had cost her Cole.

～

COLE SLID through the darkness as he moved toward the surface while the shadows churned and screamed around him. They still sought blood; it was all they craved, and they hammered incessantly at him to satisfy their hunger.

It would have been better if he stayed below, where the shadows were more suppressed, but he could never shut them out completely. He required the knowledge of their secrets if he was to protect Lexi, and recently they had started whispering about a threat to her.

There would be many threats to her, and it would be better if he were at her side to face them, but he didn't have enough control over the shadows. She'd seen enough death and destruction; she didn't need anymore, and that was what he'd become.

He was death, and he embraced it.

As the shadows carried him out of the cave, he emerged into a world of sunshine that blinded him as it chased the shadows away. Lifting his hand, he used it to block out the sun while his eyes slowly adjusted to the daylight.

He smiled as he followed the shadow's whispers toward the portal he'd opened. The shadows would take him to the threat, and he would eradicate it.

~

"You have breathed *life* back into this realm," Alina continued. "A miracle that none of us expected. It is time to start acting like a queen, and queens do *not* scrub floors."

"It's time you start getting used to a new type of queen," Lexi said.

Before Alina could reply, a loud thud came from outside, and the earth shook. When the walls rattled, Lexi's head lifted to the open ceiling above. Dragons soared overhead, but that's not where the sound and vibrations had come from.

Before she could ponder it for too long, the doors at the end of the room flew open, and Brokk rushed inside. "There's a giant in Dragonia! We have to get you somewhere safe."

Lexi scooped Belindo into her arms as she rose.

∼

Continue reading *Shadows of Light*: brendakdavies.com/SLwb

∼

Stay in touch on updates, sales, and new releases by joining to the mailing list: brendakdavies.com/ESBKDNews

Visit the Brenda K. Davies Book Club on Facebook for exclusive giveaways and all things book related. Come join the fun: brendakdavies.com/BKDBooks

FIND THE AUTHOR

Brenda K. Davies Mailing List:
brendakdavies.com/News

Facebook: brendakdavies.com/BKDfb

Brenda K. Davies Book Club:
brendakdavies.com/BKDBooks

Instagram: brendakdavies.com/BKDInsta
Twitter: brendakdavies.com/BKDTweet
Website: www.brendakdavies.com

ALSO FROM THE AUTHOR

**Books written under the pen name
Brenda K. Davies**

The Vampire Awakenings Series

Awakened (Book 1)

Destined (Book 2)

Untamed (Book 3)

Enraptured (Book 4)

Undone (Book 5)

Fractured (Book 6)

Ravaged (Book 7)

Consumed (Book 8)

Unforeseen (Book 9)

Forsaken (Book 10)

Relentless (Book 11)

Legacy (Book 12)

The Alliance Series

Eternally Bound (Book 1)

Bound by Vengeance (Book 2)

Bound by Darkness (Book 3)

Bound by Passion (Book 4)

Bound by Torment (Book 5)

Bound by Danger (Book 6)

Bound by Deception (Book 7)

Bound by Fate (Book 8)

Bound by Blood (Book 9)

Bound by Love (Book 10)

The Road to Hell Series

Good Intentions (Book 1)

Carved (Book 2)

The Road (Book 3)

Into Hell (Book 4)

Hell on Earth (Book 5)

Into the Abyss (Book 6)

Kiss of Death (Book 7)

Edge of the Darkness (Book 8)

The Shadow Realms

Shadows of Fire (Book 1)

Shadows of Discovery (Book 2)

Shadows of Betrayal (Book 3)

Shadows of Fury (Book 4)

Shadows of Destiny (Book 5)

Shadows of Light (Book 6)

Wicked Curses (Book 7)

Sinful Curses (Book 8)

Gilded Curses (Book 9)

Whispers of Ruin (Book 10)

Secrets of Ruin (Book 11)

Tempest of Shadows

A Tempest of Shadows (Book 1)

A Tempest of Thieves (Book 2)

A Tempest of Revelations (Book 3)

A Tempest of Intrigue (Book 4)

A Tempest of Chaos (Book 5)

Historical Romance

A Stolen Heart

Books written under the pen name

Erica Stevens

The Coven Series

Nightmares (Book 1)

The Maze (Book 2)

Dream Walker (Book 3)

The Captive Series

Captured (Book 1)

Renegade (Book 2)

Refugee (Book 3)

Salvation (Book 4)

Redemption (Book 5)

Vengeance (Book 6)

Unbound (Book 7)

Broken (Book 8 - Prequel)

The Kindred Series

Kindred (Book 1)

Ashes (Book 2)

Kindled (Book 3)

Inferno (Book 4)

Phoenix Rising (Book 5)

The Fire & Ice Series

Frost Burn (Book 1)

Arctic Fire (Book 2)

Scorched Ice (Book 3)

The Ravening Series

The Ravening (Book 1)

Taken Over (Book 2)

Reclamation (Book 3)

The Survivor Chronicles

The Upheaval (Book 1)

The Divide (Book 2)

The Forsaken (Book 3)

The Risen (Book 4)

ABOUT THE AUTHOR

Brenda K. Davies is the USA Today Bestselling author of the Vampire Awakening Series, Alliance Series, Road to Hell Series, Hell on Earth Series, The Shadow Realms Series, A Tempest of Shadows Series, and historical romantic fiction. She also writes under the pen name, Erica Stevens. When not out with friends and family, she can be found at home with her husband, son, and pets.

Printed in Dunstable, United Kingdom